High Stakes

Susanne Bellamy

DEDICATION

To my mountain man, whose love for the Himalayas and the people have drawn him back time after time.

ACKNOWLEDGEMENTS

With thanks to my wonderful husband, who first took me to Nepal many years ago, and whose subsequent trips provided inspiration for this story.
And to Annie Seaton, good friend and fabulous editor. Thank you.

Prologue

Sydney, Australia

John Chan faced his father across the antique rosewood desk. Eyes black and lustreless as coal pinned him to the parquet floor. Sleek, satin lapels contrasted with his snow-white tuxedo, and the benign smile he'd bestowed on guests gathered to celebrate his birthday in the marquee below was wiped from his face. Loss of face, especially for the eldest son of the head of family, was unacceptable. He bowed his head and waited for his father to pronounce sentence.

"You allowed her into your office because you let desire for this woman overrule your head. The woman accessed your computer. She escaped. We may be compromised."

"Father, I regret—"

"For a woman." Disgust leached through his words, pitching his voice higher than normal.

It didn't matter that John had increased profits since taking over operations in Sydney. Endangering the family and the business meant his life was forfeit. If his father so wished.

"Third Uncle wants your balls stuffed in your mouth.

Second Uncle prefers a visit to the shark tank."

Of course. A bullet to his temple would be considered weakness.

Bile rose in John's throat. Hands gripped tightly together, he tried to swallow the lump of fear threatening to block his response. Now was not the time to show emotion. Now was the time for quick thinking, and for negotiation. What could he offer in exchange for his life?

"I have a contact in the Bureau. May I protect my family by accessing my resources?"

His father shifted on his seat. Red and gold brocade rustled, and shimmered in the low light preferred by his ageing eyes. He tapped one gnarled index finger on the wooden arm of the chair. When it stopped, John raised his eyes to meet his father's.

"Do this, and perhaps your uncles and I will let you live." His father dismissed him with a single flick of his hand. As though he was no more than a fly.

The woman he had sought to win as his mistress had brought him to this.

Anger seared his gut as John bowed and backed out of his father's office. Luxury and all the clothes wealth could afford had been offered but the woman had played him for a fool. Humiliation would be heaped on her tenfold. She would pay dearly.

He pulled his phone from his pocket and unlocked it with his thumbprint. Scrolling through his contacts, the tremor in his fingers filled him with shame. When the code name appeared, he stabbed the screen and waited. Hand in pocket, he peered through the window. Rivulets of rain blurred his view of the formal garden, and red Poinciana leaves bled into a green bush.

The connection rang four times, as it always did. "What do you want now? I told you, she went to the airport where our tail lost her."

His contact had never shown him respect. One day, when his usefulness was over, John would take pleasure in putting a bullet into Iceman's brain.

But not yet.

"You have one chance. Find her. Kill her."

Chapter One

Jake Harris crossed his scuffed trekking boots and touched his whisky glass to the UN commissioner's. Damn if the man didn't keep the best supply this side of Everest. He sipped, welcoming the burn of island peat on his tongue, down his throat, in his gut. Not one drop had touched his lips in two months. Not since he'd found his brother in the garage.

Hanging like a frozen side of beef.

Dead.

The memory slammed through him with the force of an avalanche, and the whisky soured in the black pit of his soul.

Peter. Baby brother. Coke-head.

Dead.

He set the crystal tumbler on the mahogany desk with a thunk. Lamplight lit the lower half of his body and he leaned back, praying his face was in deep shadow. If—when—he got his hands on those responsible for Pete's death, he'd bring them down. By any means. "What do you need from me, Mr Nicholls?"

Grey jacket sleeves rode up and revealed pristine white cuffs. The commissioner folded soft hands on the desk, and his socially-polite, upwardly-mobile smile, the smile of the career diplomat, was packed away. "I understand you're a man of few words. I suppose that's why you chose field work over the diplomatic corps."

The commissioner's plummy tones grated. Jake preferred lilting Nepalese voices to Oxford city-slickness. "I'm leaving Kathmandu in the morning."

"Impatient, Mr Harris?"

"I have new field agents to train." In truth, his second-in-charge in the south-east Asia division of the Bureau was responsible for inductions, but Jake needed space. Room to breathe, open air, and pushing himself to the limit so he could snatch a few hours of dreamless sleep. So far the plan had failed more than it had succeeded.

"Fine, let's cut to the chase. Doctor Westcott is heading up the trail towards Everest Base Camp. Ostensibly on holiday." Nicholls drew a folder towards him.

"And?"

"It's the second part of her trip we hold concerns about."

"Congratulations on solving all the major world problems." He didn't bother trying to subdue his sarcastic side. Sarcasm was good. Sarcasm masked his I'm-going-through-hell face and made taking his next breath, and the next, and the next, possible.

Bitter sarcasm was all he had left.

Because he'd failed. Failed to protect one of the few people he cared about.

Nicholls' hooded eyes fixed on Jake and the sharp plane of

his nose lowered as if he were a bird dropping from the sky on hapless prey. Jake glared right back at the commissioner and to hell with protocol. He didn't give a damn if he pissed the man off. He didn't give a damn about anything.

Nicholls fiddled with the knot of his tie. "Doctor Westcott has applied for a research permit to visit the Dolpa region." Jake flicked through memories of his only trip to the central province. "It's remote, difficult to access, and entry permits are expensive and restricted. Not many trekkers go there. What's the concern?"

"Her specialty. Biological chemistry."

"So? I don't see the connection."

Nicholls leaned back and a smug smile tugged at the corners of his mouth. "Need to know basis, Harris."

Jake thought about telling Nicholls to take his intrigue and shove it where the sun didn't shine. The words teetered on the springboard of his tongue, raw, harsh, bitter. He couldn't give a flying fuck. Not when he had a mountain of paperwork, and a group of raw recruits to whip into shape. "I'm head of drug enforcement operations for the region. Who the hell do you think needs to know if not me?"

Nicholls pursed his lips and tapped his fingers on the closed folder. "This case requires top security clearance."

"Which I have. So—she's a biological chemist. What's the connection?"

"Her work involves research and synthesising compounds."

"Making what? Who for, and why here?"

"That's the problem; we don't know."

"Is Doctor Westcott flying in or trekking?"

Nicholls' internal struggle—to stand firm or answer—drew twin lines of battle between his eyebrows. "What difference does it make?"

A flicker of pleasure licked through Jake. Poncy desk jockey didn't know everything. "Have you ever trekked, Mr Nicholls?"

"Not really my cup of tea." Nicholls' clipped tone dismissed the absurd notion. He picked up a pen and patterned the print label on the folder in a series of jabs. The pen stopped, point down amid a mess of blue dots.

"Why is her mode of travel important?" The question was dragged from him like a dentist pulling a bad tooth.

Jake reached for his glass and took a leisurely mouthful. Nicholls' ignorance of transport within Nepal betrayed his inexperience, but it gave Jake the edge to prise out more details about the woman.

"How she travels determines how much and what can be carried. Unless I know more about what I'm meant to be looking for, I can't help you." He tossed back the last mouthful of whisky. "That's a smooth drop. Don't mind if I have another." Warmth spread through his belly and he poured two fingers' into his glass and sat back.

An antique clock chimed the quarter hour and the echoes hung heavily as Nicholls appeared to deliberate. Finally, he spoke.

"Drugs."

The single word blazed like a neon light in the night. Jake's breath caught on the sharp rock of grief lodged in his throat, his stomach clenched. His hands fisted on his knees, and a bongo-beat accelerated in his brain: *Revenge—Peter—revenge—Peter—revenge.*

"You were instrumental in breaking up an international supply line out of Afghanistan last month. I believe the leader, Al-Kohari was killed?"

"Yes." The word shot out like the bullet that put the drug lord beyond reach of justice. The legal kind, at least. Jake's only regret was Al-Kohari had been the key to finding and proving the Australian connection. Without him . . .

Nicholls leaned back. "Nepal isn't exactly drug territory but if Doctor Westcott is involved, we need to know."

"If she's involved, I'll bring her in."

Nicholls capped the pen. "The doctor dined with John Chan in Sydney a few days before she arrived in Kathmandu. Chan is the eldest son of a family with Asian drug links. He met the doctor at an upmarket restaurant on Sydney's Circular Quay."

Jake's heart stuttered then began a mad thumping. The Chan cartel was likely Peter's supplier. He could still see his younger brother's face, purple and obscene above the noose. Jake forced his lungs to breathe. His hand clenched the glass and he downed the whisky in a single mouthful.

"This was taken by an undercover agent tailing Chan."

Nicholls opened the folder and handed over an enlarged photo.

Beneath heavy, long, black curls, the woman's delicate expression appeared intent on her dinner companion. She was beautiful. His dispassionate gaze began cataloguing details; from the tilt of her head to the thigh-high slit in her black dress, sex appeal oozed from the woman.

"You said she was dining with Chan. Do you think it was business or pleasure?" Jake tipped the photo towards the desk lamp. "Have you got a magnifier?"

Nicholls took an old-fashioned magnifying glass from his drawer and handed it across the desk. "By the look of her I'd say pleasure, but this was the only time the operative saw them alone together."

Jake examined the photograph closely, paying attention to a mark on the woman's thigh, visible in the thigh-split of the slim-fitting black dress.

A tattoo. Maybe a snake or a gecko. He studied her features, memorising them. Any link to the Chans ensured he would take on this assignment. "So how does her trip to Dolpa fit in with this Sydney drug cartel?"

"We suspect a connection. Her visa states the trip is for research. Loopholes in the laws of both our countries allow the legal importation of certain *natural* drugs, which are then recombined. Some of the ingredients in recombined form are responsible for the recent spate of deaths in your capital cities. And mine."

Jake set the photo and magnifier on the desk. "The Chans are at the centre of it?"

"In Sydney, almost certainly."

"Paul Rimmer and I worked undercover in Sydney before I was promoted to head up the Asian bureau. At last contact, he hinted he was onto someone involved in the local trade."

And now Nicholls was handing him a connection to that underworld family. If it was the last thing he did he would find this woman who had allied herself with the Chinese drug cartel and he would extract the truth. And if she was involved in manufacturing and research . . . Jake's hand fisted on his knee.

"Too many young lives are being cut short." Nicholls' comment lacked real emotion. But bureaucratic say-the-right-thing blah hit Jake hard.

Peter would never grow up, grow old, grow anything. He had ceased to exist except in Jake's memory, and as a black and white statistic on a government department's page.

Grief sank in Paul's gut like a boulder, free-falling down— down—down—into a bottomless chasm.

But he couldn't afford the luxury of time to grieve. Time in which the drug family would set up a new supplier, find new supply lines, shatter more families. He pulled himself together, locked his grief down tighter than an airport on terrorist alert. Peter's death would not go unavenged.

"So this doctor is working for the cartel?"

"That, Harris, is what we want you to find out. Observation

only for the time being, but we want to know what the Dolpa connection is. If you confirm a link to the Chans, bring her in." Nicholls closed the folder and shoved it across the desk. "We want eyes on her as soon as possible, before she makes contact with anyone. How quickly can you reach Everest Base Camp?"

"I'll fly in by helicopter tomorrow and backtrack until I find her. Before she reaches Everest, I'll catch her."

And if the doctor was working for the drug family, he would make her pay.

Chapter Two

Marcy Westcott stepped out of the primitive Nepalese outhouse behind Peaceful Lodge and skidded on a patch of ice. Her breath huffed out in puffs of white, her arms windmilled then angled out like a tightrope walker. With a sigh of relief she regained her balance.

Before she took another step, a distant crack shattered the night. She flattened herself against the stone wall of the outhouse. Her heart thudded so hard it could set off an avalanche by itself. Fear rose in her throat, bigger, harder and sharper than the mountain.

She dug her fingertips into the cracks of the outhouse wall and peered up the track. Moonlight revealed nothing more than crouching rocks and curving dirt path, but her trembling legs barely held her up.

Stop jumping at shadows. No one's out there.

A chill wind sneaked through her open anorak and into the gap between her sleep top and track pants. She tugged the flapping jacket across her chest and wrapped her arms around her waist, her gaze drawn to the mountain towering above the rocky landscape.

Plumes of snow streamed off the peak like a bridal veil under misty moonlight. One more day of acclimatisation in the last village on the trail would reduce the chance of altitude sickness. After that, she'd finally get to visit Base Camp. Chatting with climbers attempting the ascent of Everest was as close as she could afford to go, but one day, she would climb the highest mountain and stand on top of the world. Like her father.

One day. She clutched the promise like a talisman to her heart.

Her midnight flight from Sydney and her sister's odd behaviour at their last meeting buzzed in her mind. Leaving Tamsin in Sydney had been hard. There were unresolved issues there, and she needed to sort them out when she came home.

Numb fingers struggled to hold the sides of her down jacket together. She jogged on the spot, her sluggish blood stirring with each slamming sole against stone. The mountain would be there in the morning. Right now, there was a warm sleeping bag inside with her name on it and a few more hours of sleep beckoned.

Clouds scudded across the moon, and darkness covered the landscape. Another crack like a gunshot erupted, much closer. Her stomach clenched. She tried to take shallow breaths, tried to listen, but the pounding in her ears grew stronger with every heartbeat. Echoes rolled through the mountains.

So close, so close, so close.

Marcy pushed off the wall and scrambled over the rocky ground towards the faint strip of light beneath the teahouse door.

Her boot clipped a rock, and her frozen fingers couldn't find the on button of her torch. She crashed into a wall and swore, the word short and harsh and necessary. The wind caught it, and carried her fear into the darkness. The torch dangling from her wrist scraped along cold stone as she felt her way to the door. Touching wood she pushed, and stumbled through the opening.

#

Jake waited, blending with the rocks above the teahouse, and watched the woman plastered against the wall of the outhouse until clouds covered the moon. He lowered his night scope, flexing an itchy trigger finger and peering into the inky darkness.

A second avalanche cracked and rumbled. Amid the rolling echoes, the woman's choked gasp was almost lost. But not the swear word that was followed by the sound of the outer door slamming shut.

Moments later, Jake followed her into the teahouse and shut the front door quietly behind him. He felt his way through the common area. When he heard an internal door click shut, he switched on his torch. Several guest rooms opened off the narrow corridor. A sliver of pale light slid under one door, marking her room. He stepped silently forwards and pressed his ear to her door. The soft slither of a body nestling into a silk liner, the metallic hiss of a zipper—she had climbed into her sleeping bag. The light winked out, she sighed softly, and he turned back to reception.

A note addressed to Jake lay weighed down by a statue of Buddha. He read his host's message and grinned. Chandra had given him the room next door to Doctor Westcott. He'd made the call to reserve a room at the teahouse before the helicopter arranged by Nicholls finally got off the ground mid-afternoon.

He located his room, dropped his backpack onto the floor and removed his boots and jacket. As he lay on the narrow bed and pulled his unzipped sleeping bag over his body like a blanket, his feet hung over the end. The one certainty about flights from Kathmandu onto the mountain was that delays were more common than departing on time. This morning had been no exception. Suppressing an audible groan he rubbed his gritty eyes.

On the other side of the thin wall mere centimetres from him, his target lay in bed. She murmured something, her words indistinct, husky. The soft sound tip-toed through his tired brain, and shivered down his spine like spider-legs over bare skin. He linked his hands under his head and considered this first contact with his assignment. He'd had her in his sight—an easy shot even at night—but wrestled the compulsion to squeeze the trigger into submission. She wasn't Al-Kohari. This time, he didn't plan on losing a link to the Chan cartel. This time, he'd play a different game. Morning couldn't come soon enough to meet Doctor Westcott, face-to-face.

##

Breakfast was almost over when Marcy walked into the communal dining area. A faint headache buzzed and, when she tried to draw a deep breath, her chest was tight. Was altitude sickness or her nightmare-ravaged sleep responsible for the heaviness? Blaming last night's avalanches, she rubbed her temples. Uneasiness niggled like too-hot curry in her stomach. Not since Tamsin had fallen down the old well on their property as a young teen had she felt this sense of impending disaster. Not even when her father had been …

Enough.

Marcy shook her head and instantly regretted the motion. She groaned softly and closed her eyes. A male chuckle, deep and faintly mocking, sounded beside her.

"Altitude sickness is the pits, isn't it?"

Half-opening her eyes, she peered down at the newcomer seated at the end of the long wooden table. Her gaze roamed over the trekker's rugged face.

Several days' growth of dark-blond stubble defined a strong jaw and sculpted cheekbones. He leaned against the wall and eyes the colour of dark chocolate studied her in return.

The uneasy sense of being watched when she'd ventured to the outhouse last night returned. When had he checked in? He hadn't been at dinner last night or later when she'd chatted with her host, Chandra.

She moistened her lips and blinked slowly. "When did you arrive?"

"Here. Sit before you fall down." He slid along the bench and patted the wood beside him.

It hurt to think, but had he avoided answering her question or had she zoned out? Wooziness and a nagging headache won out.

She sat and leaned her head against the wall until her brain kicked back into gear. "I was feeling okay last night." After a single night in Gorak Shep, every part of her body felt twice its weight and her lungs struggled to find enough air. Unable to keep her eyes open, she closed them and shut out the man's scrutiny.

"That's how it hits some people. Hey, look at me." A calloused finger scraped her jaw but his touch was light, impersonal.

She forced her eyes to open. The man occupied her field of vision. Up close, his irises were darker than her first impression of them. As his gaze drilled into hers, her breath caught in her throat. That look—as though he would wrench every last secret from her—sent a frisson of fear down her spine. She turned her head and lifted her chin out of his grip.

He sat back and she sagged against the wall, her hands trembling as though she had confronted her father in one of his moods and lost the argument. Abruptly, she sat on her hands and sucked in a painful breath.

"So, Diamox? I have some in my backpack if you need them."

Heat raced up her cheeks and Marcy cleared her throat. "Um, as a matter of fact, I've brought a good supply of medication but thank you—?" She paused on an upward inflection.

He looked at her before responding to the unspoken invitation. "Jake. Jake Harris. And you are—?"

She pressed her lips together and cursed her sluggish brain.

Of course he would want to know her name after giving his. Reluctantly she opened her mouth. "Marcy Westcott. So—are you going to Base Camp or on your way back down?" She prayed it was the latter. The intensity of that look had unnerved her. He would be an uncomfortable trekking companion and her pilgrimage to Base Camp was too important for distractions.

"Up. What about you?"

Sighing, she cursed Murphy's Law and its attachment to her life. "If I get over this headache, I'm hoping to see Base Camp tomorrow. My guide has promised we'll go up via Kala Patthar and watch the sunrise over Everest." Maybe her guide, Chewang, would allow her an extra day of acclimatisation and she wouldn't have to worry about Jake Harris' brooding eyes.

"We? You're here with your husband or boyfriend?" A flicker of something—disappointment, perhaps?—roughened his tone and his voice. He looked around the room before his gaze returned to her face.

Disappointment, Marcy? Don't be ridiculous. He unsettled you enough that you considered changing your plans.

Moistening her dry lips, she edged closer to the end of the bench and cast a glance at the Sherpas, hoping to catch Chewang's attention and call him over. "No, just with my guide and porters. Are you—travelling with a group?"

Jake flicked a glance at the group of Sherpas gathered at the other end of the communal dining area. "Nope. Solo trek. Since we're heading to the same place would you like some company?"

His smile, a slow upturn of his mouth as though he was unfamiliar with the expression, transformed his face and lightened his dark gaze. That smile took the edge off her distrust and replaced it with an unexpected shaft of sympathy. She loved her solo trek, but kind as her guide and porters were, conversations in fractured English weren't wholly satisfactory. Maybe Jake's initial intensity was simple loneliness?

Pleasant male company had been thin on the ground as she worked long hours to complete her doctorate. Now, Jake appeared to be interested in sensible, level-headed, *I'm-letting-my-hair-down*, scientist-on-holiday Marcy. Her gaze shifted to his mouth. Full lower lips were supposed to mean a sensuous nature, weren't they? A possibility stretched out before her, if she accepted his offer. Would she get the chance to test that theory? All in the name of research.

She shook her head at her see-sawing reactions to the man—and groaned.

Chandra moved along the table carrying a huge teapot and stopped in front of them. "Sorry to disturb. Marcy, you not well?"

Marcy nodded and winced again at the movement. "The altitude is getting to me."

Jake handed two mugs to Chandra. He filled them and Jake passed one to her.

She wrapped her hands around it, welcoming the heat on her cool fingers. She sipped the strong brew and pressed the hot ceramic mug to her forehead, rolling it across her skin in an attempt to massage away the tension of her headache.

"Come for a walk with me. Fresh air will make you feel better." Jake didn't ask. She knew he was right, but her head throbbed and her lungs ached and she couldn't decide whether Jake was a nice guy, but a little intense, or whether steering clear of him was a better idea.

"Thanks, but I'm going to take a tablet and lie down."

"Good idea. Sleep then a walk. How about I pick you up in an hour?"

He smiled again, a broad smile that crinkled the skin at the corners of his eyes. It should have made her feel on top of the world because it was for her alone, but she had the oddest feeling it didn't quite reach his eyes.

##

Jake poured another cup of tea, and sifted through what he had gleaned from their first encounter. Gut instinct told him the Dolpa trip was key to the drugs, but was this trip to Everest a red herring, or a contact point? Gear for her alleged research trip would be in storage in Kathmandu, but she might keep sensitive details about contacts on her person. He would search her room, and if nothing turned up there, he'd have to get up close and personal.

The idea of being nice to this woman suffocated him. Like being caught in a snowstorm, it stopped his breath and twisted his gut. He didn't want to observe. He wanted to shake her until she gave up the truth, spilled the names of her contacts, offered up

John Chan on a plate.

He slammed the mug on the table. Hot tea spilled over his hand. It was enough to clear the red mist from his eyes and bring the room back into focus. Shaking off droplets of tea, he wiped his hand on his trousers. Allowing the raw guilt and anger clawing at his insides to blind him would achieve nothing. Cool, dispassionate analysis was his first tool. So . . . he leaned against the wall and swallowed a mouthful of tea. What had he learned from his first contact with his assignment?

Doctor Westcott wasn't what he'd expected from the photo. The woman in the photo had screamed sex in every line of her body and come-on look in her eyes. In person, the doctor gave off a different vibe. Grey eyes like a Sydney sky in a summer storm flared with awareness when their gazes met. Not with invitation—yet. He'd make use of that attraction to win her trust if he had to. But something else bugged him.

Why had she cut her hair? Those sexy curls had gone, replaced by a short, practical cut. He set the oddity to one side and continued cataloguing details.

She claimed to be unattached and wore no ring. Her nails were neat and short, unlike those in Nicholls' photo. And she had reacted violently to the distant avalanche last night. Was that fear of place, or someone? The second possibility offered him leverage. Play on her fears, get information and cut her a deal if she proved to be small fry.

If she could deliver Chan to him . . .

He looked around the motley group of trekkers and guides, chugged the last of his tea and slid along the bench. Seated by the fire, a group of Sherpas chatted as he approached. Pressing his palms together below his chin, he greeted them. *"Namaste."*

A chorus of greetings rose from the group and the oldest Sherpa beckoned him to join them. Conversation resumed and Jake listened until the current topic petered out.

"Who's guiding the woman, Miss Westcott? I'm joining her in the morning."

"I'm guiding her but she doctor, not miss."

Marcy hadn't shared that information with him when she introduced herself. He added the small omission to the negative side of his list.

The young guide introduced himself as Chewang Sherpa, and continued. "We go to Kala Patthar then Base Camp in one day."

"That's what she said. Has she travelled alone all the way?"

"Yes, sir. Many photo stops." He grinned and pointed at Jake. "You can be in her photos instead of me, sir." The group laughed and Jake smiled wryly. It seemed Dr. Westcott was playing the typical tourist role. But he intended to avoid becoming her stand-in photo model.

"Does she make lots of stops, checking emails, that sort of thing?"

"She stop at internet cafes in Namche Bazar and Lobuche but not take long. She say she wait to hear from home."

Was she waiting for orders from John Chan, details of a contact? Manipulating the situation so they were together when she used the computer in Peaceful Lodge should be easy. Jake rose and stretched, his fingertips brushing the low ceiling. "Has she mentioned if anyone is joining her later?"

"No, sir. She trek alone. Want to climb Everest one day. You ask her about her plans."

Plans that were one hell of an incentive to acquire a lot of money fast.

A hundred thousand dollars wasn't uncommon for the privilege of climbing Everest. As a motive to be involved in drugs, it was feasible.

Jake nodded his thanks and returned to his cramped quarters.

Opening the door two inches, he checked the towel lay as he had placed it, as though casually dropped. Nobody had entered his room. He secreted his satellite phone into a day pack, re-set the towel and closed the door behind him. At the front door he looked up and down the track. A hundred metres uphill a small group of trekkers rounded a bend and disappeared. Jake followed them for a short distance before he turned off and picked his way through a loose accumulation of small boulders until he was out of sight and sound of the teahouse and passing trekkers. Then he called Nicholls. "Locate the doctor's hotel in the capital and search all her gear. I'll spend the next couple of days getting what I can out of her."

"We need answers, Harris. Don't take too long finding whatever she knows about the Chans."

"Don't tell me how to do my job." He ground his teeth and bit off the desire to tell the commissioner to piss off. Whatever it took, he'd uncover the doctor's secrets. But the idea of pretending he liked her rankled. He loathed her. She was a doctor, for God's sake, meant to be helping people. Not manufacturing misery. White-hot anger ran through his veins. Thumping his thigh with his fist, he forced himself to draw steadying breaths.

He sat on a small boulder and rested an arm across his knee. His wallet formed an uncomfortable bulge and he took it out and flipped it open. Tucked behind his driver's licence was a photo of the two brothers at Bondi Beach last Christmas. Jake stared at his brother's face, his sun-bleached hair wet and sticking out in all directions.

Aching, empty darkness filled him, expanding until he was no more than a shell of skin and bone. How had he missed signs of drug abuse in Pete?

He'd failed his brother. But the woman in the room next to his could lead him to Chan and if Jake had to make nice with her to get to the drug lord, he'd make nice.

Whatever it takes . . .

Two minutes short of the hour, Jake knocked on the door. "Marcy? It's Jake. Are you ready for our walk?"

A muffled groan was followed by sounds of creaking wood

and a thump. Possibly a pair of boots being dropped. It seemed Dr. Westcott hadn't lied about her headache. Jake might almost feel sorry if he didn't know what she was. He slammed the shutters on those thoughts. Right now, he had a role to play and that meant playing nice. For Peter. He softened his tone. "Marcy?"

"I'm coming. Just give me a minute." Muttered oaths filtered out before Marcy appeared in the doorway. Heavy-lidded, a fine pink line crossed her right cheek where it had rested on a crease. She turned a half circle as she struggled to put her arm into her jacket sleeve.

"Let me help. It's twisted." Jake straightened her sleeve and held the jacket while Marcy shoved her arm into it. As she faced him, he took hold of both sides of her zipper and fiddled until it locked together then slid the zipper up to mid-chest.

She blinked slowly as though not fully awake and turned the full force of her wide-eyed gaze on him. "I'm not a child, Mr Harris. Mild altitude sickness does not render me incapable, merely slower than normal."

His lips twitched with a fleeting desire to laugh at her school teacher formality. "My apologies, Miss Westcott. I won't make that mistake again." He gestured for her to precede him down the hallway. She swayed a little as she walked and fumbled with the door handle. He stood back and waited until, finally, she turned the handle the right way. They stepped out into the white-grey morning.

Sunshine could be bathing the peaks in gold but here, at

over five thousand metres, chill clouds curled around buildings and softened sharp outlines. Patches of ice dotted the rough track and within a few steps their breath was visible before merging into cloud. Marcy shoved her hands into her pockets and trudged as though in slow motion up the path and around the bend. After another dozen or so steps she stopped and rested against a rock wall. Peaceful Lodge had disappeared and mist muffled the sounds of activity around the teahouse.

She leaned back on her hands and bowed her head. "I didn't realise how challenging lack of oxygen would be. I trained on one of those altitude machines in the gym back home but nothing prepares you for the reality."

"Especially if you've been living at sea level. Where's home?"

"Sydney now. I grew up on a banana farm on the mid north coast of New South Wales. What about you?"

He shrugged. "I move around a lot."

She waited, patient, expectant. "Is that it?"

"Uh, sorry. Conversations with beautiful women have been few and far between in the past year." More like zero as he built up evidence against Al-Kohari. Before Pete's suicide, Jake had been offered a promotion to head office. Second-in-charge would have taken him out of the field. Slow suffocation behind a desk wasn't his idea of living and he turned it down.

But I could have been home. If I'd been at home, I could have saved Pete.

Now, only tracking down those responsible for his brother's death gave him purpose. And the doctor was his first solid lead.

He expelled an audible breath. If he expected this woman to open up, he had to offer more. Hell, she hadn't even shared the fact she was a doctor. He settled beside her on the wall and folded his arms across his chest. "I'm from Sydney originally, but I've been in Nepal a while. I prefer being outdoors."

"You're very lucky. I'd love to spend more time here." She peered up at him. "So does your family still live in Sydney?"

Shit. Marcy was only asking questions that *normal* people asked in conversation, but talking about Sydney meant thinking about Pete, and thinking about Pete would unlock memories he couldn't deal with.

Not yet.

Not now.

Not when he needed to be on his game with the doctor.

Attending his brother's funeral didn't count as going home. Jake swallowed bitterness and prepared to lie. "I haven't been home in a year. My parents took off in their caravan. I imagine they're somewhere in Western Australia by now."

"Joined the Grey Nomads, have they?" Marcy gave him a sweet smile, the first he'd seen from her. Dammit, there was even a twinkle of mischief in her grey eyes. She was attractive and, under other circumstances, appealing. Photos hadn't prepared him for the reality of Dr. Westcott.

He gripped the wall, pressing his palms into sharp stones, relishing the bite as they dug into his flesh. This woman worked for the Chans. He knew her for what she was, regardless of how sweet and innocent and good she looked. He shook his head.

"Haven't you heard that term? Over fifties who head off to explore Australia in campervans and caravans." Light and musical, her voice didn't match the sexy image in Nicholls' photo. It didn't belong to someone involved with the dark trade in drugs. It was sunshine and fresh air and it was dangerous.

The Bureau knew what it was doing when it banned getting up close and personal with suspects. Close contact humanised the target. Wrenching his focus back to his job, he grasped at the thread of conversation. "Yeah, I got it. I hadn't thought of my parents as belonging to that group."

"I'm sorry. I didn't mean to offend you. It's just—"

"No offence. Guess it's a matter of perspective. What do you do, Marcy?"

Her gaze slipped away and she hesitated a fraction too long. "I'm—an events coordinator. In Sydney."

Her lie sank like a lead weight in his stomach. That sweet smile could almost have seduced him into thinking she was naïve, but he knew it for an act.

So be it. He'd play along.

For now.

"I bet you meet all sorts of important people in that line of work. What sorts of events have you organised?"

"A car show for a major importer at the showground. It was a circus theme with precision acts to highlight that feature of the car. Did you see it in the newspapers?"

"No." But he'd be looking it up online first chance he had. Her answer had been quick and informed. She knew about it, had maybe even attended the function. But she was hiding her real profession. Why? Did she suspect him? Or assume she might be followed?

"Come on. Let's walk out on the ridge. If the mist lifts, it's a fantastic view and we won't be interrupted." He picked up her hand and took one step up the path. His arm was tugged back. Surprised by her resistance, he stopped.

Marcy stood in the middle of the path looking up at him. The heaviness of her breathing wasn't entirely due to thin air. Eyes wide, her tongue swept across her upper lip with a nervous flick. "What do you mean we won't be interrupted? From what?"

Shit. He hadn't meant to scare her. Grief for his brother had thrown him off balance. He had to do better than this. He was *better* than this. Somewhere there was a fine line he had to tread. A line between keeping his focus and playing the role of a man attracted to a woman.

Her.

"Sorry. I forgot you're not feeling one hundred per cent but mild exercise will help clear your head."

Intelligence and suspicion vied in the straight look she levelled at him. Despite her youthful appearance, she was a well-educated woman with a doctoral degree. He gentled his voice and softened his expression. "Walk with me, Marcy?"

She didn't budge. "Tell me what you do, Jake. You sound like you know about the mountains." Her eyes narrowed and he sensed she'd clam up at the slightest hint of lying from him. She wiggled her fingers and he was surprised to discover he was still holding her hand. He relaxed his hold.

A gleam of sunlight broke through the cloud cover. Soon the mist would lift and the valley would be visible. He shoved his hands into his pockets and met her gaze. "I'm in tourism. I lead groups into remote areas like Manasalu and Dolpa. Occasionally Everest too."

"Dolpa?" Her chin rose, interest piqued by mention of the remote region.

"Have you heard of it? It's quite remote and the permits are expensive although the government is making moves to reduce the costs."

"Um, yes, I've heard of it." She shook her head. "Maybe I'm misunderstanding this but isn't it a bad idea to reduce permit costs? I mean, here in Sagarmatha Park for instance, aren't there already too many climbers attempting Everest and dying because of traffic congestion in the death zone?"

Impressed by her grasp of the problem, it took him a moment to recall her guide's comment. "Wouldn't you like to climb the mountain?"

"Of course. But opening the floodgates will lead to more

deaths and people taking silly risks. It's an unscientific approach and more about money than safety."

Damn being an events coordinator. The scientist in her had jumped in, analysed the problem and offered logical opinion before he drew another breath. It was a timely reminder not to underestimate her.

"That's a practical way to look at it. Most people would be pleased to see the permit costs reduced. You're unusual in seeing through to the heart of the issue."

A soft blush rose in her cheeks and her gaze slid away again.

Surprised by that blush, he held out his hand for a second time and waited. Soon, the track would become busy with trekkers heading up to Base Camp and he wanted privacy. "Shall we continue our walk?"

She looked at his hand, cleared her throat and tentatively placed her hand in his. He curled his fingers around hers and smiled. Facial muscles unused to the expression protested. He relaxed a little as they strolled off the track.

It was time to dust off his rusty charm.

Chapter Three

Marcy pushed away the niggling thought she hadn't exactly told him the truth. White lies didn't sit comfortably with her, even those told in childhood to protect her twin sister from their father's anger. But there was something in Jake's eyes—correction, missing from his look—that made her wary.

And so she'd given Tamsin's job instead of her own. Pharmaceutical espionage was a fact of working in the industry and even though Jake was an unlikely spy, keeping quiet about her research was sensible.

Mist swirled and began to thin as they stopped beside a flat-topped boulder. Marcy scrambled up and wriggled across to make room for Jake. He hoisted himself beside her, bumping shoulders on the way up. No more than an inch separated their hips and the length of their thighs. Leashed power emanated from his muscular body, dangerous and exciting.

He leaned back on straight arms and crossed his booted ankles. "From here you'll see the valley spread out before you."

"You know this area so well. Why do you want to tag along

with me?"

Shut up, Marcy. Don't push it. Don't push it. Don't be the scientist.

He looked at her, his gaze teasing, testing the waters. "Why wouldn't I take the opportunity to walk with the prettiest woman I've seen?"

Okay, it wasn't the smoothest of pick up lines but for someone who'd spent so many lonely hours completing her doctoral thesis, it breathed a warm glow into her recent dateless existence. "That's the second time you've said that. I kind of like it."

Out here with the sun brightening the morning air, she noticed flecks of gold in his irises. Her gaze fluttered to his mouth. Firm lips looked like they knew how to bring a woman pleasure. Danger—pleasure. Which was the real man? The odd push-pull she felt around Jake roused her curiosity. Was he was playing a role simply to see if she wanted to hook up? Marcy couldn't tell, but there was a darkness in him that her cautious nature recognised even while she couldn't name it. It would be much safer to have nothing more to do with the mountain man.

"What do you say we do some exploring together?" His fingers brushed her cheek, held her chin.

A rush of heat flooded her belly, and ran between her thighs and safety began to seem overrated. Conducting a simple experiment seemed like a good start. She closed her eyes. Any second now his lips would meet hers and—

"Marcy, look. The cloud is lifting."

Her eyelids flew up. Jake was looking out beyond the rocky edge, his profile sharp against a blinding shaft of sunlight that pierced the swirling clouds and warmed her face.

The almost-kiss hung in the air between them, shimmering with possibility and hope. Jake turned to her, his eyes almost black. A reaction that could be associated with heightened sexual awareness. If that was so, why had he retreated? She drew back and hope dissolved like clouds burned off by sunlight.

A different heat crept up her face. Even without the *brainiac* tag to frighten him off, what had she expected? She jumped off the boulder and strode the few paces to the rocky edge. Stiff-legged, fists clenched, she sucked air into a painfully tight chest and looked over the valley without seeing what was before her.

Fuming. Embarrassed. Deflated.

She didn't need a clearer reminder of her undesirability. And she didn't need to look at Jake Harris to know he'd be either smirking or sympathising.

Neither was palatable.

He was playing her and that she wouldn't forgive. Hair rose on the back of her neck and prickles of heat ran down her spine.

Jake's hand landed on her shoulder and the other pointed out some distant feature. His baritone rumbled beside her but nothing he said registered.

She shrugged off his hand and stepped away.

Loose stones rolled towards the edge and her boots lost their grip. Arms wide, she slid towards open air. A scream tore from her throat.

Jake grabbed her elbow and hauled her to safety. If that's what being plastered against his chest could be called. Her legs were tangled with his, and arms like bands of steel held her fast. Everything about him was hard, including the gaze he levelled on her. Heart racing like a snowball down the mountain, she clung to his jacket.

"Hey, watch where you step, Marcy. I don't want you taking the quick route down. Not when we're just getting to know one another."

"Gee, you're a comedian." Her breath caught in her throat and she pushed against his chest.

He didn't budge.

"Two left feet are dangerous even off the dance floor. I'm fine now." Innate klutziness and her subconscious had pushed her into Jake's arms. She didn't need to stay there.

He relaxed his hold but didn't release her. "Did I do something wrong?"

Did he? Or was that just her going ape with frustration? "I wasn't the one who pulled away from—forget it."

"Ah, that." He looked her straight in the eye. "What sort of man would I be if I made advances on a woman with altitude sickness? Besides, I prefer to be the reason for your light-headedness, not taking advantage of it."

She swallowed her snarky comment. What had the poor guy done after all except bring her out for a walk and a look at the view? Oh, and saving her life. He wasn't responsible for her lacklustre love life, nor for her weird reaction to him. Ashamed of herself for attempting such a silly experiment, she brushed away his pathetic pickup line. "Thanks. I mean for saving me. You can let go of me now."

He backed her away from the edge and seated her before releasing his hold on her arms. "You're welcome. And you didn't answer my question."

Pinned by his gaze, his body blocking her retreat, she huffed and tried to recall what he'd asked. Maybe her timing was off, or maybe the altitude had messed with more than her balance. Her breath caught all over again; interest sparked in Jake's eyes, enough to fog up her safety goggles if she were in her lab.

"Sorry, I'm a bit light-headed. What was the question?"

"I thought we made a connection. Was I wrong?"

Unwilling to commit, she hedged. "Would that be a good thing?"

"Yes. Do you?"

Okay, Marcy, he's interested. Go with the flow. Do not blow this. "We could explore the connection and see what happens. I'm—open to the idea."

One side of his mouth rose and crinkles appeared beside his eyes. "Good. Since we're both *open* to the idea then, today, we're going to kick back, get to know one another and give you a chance to acclimatise."

With the opportunity for light hearted flirtation salvaged, she smiled and leaned back on her hands. "R and R sounds good. I'd like to check my emails before we head off anywhere though."

"Expecting to hear from someone special? Should I be jealous?" Definite interest sparked in his eyes.

Home and its problems, the worries she carried, faded. "Just—business."

Jake's crinkly smile dimmed. "The teahouse has a solar powered computer."

"Great. By the way, I didn't see you last night. Did you—?"

"I visited a friend down the track. Chandra knew I was coming in late and kept a room for me. But if I'd known who I'd meet here, I'd have arrived earlier." Jake leaned against the rock at her side and folded his arms across his chest. "Much earlier." The half smile that had begun with her agreement blossomed into a shattering, fully formed grin.

Despite the cool morning air, Marcy had an urge to fan herself. Including a trek up to Base Camp before her Dolpa research trip was one of her better decisions. She peeked at her new companion. Present view included.

They wandered back to the teahouse, passing several groups bound for Base Camp followed by a line of heavily laden yaks. Her heart knocked in her chest as the animals drew near. They might be placid but she quickened her pace and detoured up the incline, giving the beasts a wide berth. Cattle of any kind scared the bejeezus out of her.

She thrust the front door open and stumbled against their host. Embarrassment was a small price to pay for escape from the beasts. Chandra caught one arm and Jake grabbed the other. Muttering profuse apologies, she straightened her jacket and headed for the computer set up in pride of place outside the kitchen.

Jake slid along a nearby bench and leaned his back against the table. "You go first, Marcy. I've no pressing need."

"Are you sure?"

"Frankly, I love it when I can disconnect from all that stuff."

"I won't be long." She pulled out the wooden stool, sat and logged in. The internet connection was slow, as it had been at several stops along the track. She shook out her fingers and began playing a rock song on an imaginary keyboard while the computer whirred.

Her inbox appeared. She scrolled through work related names and clicked on an email from Tam.

Chandra placed a mug of tea beside her right hand.

Mumbling her thanks, she picked up the drink. Steam rose in welcome warmth around her nose and she blew across the surface before sipping. Through the steam, she read the message. Lowering the mug before she spilled tea over the keyboard, she read it again.

Sparse with details, the message was clear. Tam had left Sydney and her fiancé had disappeared.

Her emotional, big-sisterly self considered cutting short her trip to be with her sister. As she tapped a segment of Beethoven's Fifth Symphony with her left hand, her right curled around her mug and her mind churned through possibilities. Drawing a deep breath into her tight lungs, she set down her mug, typed a short reply and pressed send. The connection froze.

"Marcy?" Jake touched her shoulder and she frowned at the intrusion. "Chewang wants to speak to you when you've finished."

Her gaze slid past his hip to her guide waiting respectfully near the door. "I'll come back later and check if my message sent." She closed her account and pushed away from the table. "All yours."

##

Jake watched Marcy and her guide disappear into the communal dining area. It bought him time to check her story. Typing two-fingered, he entered his search parameters.

While he waited for the connection, he reviewed Marcy's reaction to the email. The short message had made her cheeks pale. She hadn't noticed his approach and he'd managed to read the sender's name, but not the message. Was Tam a member of the Chan family? Another question for Nicholls to answer.

When the page loaded, he whistled long and low. An image of Marcy with long, dark curls smiled invitingly at him. He checked the date. Two weeks ago.

So, she'd attended the car launch just as she said. Quickly, he scanned the paragraphs beside the uncaptioned photo. Media handout stuff and no mention of her name or title.

He enlarged the photo and studied it closely. Occupying the central position and leaning on the hood of a display car, Marcy gave the photographer a sultry look at odds with the woman Jake had taken for a walk. A little black dress hugged curves he'd only guessed at beneath her trekking gear and the plunging neckline revealed a small birthmark on her left breast.

He moved on from his examination of Dr. Marcia Westcott's shapely curves to two slightly out of focus figures in the background. Dressed in tuxedos, the men appeared to be deep in conversation. Almost certain one was John Chan, Jake tried to recall details of the man. Nicholls's photo had been snapped from Chan's right side. Chan's right hand clasped the shoulder of the other man as a friend might. His other hand held a champagne flute. The photographer's flash created a miniature starburst around what was probably a large gemstone on his little finger. Worth a fortune, but a drop in the bucket for a major drug dealer.

Jake moved on to examine Chan's companion and his breath caught in his throat. Anger seared Jake's gut and his hand curled into a fist.

'Never get familiar with your target; that's the first rule of undercover work.'

He'd berated himself for losing focus with Marcy, but proximity was a necessary part of his brief.

But there was Paul Rimmer, his good mate and former partner, talking animatedly with John Chan.

Red haze swirled in Jake's mind and bile rose in his throat. Paul knew who Chan was. A top agent, Paul's open association with the Chans made no sense.

Unless—

Suspicion sank like a stone in his stomach even as his mind rejected the possibility. It was ludicrous to contemplate that Paul knew who Chan was and failed to act. Only ten days ago, Paul had alerted Jake he was close to uncovering one of Chan's contacts.

Jake rested his chin on his hand.

Had Paul gone rogue?

Every fibre of his being shouted denial. He knew Paul too well. Lies and corruption linked Marcia Westcott to the Chan family but—Paul? How did he fit into the picture? Until Jake knew more about this woman, he couldn't afford to contact his former partner.

Mired in frustrating and incomplete links between his best friend, the doctor and the Chans, Jake stared at the screen.

Voices rose in laughter from reception as a large group tramped into the teahouse and dumped backpacks inside the door. Calling for the owner, two German men clumped over to him.

"*Guten tag.* Have you finished on the computer?"

Jake nodded and ended his session. He forced his fists to unclench and rose from the stool. "Be my guest."

"*Danke.*"

Jake shoved his hands into his pockets and slipped out the back door. Space to think and a few quiet moments to plan his next step were essential. His jaw tightened until it hurt. Was his best mate playing a double game?

#

Wondering what the urgency had been about, Marcy left Chewang. Their plans required minimal changes to accommodate Jake's company but her guide had itemised each detail again.

Marcy stretched and realised her headache had eased. Fresh, cold air and the promise of a hot man for company were a winning combination. Her lips stretched into a smile.

The trekker who had half turned when she passed him leaned on the counter and eyed her with more interest. She tossed him a casual hello before heading to the computer station.

Jake had vanished and two blond Germans sat in his place. She checked out the main rooms of the teahouse before knocking on Jake's door. Puzzled and a little disappointed that he had disappeared, she wandered outside.

Smoke drifted on the cool air, children played a game rolling a hoop with a stick but Jake was nowhere to be seen. Deflated, Marcy toed a stone out of the dirt, shoved her hands in her pockets and wandered off towards the lower section of Gorak Shep. Not that there was much to differentiate it from most other small villages en route to Base Camp, but it gave her something to do.

Pleased with her recovery, she maintained a slow pace. At

the end of the village, stone walls gave way to natural rock outcrops. Where the main path turned left, a smaller path led off at an angle from the well-trampled track. Half forgotten lines of a poem floated through her memory, about two roads diverging. Softly humming "Long and Winding Road", she chuckled at the butterfly choices her mind had made and turned back. Maybe the altitude had affected her after all.

# #

Jake pushed himself up the track in an effort to clear his mind. Coincidences didn't happen. He knew Paul, for God's sake, but his mate's relationship with Marcy had to be called in. Had Marcy beguiled his friend to the dark side? The Bureau would pull Paul off the case if he'd been compromised, and a prison term loomed if he was found to have knowingly aided the cartel. There must be something Jake could do . . .

Unless Paul was beyond saving.

Jake's gut roiled and his fingers itched to shake the truth out of Marcy. Peter was dead and Paul may be compromised while the doctor amused herself playing tourist. He rounded the path above the teahouse. Below him, the village buildings lined the track and there, heading away from the far end of the spill of houses, was Marcy. He hurried into Peaceful Lodge, aware that he might not get such a good opportunity again.

Small, like all teahouse accommodation, Marcy's room was the neatest he'd seen. All that scientific training in laboratories perhaps? Methodically, he searched her gear. Nothing out of the ordinary except—his finger hooked a pair of black, lacy undies. He raised his hand and checked them out. Very lacy.

An odd choice; Nepal wasn't exactly Romance Central. He replaced the lingerie and cast a final check around her room. Satisfied she would be unaware of his visit, he cracked open the door and listened.

Her passport would be in Chandra's safekeeping.

Jake slipped from her room and reached reception without encountering anyone. Chandra was in the kitchen with his wife. Their voices rose and fell in universal patterns of domesticity. The German contingent had settled outside with cans of beer and looked likely to spend the remainder of the day soaking up what sun there was.

Jake pulled out Chandra's safe box and picked the lock. He flicked through a stack of passports until he found an Australian coat of arms on a navy cover and flipped it open. Marcia Jane Westcott, twenty-seven, Sydney, Australia. What a pity passports didn't still include distinguishing marks. Nothing like permanent marks on the body to verify one's identity.

He mentally reviewed the photo Nicholls had shown him in Kathmandu. Under magnification, he'd seen the tattoo that graced her thigh and the online photo had revealed a birthmark on her left breast. The easiest way to check her bare skin was by seducing her. But her reaction to him on their morning walk didn't match the image of Marcy draped across the bonnet of a sleek sports car.

He checked the date on her passport. September of the

previous year. He skipped past the Nepalese visa until he found two pages with Immigration stamps—Fiji last Christmas and Bangkok as she transited through Thailand.

The front door of the teahouse squeaked as it was pushed open. He tossed Marcy's passport into the box, dropped the lid and pushed it quickly back below the counter before meeting Marcy's gaze. "Well, well, the wanderer has returned."

Marcy's face lit up as he leaned on the countertop and gave her a smile; it would be like taking candy from a baby. "Looking for a room, madam? I have a double with ensuite and views of the ocean if you wish."

She giggled, the sound delicious as ice cream in summer, and leaned on the counter facing him. She was a damned good actress; he'd give her that. She'd nailed the sweet and innocent look. "Got one, thanks. I—um, went for a walk."

Determined not to leave her alone until he'd worked out what was going on, he dug deep for the charm he'd once been told he had by the bucket load. Not his usual weapon in the field, but he'd leverage whatever worked. "I noticed. Fancy a beer before the guys out back run this place dry?" His smile came easier, and he jerked his thumb towards the back of the lodge.

What sounded like a beer-drinking song barrelled forth in lusty rounds.

She nodded and he fell into step beside her. Cold air clung to her jacket, chill on his fingers when his hand brushed her sleeve.

Pink-cheeked after her walk, her gaze sparkled. "Your

shout."

Chapter Four

Jake returned from a lukewarm shower and knocked on Marcy's door. Damp hair curled onto his collar and he pushed a wayward strand off his face. "Marcy? Are you ready for dinner?"

There was no answer.

Thinking she'd fallen asleep again, he tapped louder and cracked the door open. Her bed was neatly made, and her jacket folded on the end. He called again and pushed the door wide, but her room was empty. Her belongings were in the same place as earlier in the day. Only Marcy was missing.

Dammit. He'd taken ten minutes to have a shower and change and now he'd lost the damned woman. He strode down the hall and entered the communal area. The German contingent was grouped around one corner. Good-natured joshing and hands clamped around beer bottles suggested their afternoon session had continued into the evening.

Subtle jockeying for position opened a gap between bodies. In that split second, Jake spied Marcy before the Germans closed ranks around her.

Rivalry for her attention hadn't factored into his plans.

What did that say about him as an agent?

And as a man.

This morning, interest had sparked in her eyes and she'd been willing to kiss him in a holiday-romance kind of way. Her lacy black knickers reinforced the perception she was open to some fun. All he had to do was exhibit interest in her and he'd find out what he needed to know. But if he didn't lift his game, the small advantage of being first on the scene would become worthless.

Jake clapped a hand on the nearest shoulder. "Good evening."

The young man turned and saluted him with his beer. "*Guten abend.* Join us and the *schöne fraulein.*" He shuffled a half step and made a small space for Jake.

Across the table, Marcy was the focus of every male in the group. Mindful of the competition and the threat it posed to his plans, Jake parked his dark knowledge of her involvement with the Chans, and looked at her. Really looked.

Hands wrapped around a bottle of beer, her smile clung to her lips and her gaze flitted from face to face as though in disbelief at being the centre of attention.

God, what an actress.

He felt the sneer taking over his face and slapped a hand over his mouth.

Marcy spotted him. Her lips curved up in invitation, grey eyes wide and welcoming.

He hadn't left his run too late. He could play a role too if only he kept control of his anger and the grief that lay at its heart.

For Pete.

She slid along the bench and patted the spot next to her, as he'd done this morning.

His squeezed past the big, blond trekker and sat beside her. Several faces around the group revealed disappointment when Marcy's preference registered. He needed to stake his claim clearly. A burst of testosterone made him edge closer.

Marcy pushed a bottle beaded with drops of condensation towards him. "I thought you'd never get here."

"You mean you missed me? With this crowd of admirers, I'm surprised. And flattered." He smiled to take any sting out of his words, tapped his bottle against hers and drank.

"Frankly"— she leaned closer and placed her mouth near his ear. The scent of coconut shampoo teased his nose as she whispered—"they're a little overwhelming. I'm used to quieter places."

"Really? Aren't those events you plan big and noisy and crowded?"

She turned abruptly as though bitten and dropped eye contact. "Yes, of course. I just meant—I prefer to be able to hear myself think." She quickly tipped her bottle to her mouth and set it back on the table.

Her bottle was almost full, and he wondered about the party girl he'd seen online. Cleavage and long, dark curls.

He lifted his bottle.

And stopped halfway to his mouth.

Long, dark curls.

Her passport was over a year old. The photo sanctioned by officialdom showed Marcy with short, feathery hair. Just like now.

He leaned against the wall and stared at the scrubbed wooden table top. Mentally he placed the two photos of Marcy with Chan side by side.

The snake tattoo on her thigh could have been a temporary tatt but a birthmark on her breast would be difficult to fake. Something was wrong.

I've got to check out her birthmark.

His focus clicked back onto Marcy's face. Was she a superb actress, or had someone in the Bureau security stuffed up?

Seducing Marcy had just become the only means to his end.

Dinner arrived, carried on trays by Chandra and his wife. Bowls of dahl baht, rice, and chicken curry were set at intervals along the table and everyone piled their plates high.

Jake passed on the curry. Cast iron stomachs were no guarantee against a bout of food poisoning and he couldn't afford down time. Not when the number of questions thrown up about Marcy and where she fitted into the picture doubled with each piece of information he uncovered.

What was her role in the Chan organisation? Where did her *research* fit? If he was to stop the Chans once and for all, he had to extract whatever she knew.

And quickly.

"What's up, Jake? You look rather grim."

She had no idea how dark his soul was.

Peter might not have died if his big brother had been home. Or if Jake had taken time to get to know Pete's girlfriend. Dismissing the first year Arts student as a ditzy blonde had been a huge error of judgement.

Too late, he'd seen evidence of her addiction, discovered she was dealing to Pete and his brother's mates. He wouldn't allow that to happen to more families. He *would* stop the cartel's operation and take down anyone associated with it.

Including Marcy.

She pointed at his plate of dahl baht with her fork. "You should have tried some chicken. It's delicious."

"Bit of a stomach ache. Thought I'd play it safe tonight." His stomach roiled for real and he pushed his plate away. That sixth sense he'd learned to listen to raised its head. What was he missing?

"I've medication if you want it. I've brought standard treatments for a range of illnesses. Given that medical help is in short supply up here, it's better to be prepared."

"Girl Scout, were you? I'll be fine, thanks." He downed the rest of his beer and drew his plate back. Keeping his mouth occupied avoided conversation and gave him time to lock away dark memories.

The Germans on Marcy's other side drew her into their conversation and Jake dropped his fork onto the plate, sat back, and nursed a second beer.

Chewang joined them for a post-dinner cup of tea. "I wake you at five in the morning and you see sunrise from top of Kala Patthar. Okay?"

Marcy's eyes brightened and she nodded. "Five a.m. I'll be ready." She turned to Jake. "Are you sure you want to join us? I mean, I guess you've seen it dozens of times and you *are* on holiday."

The tentative attempt to stop him accompanying her was all the more reason to stay by her side. "I wouldn't miss seeing it with you. Chewang, wake me at five too, please."

"Will do, sir. Sleep well." Chewang ambled over and joined the group of guides and porters singing by the fire.

"I don't think I'm going to sleep, I'm so excited." She clasped her hands in front of her mouth. Excitement quivered through her body and her eyes shone like a child's at Christmas.

Her excitement was so natural and child-like Jake marvelled at how easy her seduction would be. He gripped his post-dinner cuppa and finished his tea. There was no better time than the present.

He wiped his mouth and leaned in close, his words for her ears alone. His breath stirred her hair and he slid a hand up her spine, resting it on the nape of her neck.

Like a cat being stroked, she arched her back.

"I've a sure-fire way to help you sleep if you want."
Gently, he rubbed his thumb across her bare nape.

Her eyes fluttered closed and she pressed into his touch. "I don't want to be drowsy from medication in the morning. I want to have every single sense alive and kicking when I see Mount Everest in the sunrise."

His hand stilled on her neck. He'd worried his suggestion was too obvious, but somehow, she'd misunderstood it. Or had she?

"I'm not talking pharmaceutical interventions, Marcy."

"Then what did you—oh." Her eyelids flew open and pink limned her cheeks as his meaning hit home. Her tongue touched the corner of her lips, focussing his attention there.

Beneath his thumb casually brushing across her skin, her pulse rate accelerated. She lowered her gaze, grabbed her mug of tea with both hands and buried her face in it.

Had he pushed her too far, too quickly with his suggestion? Did it matter if he waited a day or two to check out her birthmark? Yes, it did.

Dieter and Friedrich, the guys he had figured were a couple, strolled over and leaned on the table. "Marcy, *liebling*, we want you to play for us." Dieter held out a guitar.

Jake frowned. Could Marcy play? When had the Germans discovered that fact and why didn't he know it? What else had he missed? "Looks like you're needed." He slid along the seat and held out a hand, leaving her minimal room to pass.

Tremors transmitted through her fingers when she took his hand. She avoided making eye contact but as she squeezed past, her hip brushed his groin.

He bit back a groan. Needing to stake a claim in front of the other men, it was his fault for crowding her, but no one would muscle in on her this evening. He folded his arms and leaned against the wall.

Marcy picked up the guitar. Someone pulled out a stool and she sat and bent over the body of the instrument. She strummed the strings, adjusted a couple of tuning pegs and tried again. Satisfied with its pitch, she looked up. "What do you want to hear?"

Several voices called out pop tunes. She launched into a skilful rendition of a current Adele song and her audience enthusiastically joined in. Song followed song until an older Japanese man stepped forward and made a soft request. Marcy smiled and nodded before turning to the group. "Mr. Ishikawa would like to sing this in honour of our newest arrivals."

The room quietened down as Marcy plucked the opening notes and Mr. Ishikawa began to sing *Edelweiss* in a slightly tremulous but tuneful tenor.

Jake shook his head. A Japanese man accompanied by an Australian woman, singing an Austrian song to an international audience. It never ceased to amaze him how Nepal blurred nationalistic tendencies.

Marcy strummed the final chords. Mr. Ishikawa bowed low to his audience and acknowledged his accompanist. Uproarious applause unleashed a self-conscious smile and she inclined her head and returned the guitar to its owner.

Jake hung at the back of the circle of trekkers surrounding her. Finally the group dispersed, and he stepped up beside her. "You're a talented performer. That was great."

Her eyes were shadowed as she tipped her head and looked up at him. "Thank you. I really enjoyed playing again." She caught her lower lip in her teeth and drew an audible breath. "Jake—about your offer. I'm exhausted just breathing at the moment. I'm going to bed. Alone."

Without creating a scene, all he could do was accept her withdrawal. "Sorry, I didn't mean to come on so strong, but you're incredibly attractive. Can we take a rain check?"

Relief shone in her eyes and the tense line of her shoulders relaxed. She touched his arm and nodded. "Might be a good idea. Thanks. Good night, Jake."

"Sleep well." He watched her walk across the room and disappear down the hall.

Dieter thumped a heavy hand on his shoulder and jerked a thumb in the direction Marcy had taken. "Never mind, my friend. If not tonight, she will have you another night." He winked at Jake as Friedrich touched his partner's arm. "*Gute nacht.*"

Jake retired to his hard, narrow bed—alone—folded his arms behind his head and willed his body to rest. But his brain refused him sleep.

Inches away, separated from him by a thin partition, Marcy

lay curled in her sleeping bag. Barely muffled by the thin wood, she sniffed and sighed. Was she asleep already?

Dr. Westcott appeared to be sassy, sweet, sexy—and intelligent. Intelligent enough to hide in deep cover? Somehow he had to uncover the truth, starting with discovering if she was the same woman flagged by the Bureau. His gut instinct said she wasn't.

But if the woman in the photo with Chan wasn't Marcy, could it be her sister? And if that were the case, the inexperienced sexy woman next door might be in danger if the Chans knew of her specialty area.

A pair of lacy black undies floated through his imagination. He groaned and thumped his head against his arms.

It was going to be a long night.

Chapter Five

The mountain peak towered, silhouetted as dawn crept up the eastern sky in layers of pink and gold. Marcy turned back to the track, walked another dozen paces and stopped. Chest heavy, her lungs worked overtime as they climbed the last few metres to the top of Kala Patthar. Jake followed while ahead, Chewang picked out the easiest route. One more set of steps would bring her to her first goal—watching the sun rise over Mount Everest. Determined not to miss a second of the unfolding day, she hauled her protesting body to the top of the dark rock.

Chewang pulled out a flask, poured a cup of tea and placed it beside her. Jake helped take off her backpack. Although he breathed heavily in the thin air, his energy appeared undiminished. She, on the other hand, couldn't recall a time she'd been more tired.

She turned to the east. Haloed by the rising sun, Mount Everest reared up, its peak touching heaven. A sigh escaped and she blinked away moisture threatening to blur her view. Had her father seen the glory of such a sunrise the day he died? What if it had been the last thing he'd seen before the avalanche?

Tamsin, for all her strength of character, hadn't wanted to

visit, but to Marcy, the pilgrimage honoured the memory of their father.

"Does it live up to your expectations?" Jake's voice was pitched low, as though he didn't want to intrude into her special moment.

Without taking her eyes off the dawn blush beyond the range of mountains, she swallowed the lump in her throat. "All that and more."

"Where's your camera?"

A stab of disappointment pierced Marcy's communion with nature. She hadn't expected Jake to be one of those if-you-don't-have-the-photos-you-weren't-really-there people.

Without taking her eyes off the high peak, she pulled her digital camera from her pocket and offered it. "If you want to take a few shots, be my guest."

Bet he's seen this more than a few times already.

No matter how many times she saw it, the Himalayan sunrise would never lose its bittersweet magic for her. Past hurts disappeared as she imagined her father turning his face to the rising sun, imagined sharing the moment with him. Did the sun touch his final resting place somewhere on the mountain even now? Her throat closed around a lump of emotion she hadn't anticipated.

Beside her, Jake fiddled with her camera. There followed several bursts of clicks, then silence.

Chewang appeared on her other side and held his hand out

for the camera. "Sir, miss, I take photo of you two?"

"I'll get another of Miss Westcott, Chewang."

"Dr. Westcott, sir."

Silence, hard and cold as the glacier ahead shrouded them.

No, no, no, no. Marcy froze, her hands clinging to her rocky perch.

Now Jake would know she'd lied about her job. Guilt and embarrassment heated her cheeks and her pleasure in the morning dimmed.

He was going to turn tail and run. She knew it.

She turned to Jake. He'd been open about his job and she'd repaid him with a lie. Her innate caution coupled with a feeble attempt to shrug off the spectre of her university days had backfired. Big time.

Clever move, Marcy.

"Give us a moment, will you, Chewang." Was that a hint of frost in Jake's words, or her own sense of guilt looming over her head?

Her guide moved a few metres away.

Jake turned off her camera, shoved it in his pocket and raised an eyebrow. The unspoken question in his eyes accused her. And why wouldn't it? Finally, he sat on the rock at her side. "I'm guessing you wanted to avoid medical consultations while you're on holiday?"

Seconds passed. Should she reveal her specialty? Plumping for half-truth by omission, she lowered her gaze. "It can be awkward when I tell people what I do. Sorry about that."

He shrugged. "Hey, no big deal. I don't always reveal my job. When you're on holiday, you just want to kick back and not have to answer a lot of questions."

She pressed her lips together and looked sideways at him. "Does that mean I can't ask you to name the mountains for me or tell me the real legend of the Yeti?"

He folded his arms and pretended to consider. "Well, if I answer your questions, you should answer some of mine in return. Deal?"

"Deal." Agreement slipped easily from her lips. "I think."

"Hey, no backing out now. A deal's a deal. So"—he took her hand and led her to a small patch of level ground, stepped in behind her and rested his hands on her shoulders—"let's start with that one that looks a bit like a fish tail."

He pointed out and named major peaks, adding details about each. As he directed her attention to the far right of the mountain range, he brushed against her. Hard against soft, his body cocooned her back. Warm breath tickled her ear and his thigh connected with her butt. If she leaned back, she'd rest against his broad chest.

Anticipation stole what little breath she had, but as far as distractions went, she would file this moment under best holiday memories.

She peeped up at the square, stubbled line of his jaw and her chest constricted. Breathless seemed to be her new permanent state around Jake.

His hip connected with her bottom and a jolt of desire kicked in. Had she been right to refuse the mountain man's offer last night? Lean dating months as she worked on her doctoral thesis and wrote submissions for research grants had skewed her priorities.

What was I thinking to refuse him?

She had to remind herself she'd known him barely twenty-four hours and caution was her middle name. Jumping in the sack with a guy on such short acquaintance wasn't her style. But if he accompanied her down to Lukla—she grinned at the thought—all bets were off.

Buoyed by renewed optimism about Jake, her white lie seemed irrelevant.

And as he took her hand and helped her traverse a tricky stretch of path in an area flattened by long ago glacial movement, she all but burst into song.

##

Jake relaxed as they walked along the boulder-strewn path of the glacier towards Base Camp. Chewang's innocent revelation of Marcy's deception had handed him an opportunity to dig for answers. In return for his travelogue skills, he could ask questions.

Not about the email though. Nicholls would have to dig into Marcy's email records for those details. But that email and her odd reaction to it gnawed at his brain. Was *Tam* a code name for John Chan or one of his minions?

When the route they traversed levelled out, Marcy hummed snatches of old Beatles' songs. If he didn't know better, he'd say she hadn't a care in the world.

"You sound happy, Marcy."

In spite of a passing frown as she sucked in an audible breath, her smile was dreamy. "Today's the culmination of years of dreaming and saving."

Earnest and innocent. The two descriptors fitted Marcy in a way that contradicted Nicholls' sparse evidence.

And the sex siren in the online photo.

How could he reconcile this woman with that image? Was the trekker happily humming Beatles' songs the real Marcy, or was she an accomplished actress? His gut feeling tended towards the former. So what the hell was going on? Had she dined with Chan?

"Dreaming? Is that why you were humming *Lucy in the Sky with Diamonds*? That whole surreal dream world Lennon created?" Or was Jake reading drugs into everything about Marcy?

"Was I? Maybe subconsciously I picked up on the dream part."

"Some people claimed it was about LSD. You're a musician, what do you think?"

She pulled up, drew a few breaths and perched, easing the weight of her pack onto a boulder. He'd expected more of a reaction when he raised the issue of drugs, but she smiled as she rested against the rock. "People claimed there were drug references in lots of the Beatles' music and hey, it was the 1960's after all.

But I think drugs were the last thing on their minds." She stepped away and stumbled over a rock.

He grabbed her elbow and steadied her. "Watch where you're going. It's easy to fall when your muscles are tired."

"Thanks." She adjusted her backpack and stepped carefully over the next hundred metres before flopping onto a largish rock. "Phew. I need to stop again."

She drank from her Camel pack and toyed with her jacket zipper. "I read somewhere that song was inspired by Lennon's son, Julian's painting at preschool. It wasn't about drugs at all, just a child's painting combined with Lennon's memories of Lewis Carroll's *Alice*. I suspect people see what they're looking for rather than what's there."

Jake stared at her and something shifted inside him. The idea of cold-blooded seduction shouldn't affect him.

But with Marcy, it did.

Had he allowed emotion to cloud his judgement? His gut told him Marcy was clean but the evidence from Nicholls' file told a different story. He had to see her body. That was the only way to see if she was the woman who had dined with Chan. And that meant seducing her.

Marcy tipped her head back and looked up at the summit towering above them. Longing to reach the peak was clear in every yearning line of her body.

He beat back the little voice of conscience with cold logic. She'd quickly forget a casual affair on the track to Everest when she left.

"Shall we continue?" She pushed off the rock and followed Chewang.

Jake nodded and slung his pack over his shoulder, following at a distance. Right now, he didn't trust himself to maintain the façade of camaraderie with Marcy.

Base Camp came into view and Chewang guided them to a group led by one of his cousins. A small ethnic group, the Sherpas were close-knit and inter-related. Jake excused himself on the pretext of visiting a fellow guide and wandered off.

Once out of sight, he shrugged off his pack and pulled Marcy's camera from his pocket. Quickly, he flicked through the shots he'd snapped earlier, not lingering over those she'd taken during her stopover in Bangkok. Typical first-time traveller shots.

Flicking further back, he reached a series of photos from the car launch. Sexy as all hell, long, black hair curled onto her breasts and the little black dress was slit high up the thigh revealing her tattoo.

Her gaze connected with the photographer, and she smiled as though they shared a secret joke.

In the frame a little way behind her were his best friend and John Chan. Both men watched her posing for the camera. Paul's expression was like any man's looking at a beautiful woman but Chan's face had been caught in a moment of predatory intent. Like a snake waiting for the moment to strike, his eyes glittered.

Jake zoomed in on the photo, trying to pick up any clue on

the situation. Why did it keep coming back to Paul? Was it possible his mate had hooked up with Chan in order to infiltrate the drug trade? But if so, why wasn't Paul here with Marcy, following the trail to Everest, then on to Dolpa?

And why the hell Dolpa? What was Marcy looking for on the remote plateau? Almost nothing grew and there was little to attract people to the desolate area. Aside from the annual harvest of fungi for the Chinese herbal market. Casual conversation about drugs hadn't provoked a reaction but she'd been interested when he mentioned Dolpa.

Was there a possibility she'd discovered a new source of materials in the region, or another method to manufacture synthetic drugs? Nicholls had referred to natural drugs able to be legally imported into most countries. That seemed more likely.

Satisfied he'd gleaned all he could from Marcy's camera, he picked his way through the bright yellow and orange tents grouped along the rocky site. He headed for the larger of two circles, certain he'd find her at its centre. Her natural warmth and interest in others drew them to her like a magnet.

She caught sight of him and grinned. "Jake. Glad you made it back. Nathan here is about to leave for First Camp and was anxious to catch up when he heard I'm travelling with you."

His focus had been entirely on Marcy but he switched his attention to a young man with a shock of red dreadlocks and an electric blue jacket. "Hello, Nathan."

His brother's best and oldest schoolmate strode over and

pumped Jake's hand. "Hi, Jake. I hoped I might meet up with you while I was here. Mum and Dad said to say hello if I did. I haven't seen you since—"

"Yeah." His jaw tightened and his throat closed over the words he still couldn't speak. He clamped a lid on the image, never far from his mind.

Two months since Pete's death.

He didn't want Marcy to hear any mention of his brother. He jerked his head towards the upper trail. "So, you're attempting the mountain?"

Nathan shuffled his feet and Jake remembered how close Pete and Nathan had been. The lad was still hurting. "Yeah. My graduation present from the oldies."

"Good luck. Fine weather's been predicted for the next few days."

Nathan's throat rippled and his lips clamped together before he thrust a hand into an inside pocket and pulled out a photo. "I've brought Pete with me. We were going to see the world together."

Jake's stomach gripped like he'd been sucker-punched.

Whatever it takes, I'll bring them to justice.

He gripped Nathan's shoulder. "Thanks, Nathan."

Chewang stepped into view and brought his hands together in the traditional manner. "Excuse me, Doctor, sir. We depart soon and walk in daylight."

Marcy acknowledged her guide and rose from her seat.

"It's been wonderful to meet all of you. Best of luck."

A middle-aged woman came forward and hugged her. "One day it will be your turn, Marcy. Believe that and keep your eye on the goal."

"Thanks, Janet. I will. And I'll be looking for your posts about what it's like on top of the world. Good luck with breaking that record." Marcy picked up her pack, hitched it into place and waved goodbye, then followed Chewang out of the campsite.

On the return trip, Marcy needed to rest several times, and a frown puckered her brow. Altitude sickness had returned, but Jake's offer to carry her pack was met with a determined refusal. By the time the lights of Peaceful Lodge appeared, it was nearly dusk.

He followed her to her room and helped ease off her boots and jacket. As he tugged her shirt out of her trousers, she fell back onto the bed. With a groan, she flung an arm across her eyes.

"I'll be right back." Frustration gnawed at Jake, but he put his plans for the evening on hold and slipped out to the kitchen. He wasn't such a bastard that he'd attempt seduction of an ill woman. Playing nice tonight would reap rewards tomorrow.

Softly, he knocked and pushed the door open. "I've brought you a cuppa. There's a couple of biscuits if you can manage them but I'm staying put until you've drunk your tea."

She peeped beneath her hand. "Thanks. Would you mind diving into my bag—the top pocket—and finding my first aid kit please?"

Yesterday he'd searched the contents of her bag. He knew exactly where her medi-kit was but he made a show of looking before triumphantly holding the zippered bag aloft. "You want Diamox tablets?"

"Yes, please." She gave him a half smile when he popped the blister pack and the tablet fell into her hand. "Thanks. Tea and sympathy for supper and a good sleep and I'll be fine tomorrow." She swallowed the medication and the rest of her tea and lay back.

"I can't be bothered undressing. See you in the morning, Jake." Her words slurred and her eyelids fluttered down like a dark fan on pale cheeks.

He opened the zipper of her sleeping bag and spread it over her. "We'll take it easy heading back tomorrow. Night, Marcy."

Deep in thought, he returned to the dining area and stood looking through the window. Judging character, sifting lies from truth, these were his strengths. But at the end of his second day with Marcy, he felt no closer to unravelling the mystery of her.

A half moon hung low on the horizon, silver-bright in the dark sky. Too restless to sleep, he wandered outside, needing the cold, empty night to smother an out-of-character surge of sympathy. The woman might be making drugs for the cartel. Voices argued in his head.

She's not.

But the proof is in the photo.

Is it?

The proof was in twin marks on her body, which he had no hope of uncovering tonight. Proof she was the woman who had met John Chan.

Or that she isn't?

Chapter Six

Sydney, Australia

John Chan snapped open his phone and checked the caller ID before answering with a sharp, "Have you found her?" It wouldn't do to address his father or uncles in such an arrogant tone and sharp words. Those he paid to do his bidding didn't matter.

"I've established that she caught a flight to Kathmandu via Bangkok. I'm sending an operative in to track her down. Do you still want him to eliminate her?" Iceman's cool tone held a hint of condescension. Perhaps his arrogance now outweighed his usefulness.

Chan clenched the phone. He needed the operative within the Bureau until he had the woman in his power. After that ...

An image of the woman at his father's birthday party filled his memory. Beautiful, sensual, and stringing him along right up until she stole from him. Death was too quick and merciful for the dishonour she had inflicted on him. Dishonour demanded vengeance, as did his thwarted desire for the woman. He'd played her game and courted her, right up until Rimmer had declared himself, proposing to her in a very public way. He'd hidden his anger and congratulated the man while planning his demise. Soon she would be in his power.

"No. I want her brought to me. Untouched." He ended the call. Before he killed her himself, he planned to make the bitch pay with her body. The thought of her lush curves, what he would do to her, how he would make her beg for every indignity he heaped on her shining black head . . . He sucked in a deep breath. Anticipation made him hard.

He unzipped his trousers and stroked himself, working his hand as he pictured her plump red lips servicing him until he came down her throat. He would come . . . he would . . . He pumped harder, faster, desperate for relief.

With a groan, he leaned his forehead against the cold plate glass window. He wanted to come, but without the woman's pain, release remained out of reach.

He should never have played her game, but the tantalising offer of a woman who would choose him over her fiancé had been irresistible. At dinner the night before Honourable Father's party, she had hinted her choice was made; that he was the chosen one. His efforts should have brought her to his bed, rewarded him with her willing passion; instead, she had played him for a fool and accessed his computer.

He thumped the glass panel and roared his frustration. "Does she think she can blackmail me with what she stole?" Many would pay a high price to get their hands on information that could destroy his family and bring down the cartel.

If they got to her first.

He would find her and *he* would kill her—slowly and painfully.

Chapter Seven

Marcy slid along the wooden bench in the dining area, tucked herself into a corner and wrapped both hands around her mug. She had woken feeling marginally better but her stomach revolted at the thought of anything more than tea. Conversation rippled around the table as the German group packed up.

Dieter and Friedrich clumped over to her. She stood, ready to shake hands but they laughed and kissed her cheeks. Friedrich took both her hands in his. "Goodbye, Marcy. It was nice meeting you and hearing you play. Have a good trip back."

"Thanks."

"Have fun with your mountain man." Dieter winked and laughed as heat filled her cheeks.

They threw her a cheeky wave before joining their companions. After the departure of the large group, the teahouse fell quiet and Jake's absence became more marked.

Chandra came in with a fresh pot of tea. "*Namaste*, Marcy. How are you this morning?" He topped up her mug and set the teapot in the middle of the table.

"Better, thanks, Chandra. Have you seen Mr. Harris yet?"

Her voice tailed off into a croak. She coughed and sipped more hot tea.

"He went out early. He said you would sleep late after taking medicine last night."

"Looks like I was right." Hands in pockets, Jake sauntered into the dining area. "Did you sleep well?"

Her heartbeat kicked up a notch and a ridiculous sense of optimism filled her at the sight of him leaning against the doorframe. Dreamless, drug-induced sleep had a strange effect on her morning view of the world. But then, the sight of Jake waiting for her with a smile on his face would do any woman's heart good. "I'll be fine to walk today."

He nodded at the empty space in front of her. "Have you eaten already? I was going to join you for breakfast."

"Not really hungry, but don't let that stop you."

At least, that was true about food. Where Jake was concerned—totally different ballgame. Last night played through her mind. Jake, all concerned for her welfare and bringing her a cup of tea. Had he really tucked her in? And the night before . . .

Let's take a raincheck.

Every lean inch of Jake was temptation personified. Would tonight be rain check time?

"Breakfast for one please, Chandra." Their host headed to the kitchen and Jake joined her at the table, sliding in until his long legs invaded her space. His knee touched her thigh, sparking tingles when he didn't move away.

Sipping her tea, she tried to gather her woolly thoughts before their host returned carrying a plate of scrambled eggs, some heavy bread and a second mug.

Her gaze collided with Jake's. He pushed the plate between them and picked up a fork. "Have you tried to eat anything? You missed dinner last night."

She shook her head. "Don't want to risk it."

Jake broke off a piece of bread and forked a small amount of egg onto it. He raised it to her mouth. "Try a little sunshine power. It's delicious." Dark chocolate eyes challenged her to refuse his offer.

The aroma of fresh, scrambled eggs set her nose twitching and her mouth watered. Damn, but she was hungry after all. Giving in to temptation, she leaned in, lips parted. His fingers grazed her lower lip as he popped the morsel in and she closed her mouth, capturing the tip of one finger.

His gaze zeroed in on her mouth, his eye colour changing from chocolate brown to black velvet within a heartbeat.

She applied gentle pressure before releasing her hold. If it worked for Tam, there was no reason it couldn't work for her. Slowly, she swept her tongue over her lips and into the corner of her mouth.

Jake's eyes remained fixed on her lips, his only movement a slight shift towards her. "A few more mouthfuls like that and you won't reach Dengbouche today."

Danger and promise threaded through his words and

stroked down her spine. A night or two with Jake at a lower altitude would offer all the sensual pleasure she could want.

His mouth stretched in a smile that reminded her of the big cats at Taronga Park Zoo. "Chandra, please bring a plate of food for Dr. Westcott. Not that I mind sharing with you, but you need strength for the walk. I want to be at a more *convenient* altitude tonight."

# #

A couple of hundred metres lower and two hours into their walk, Lobuche came into view, a line of small, colourful buildings huddled along the track. They passed a bright yellow sign, its red arrow pointing the way back to Mt Everest as they entered the village. In deference to Marcy's health, Chewang called a halt and they rested a little longer than usual. But with each downward curve of the trail past the Khumbu Glacier, the tightness in her chest eased, replaced by anticipation. Tonight, she would take a leaf out of her sister's book.

Jake Harris was an opportunity not likely to cross her path again.

As they approached a Sherpa cairn, strings of prayer flags flapped in the wind. Jake shrugged off his backpack and turned to help her. "Did you stop here on the way up?"

"I did but the weather wasn't good. I'd like to take a couple of photos while the sun's out. I know my father stopped here—" She bit her lip and turned away. Her father's diary spoke of his feelings in this place where trekkers and guides alike were reminded of their mortality on their way to conquer a mountain. Had her father sent up a prayer here?

Some prayers aren't answered.

"Your father came here to climb Everest? Did he succeed?"

Sorrow exploded like a physical pain in her chest. After more than ten years, the bitter tears caught her unawares. They flowed only because she knew she was following in her father's final footsteps. Blinking furiously, she struggled to contain them. Her father had known the risks and still he had left his young family for a chance at his dream. "Not exactly. He was killed in an avalanche."

"I'm sorry." Jake gently squeezed her shoulder.

His broad chest seemed capable of absorbing all her pain and offering oblivion. If only she could bury her head against his shoulder and weep. For her father and for his lost dream, the one she was determined to fulfil one day.

"Are you okay?"

She brushed the back of her hand across her eyes and nodded. "Yes. It's just—somehow I feel nearer to him here than at home. Silly, I suppose, but seeing this country the way he did, I can almost share that last trip with him. Not that he would have allowed a girl to go with him."

Jake patted a section of smooth rock and offered her a hand. "Where's your camera?"

Fumbling, she opened her zippered pocket, extricated her camera and fiddled with the power button. She sniffed and cleared the lump in her throat that rose whenever she thought too long about her father. When she raised her eyes, Jake's were focussed on her. Strength and reliability exuded from him, but beneath the surface, she sensed something deeper, dark and dangerous.

To me? A spider-shiver tap-danced through her stomach.

Shaking her head, she stepped away. "Let me take one of you instead." She raised the camera. Anything to hide her red nose and eyes. And the frisson of fear that slipped down her spine. Jake looked every inch a mountain man, but that look in his eyes reminded her of Tamsin's Paul. Both men had the same quiet intensity.

Jake plucked the camera from her fingers.

Lips parted in surprise, she tipped her head up.

His hand slid down her arm and he squeezed her hand. "I'm not the one who's looking for closure here."

"Is that what you think I'm doing? Looking for closure?"

"You're looking for something. Your father was here. Maybe you need to deal with his loss before you can move on."

#

Jake was good at dispensing advice but damned if he could follow his own suggestion. He waited for Marcy to settle on the white-painted *stupa* and lined up the painted eyes either side of her body. A wistful look settled on her face and he clicked off a burst of shots. Moving further back, he took a couple of the whole structure then zoomed in again. Marcy's gaze was turned to the faraway mountain.

Climbing Everest was a compulsion for Marcy—Jake understood that—but on a powerful, personal level, it gave her greater motive to make big money.

He sighed and lowered the camera. The more he learned about her, the less he understood how she could be involved with the Chans.

A shuffling movement rippled through the groups taking a break at the memorial. Jake looked back along the path they'd traversed as the crowd parted to reveal a police escort cutting a swathe through the onlookers. The troop moved quickly, looking neither right nor left. Handcuffed within a human cage of policemen trudged a lone male prisoner.

Marcy jumped down from her perch and hurried to stand beside Jake. She grabbed his forearm and squeezed. "The poor man. Where are they taking him?"

Ragged and bruised, the prisoner marched past them, eyes downcast.

Sympathy oozed from her words, undeserved and ridiculous.

Jake chased criminals and locked them away, knowing his actions protected others. "Don't lose sleep over him. He's a prisoner under guard, not a charity case."

Why was Marcy upset? It was ridiculous to worry over a felon and yet—

He looked down at her hand on his arm. White knuckled, she clutched him like he was her personal life raft.

Was the prisoner an all-too-real reminder of what happened to criminals in this country? Care for others seemed to be an essential part of Marcy's character. Maybe that was what was pricking his subconscious—the implausibility of Marcy being involved in drugs. An inconvenient tendril of protectiveness curled up within him.

Tense and shaking, Marcy tore her attention from the prisoner and levelled her gaze on Jake. Was the emotion in her eyes fear or guilt?

He covered her cold hand with his warm one and patted it. "They're probably heading for Lukla and a ride to the capital where he'll stand trial."

Her cheeks paled. Abruptly, her grip on his arm relaxed and she fell against the last policeman.

Jake grabbed her arm and managed to spin her back into his chest. Accident or not, her tumble into the police officer could see her arrested if his captain chose to be difficult. Slumped against his chest, he was unsure if she was conscious. Holding her tightly, he leaned close to her ear. "Say nothing or you're likely to spend tonight in a Nepalese jail."

An officer in charge of the group called a halt and stalked back, eying Marcy with a grim expression. In Nepalese, the officer demanded to know who she was and what she was doing.

She struggled to lift her head from his chest.

Jake held her firmly, and pressed her head into his shoulder, muffling any attempt at speech. Determined to keep her in his custody, he replied in the local dialect. "She fainted. She turned too quickly and fell against the officer."

Chewang hurried forward and confirmed Marcy's recent bout of altitude sickness.

A muscle spasmed in the officer's jaw. For long seconds it was touch and go whether he believed them. "See to her." The officer turned his back and set his men marching down the track.

Jake held Marcy close as the police disappeared around the bend. She was trembling in his arms.

His hand slid from her head to her back, rubbing a small, soothing circle. As he relaxed his hold, she pushed his chest. He took a step backwards. Words of comfort died as stormy eyes glared up at him. Her lips looked as though she'd been kissed, not pressed hard into his jacket.

She jabbed a finger at his chest. "Why did you hold me back? Do you think I can't speak up for myself?"

She reminded him of his childhood pet, a small bantam hen that was a match for anyone trying to invade her nesting box. All black and white feathers, gimlet eyes, and attitude. He bit back a chuckle.

"Grabbing you seemed a good idea when you fainted. I thought you'd prefer my arms to incarceration in a Nepalese cell. In case you haven't noticed, the police here don't have a sense of humour."

"And you think you have some responsibility for me?" Arms rigid at her side, anger vibrated through her, rolling over him in waves that made a mockery of his instinct to protect.

Anger grew in Jake's chest. "What's got into you, Marcy? Was that *faint* deliberate?"

Fury flashed in her eyes before she lowered her gaze. "Don't be ridiculous. Of course not." Her chest heaved and indignation leapt out of every pore. "But I don't need some white knight charging in to rescue me. Just because I don't speak the language, you don't have to clamp me to your chest like you're my personal life preserver."

"*Doctor* Westcott, it may have escaped your notice but this is not Australia and the police take a dim view of any perceived interference in—"

"Don't talk to me. Just"—she held up a hand and backed away—"don't say another word." She stalked over to her backpack and heaved it around her shoulders. It thumped heavily and she stumbled against the stupa. She rubbed her knee, threw him an angry glare and set off down the track.

Chewang quickly followed.

Jake gritted his teeth and stalked to his backpack.

Women!

#

How dare he?

Marcy absolutely, positively wasn't going to speak another word to Jake. Ever. She marched on, barely hearing the thump of her boots on the track for the blood pounding in her ears. Chewang edged past her, taking his usual position at the head of their small group. Somewhere behind, she assumed Jake followed.

Silence she could cut with a knife stretched between them as Dengbouche came into view, its squat buildings and dry stone walls lining the path. Lower than Lobuche but still well above the tree line, the village was a welcome sight after their argument.

The constriction around her lungs and heavy head had eased but, in its place, a new heaviness lay on her spirit. Jake had taken her right to defend herself and treated her as a helpless female, just like her father had. The revelation was more bitter than the quinine solution she'd painted on her fingernails as a nervous, nail-biting teenager.

She wouldn't be spending the night with Jake, not after his macho display. Why did the men in her life think they could just take over?

Ignoring Jake, Marcy turned to her guide. "Chewang, which teahouse did we stop at last time? I'd like to use their shower."

Determined to wash away her blues and a portion of the dirt accumulating in her pores, she prayed there'd be plentiful hot water available, as advertised on the tin shed shower block. Hot water pouring over her was the only comfort she needed tonight.

Chewang indicated two houses further along. "That one, Doctor. The blue door."

"Thank you." She marched inside and waited for the owner to appear. "I'd like a room for me and one for my guide please."

"And one for me too, please." Jake leaned on the counter

beside her.

Their host looked from one to the other. "Would you like rooms together?"

"Yes." Jake's response shot out faster than her dissent.

She would show him she was more determined. "No. We don't really know one another, do we, *Mister* Harris?"

"That's not for want of trying, *Doctor* Westcott. I suggest we talk over a cold beer." His lazy gaze met hers.

Her earlier desire shot a bolt of heat low in her belly. She gripped the strap of her pack. "No, thank you. I'm going for a hot shower." She turned on her heel and followed the bemused teahouse owner to her room.

Privacy in a teahouse or tent was a relative term, but once out of sight, if not out of hearing, she slumped on her narrow bed and bowed her head into her hands. Jake lived and worked in Nepal. He must know what the Maoists had done. Reports of torture and mistreatment of prisoners were common, yet he'd done nothing when the police escort passed them by. Aside from preventing her making her feelings known. And catching her when she'd blacked out for a second or two.

Blasted altitude sickness.

She dragged her fingers through her stiff, sweaty hair and grimaced. Yanking off her jacket, she hauled her pack onto the bed. Somewhere in the second pocket lay her toiletry bag and a carefully rationed bottle of all-in-one shampoo and conditioner. Outside the back door, five dollars would buy her a short, hot shower. She pulled out her travel wallet and checked her reserve. Damn it, this was a ten-dollar shower day.

#

Jake logged off the teahouse computer and sat back. Nicholls' email confirmed Marcy had a twin sister named Tamsin—*Tam of the email*. Jake had no idea if the twins were identical or fraternal, but it was possible Marcy's sister looked enough like her to cause confusion. Had someone at the Bureau stuffed up? Could Tamsin have been the twin who met John Chan in Sydney? Were the sisters working the drugs thing together, one to make contact with the Chans, the other to do what? Research?

Every piece of information about Marcy threw up more questions. He returned to first principles; was Marcy the sibling who had met John Chan?

Proof's on her body.

And that body was currently in the shower out the back.

Jake strode through the back door and turned the corner. Snatches of *Yellow Submarine* floated from the shower shed on wisps of steam. He tapped on the wooden post then tugged the door open and stepped inside.

Bare, wet, soapy skin glistened in late afternoon sun slipping through the gap beneath the tin roof. Hands engulfed in a lather of shampoo, Marcy stood with her back to the door, a modest bikini her only clothing. As she turned, her eyes were scrunched closed against the shampoo. She tipped her face up to the bucket suspended overhead.

A flash of creamy thigh was gilded by sunlight. His voice dried in his throat and his ability to think rationally disappeared as his blood headed south.

One hand shielded her eyes from the shampoo while she groped for the rope with the other. Once, twice, she missed. "Dammit, where is the blasted thing?"

Jake reached across and silently guided it into her hand.

She pulled the rope and hot water spilled over her head and shoulders, splashing his shirt. Soap bubbles raced down her body, gliding over her hips, under the edge of her bikini bottom.

Jake swallowed and stepped back. He had to get out before she saw him. Before—

She wiped water off her face and opened her eyes. For a heartbeat or two she froze, looking at him looking at her. Her lips parted and a shriek gurgled from her. Both arms wrapped across body parts that proclaimed her sex before she spun away from him. "Get out. Good grief, what are you doing in here? Get out!" Peeping over her lightly tanned shoulder, she was a picture of demure outrage and sexy as hell.

Bemused but unable to turn away, Jake found his voice and his sense of humour at the same time. "Which do you want, Marcy? Shall I go now or stay and answer your question?"

"Go. Just hand me that towel first."

Jake looked at the exposed wooden strut from which hung a camping towel not much bigger than a hand towel. He held it out by the top two corners and shut one eye like a painter sizing up his model. "This won't hide much."

"Close your eyes."

He grinned and closed his eyes. Marcy was delusional if she thought he wouldn't still see her. The image of her delicate curves was imprinted on his brain for all time and his hands itched to shape them for real. Slim waist, softly rounded hips and breasts that would fill his hands.

Not what he should have seen, yet more than he'd expected to see.

But maybe what, subconsciously, he'd known since that first morning.

Marcy's thigh was clean. The gecko-snake could have been henna and temporary, but her arm had shielded her left breast. And any definitive birthmark.

He stepped out and shut the bath-shed door. Tattoo-free Marcy wasn't aware he knew about her sister. But the more he thought about it, the more likely it seemed she was shielding her sibling. From what he still had to discover.

Hands in pockets, he strolled down the track and considered how he would play the next few hours. It would be very satisfying to push her buttons. Unsettled, she might just let something slip.

# #

Cheeks hot but dignity restored, Marcy marched back into the common room of the teahouse.

Jake was seated beside a window, hand curled around a

mug of tea and watching passers-by on the track.

She stopped short of the table and crossed her arms over her chest. A drop of water made its way down her neck and she wriggled her shoulders at the ticklish sensation.

Jake's amused gaze met hers over his mug. He pushed a chair towards her with his foot and indicated the second mug of tea steaming on the table in front of it.

Did the man think he could waltz into her shower and take inventory of her body then sit there calmly offering her tea? Memories of desire flaring in his eyes shot tingles to every pulse point. Damn his assumptions and his smug face and damn the fact that her body still trembled with awareness of him.

Smug bastard. "What the hell did you think you were doing walking in on me like that? Is that how you treat all your clients?"

"Only one beautiful, dark-haired temptress. And you're not my client. Besides"—he sipped his tea—"you were clothed. What's the problem?"

"You're saying it's my fault that you saw me—saw—"

"Saw you in your *bikini*? Not that I'm complaining, but what's the problem?" He grinned, a full-blown, downright sexy-assin grin that heated her almost as much as his gaze, currently taking a leisurely circuit down her body. Like he was remembering and liked what he saw.

She doubted her cheeks could get any hotter. Hands fisted at her sides, she silently counted to ten. "Are you going to apologise?"

"For seeing you in your *bikini*?"

"Stop saying it like that."

"Like what? How am I saying *bikini*, Marcy?" Crinkled laughter lines beside his eyes deepened while his grin grew even wider. Devastatingly wicked, it fuelled both her anger and her desire. Damn, the man should be labelled *lethal when laughing*. How was she to give him a dressing down, as Grandma called it, when she could barely remember why she was angry with him? His smile distracted her and reminded her what it was like to be wanted.

And therein lay her dilemma. She wanted Jake.

And mountain man Jake wanted her.

The thought zapped through her veins and heated parts much further south of her cheeks. She shifted her weight from foot to foot in a bid to ease the pressure.

"Like you enjoyed it. And like you're enjoying it still. It's not gentlemanly." God, she sounded like her grandmother but Jake threw her off course when he looked at her like that. Like he wanted to gobble her up, boots and all. "So, apology?"

"I'd have to be sorry about what I did. I'm not. But if you want to get even, I'm going for a shower in a few minutes. Feel free to gate crash." He finished his drink and threw her a wink as he stood. "I promise not to scream."

Her mouth opened and closed like a goldfish. By the time she'd composed a withering retort he'd disappeared down the corridor to his room. She stamped her foot and growled.

Insufferable prick.

He had tickets on himself if he thought she'd be joining him in the shower. Or anywhere else. But her body disagreed with her brain. An image of Jake all wet and slick and soaped up for her delectation refused to budge from her imagination. Her heart hammered. She licked her lips, suspecting herself of a hitherto unrealised penchant for bad boys.

Jelly legs threatened to upset a dignified retreat from the public area. She slipped into the vacant seat and picked up the mug of tea he'd ordered for her.

Get a grip, Marcy.

Trouble was, she knew what she wanted to grip. Six feet of wet man. She buried her face in the mug and prayed for amnesia.

Marcy closed her email account and rested her elbows either side of the keyboard. Hiding her face in her hands, her heart ached as though a fist squeezed it, constricting her ability to breathe.

Tam was in trouble, though exactly what sort of trouble was frustratingly unspecified. But within the simple email, her message was clear. *Stay where you are and out of sight. Do not come home.*

Why?

Marcy's glib remarks to Jake about being an events coordinator assumed a menace beyond her simple lie. Could they endanger her sister?

I had to try to be super cool Tam instead of boring, nerdy Marcy.

Her lone hope lay in Jake not being interested enough in her crappy subterfuge to look her up online. Quietly, she promised to be good from now on if only Jake didn't check the net.

Chapter Eight

"Decided not to take me up on my offer then?"

Jake sat beside Marcy on the stone wall, leaving a person-sized gap between them now he knew what lay beneath her trekking gear. His hands itched to touch her body, to shape the curves and dip into the valleys, but even tattoo-free, Marcy may still be connected to the Chan cartel. Seduction was still on the table, but not out here. He fisted his hands in his pockets and focused on getting back into her good books.

The rise he'd expected to get out of her didn't come. She simply sat, fingers tapping a slow rhythm on her thigh. "No."

"Just as well. I ran out of hot water halfway through."

Marcy's fingers stopped abruptly. "That would have been disappointing." She wasn't going to forgive being surprised in the shower anytime soon.

"Sweetheart, if you'd been there, I wouldn't have disappointed you." Despite what he suspected her of, nothing short of a snap freeze would stop his physical response to her body.

"I didn't mean—"

"I did. And I plan on more than five minutes with you

when the water is hot and steamy."

"*Mister* Harris, I'm not interested, even if the water supply is limitless. You're not the man I thought you were."

The spark of irritation wasn't much, but it was an improvement on her indifference.

"Because I didn't let you get arrested by the police? Come on, Marcy. You're an intelligent woman. A little over-emotional with some things but you would have done more harm than good by creating a scene back there."

She hunched her shoulders and examined the ground near her boots. "I wanted to make it clear not everyone accepts torture as normal. But I blacked out."

"And I caught you before you hit your head and maybe got yourself arrested."

Scuffing the dirt, she toed a stone out of its resting spot. With a sigh, she tipped her head to look at him. "You were right. God, it's annoying to have to say that."

He chuckled. "Because I was right, or because it's me?"

She snorted self-deprecatingly. "Honestly? A bit of both, I think. I know you were right—but I hate anyone stepping in because they think I can't manage. When that burst of adrenaline hit I stopped thinking logically and now I'm embarrassed. I *should* thank you."

Her honesty was refreshing, and unusual, and his instinct was telling him this was the real Marcy. The woman who hadn't managed to tell him a successful lie.

He bumped her shoulder with his. "I couldn't let my trekking partner spend a night behind bars. Nepalese jails are bottom rung on the accommodation ladder."

"Worse than my narrow bunk in the teahouse?"

"Infinitely. By the way, that prisoner is accused of murder and headed to Kathmandu to stand trial."

Nodding, she said nothing but pressed her lips together. He sensed her reluctance to talk further about the incident. It suited him. As far as he was concerned, that chapter was closed the minute the police escort disappeared down the track. But other issues needed to be addressed.

"As for that apology—"

"You don't apologise when you don't mean it. I heard you the first time."

He chuckled. Marcy's wry sense of humour had wrung more genuine laughter from him in the past few days than he'd known in the last year. "Sweetheart, no man could be sorry if he'd seen you under that shower. But I am sorry if I embarrassed you—"

She silenced his attempted apology with a talk-to-the-hand gesture. "If you say that one more time—" For a petite woman, Marcy's glare would stop a marauding ostrich in its tracks. Or an overzealous male who'd seen her nearly in the buff.

He raised both hands in surrender. "I promise. At least, not until we're both in a more—interesting state of undress."

"Cock-sure, aren't you? What makes you think you'll

achieve that state of—Nirvana?"

"Sweet Marcy. I know you've felt the zap between us so don't try to deny it."

"Nothing more than static electricity."

"Bull."

Awareness thrummed in the air between them and in Marcy's clear grey eyes. She could refute the attraction all she liked but he knew she felt it. Their attraction would melt glaciers.

Shit, get with the programme, Harris.

Gingerly he eased his buttocks forward to relieve the pressure in his trousers. His path lay on the fine line between seduction and sexy teasing. "We have chemistry, Marcy. Have you heard of it?"

"We're people, not atoms."

"People are made up of atoms and ours are aiming to get together and party."

Pheromones flew and her eyes widened. "Party implies more than two getting together."

"Yeah, atoms bonding and recombining, creating heat and energy."

More like spontaneous combustion with Marcy.

"Any more like you at home? I can't imagine what two of you together would be like." *That came out wrong.*

Marcy's lips snapped shut and she turned to watch a group entering the lower end of the village. Tension radiated from her rigid torso. Was the ménage type quip or her sister's email responsible? For all her edgy banter, her indrawn breath sounded strained and shaky.

Great way to complicate an interrogation. Bringing kinky sex quips into the conversation.

Her shoulders straightened and she turned back, a forced smile painted on her face. Before the words left her mouth, his gut clenched, knowing truth would be a casualty of whatever was going on with her sister. "They broke the mould when they made me. What about you?"

Disappointed, he shrugged. What could he tell her? "My sister's working somewhere in England. I haven't heard from her in a while. But I am curious about something."

Head tilted, Marcy's lips twitched. "You mean there's something about me you didn't find out in the shower?"

He'd found out plenty, but getting a little of his own back until she admitted she had a sibling would be entertaining. "Marcy, my curiosity about you is insatiable. And I want to satisfy it both in the shower and out of it." Hell, he was ready to start an exploratory with her right now.

But then her gaze dropped to his groin. Her eyes widened and her lips parted and like that, he lost control.

Savagely, he wrenched his brain from images of Marcy's mouth doing pleasurable things to him and pushed to his feet. He towered over her and common sense flew out the window. "Where is your sister?"

Colour drained from Marcy's face. Gripping the stones

either side of her hips, she swayed. Her mouth opened and closed but no words formed.

He had expected surprise at his casual question, and dissembling, but not the shock evident on her face. Nor the fear in her eyes. *What the hell is going on here?*

Realisation slammed home. Her fear wasn't of him, or for herself, but for her sister. Did the Chans have a hold over her sibling? Was that why the sister had simply *disappeared*?

"How do you know about—?" Breathy and soft, he strained to hear her question.

"Are you okay? You look like you've seen the proverbial ghost."

"Were you checking up on me?"

There were times when catching a suspect's unguarded reaction gave him the break he needed and his neural pathways fist-pumped his success.

And then there was now.

He felt like a Spanish inquisitor. Applying pressure meant seeking vulnerable spots and attacking. He had to know how deeply involved Marcy was.

"When you said you were an events coordinator and mentioned that car launch, I went online and found a great snap of you. With long curls and one kickass little black dress." He traced a path along her ring finger, feeling tremors as she gripped the rock in white knuckled desperation.

"It was two weeks ago. Were you at that car launch,

Marcy?"

Statue-still, she sat while he waited several heartbeats. Heavy-lidded, almost languorous, she looked at their joined hands before raising her gaze to his face. He waited until their eyes met. Her tongue made a slow pass across her lower lip and she drew in a long, audible breath.

Chapter Nine

"Yes."

Technically, she had been at the event although that wasn't what Jake had been asking. "Why does it matter to you, Jake?"

"It doesn't, except I was wondering about your sister."

"I told you I don't have—" A bolt of angry adrenaline shot through her body. She jumped to her feet and stalked away. Damn Jake. Why did he have to go and spoil her adventure by ferreting out that photo?

Tam's message had been clear: 'Don't come home.' Her twin was in danger and refusing to let Marcy help.

Jake followed until she stopped and whirled to confront him.

"Who are the men in the photo?"

"I don't know."

Paul was Tam's man. Although she'd been introduced to the other man, his name slipped her mind but she couldn't mention Paul without risking exposing Tamsin. The closer she stuck to the truth, the more manageable this ridiculous charade would be. "I didn't take any notice of who was behind—me."

"Why did you cut your hair?"

Marcy shoved her fingers through her short hair. "Because I felt like it, okay?"

Jake hooked his thumbs in his pockets and looked at her. Just looked.

She crossed her arms and glanced away. "Women are irrational creatures when things go wrong in their lives. Some women cut their hair after the loss of someone they love." That had been her reaction after her father's death. Chopping off her long curls had felt right at the time. Discovering how much simpler it made her lab work, she'd settled on *pixie cut* as the new Marcy look. Not that it had made a difference to her love life.

"Are you saying you cut your hair and transformed yourself from an events coordinator into a doctor in the space of—what? Two weeks?"

Half-truths seemed to be the order of this bizarre day. No matter how much of a battering her self-esteem took, she had to protect Tamsin. Desperation lashed at Marcy's dormant creative side. "I've had enough. I'm going to say this once and then, so help me, if you bring it up again, I am leaving. Alone. You asked why I lied about my job. I'm a doctor, okay? Most guys get scared off when I tell them that so I *borrowed* a friend's occupation and told you I'd organised that launch. I *was* there, but only as a guest."

#

Marcy, the lioness, protecting her sister was magnificent to behold. Fascinated by the dramatic change in her confidence when she was fighting for someone dear to her, Jake folded his arms and cocked his head. "Then what, Marcy?"

Her gaze flicked from his mouth to his eyes. Hunger flared in hers and her lips parted. She stepped into his personal space and rested her hands on his shoulders. "Shut up and kiss me."

He didn't need to be asked twice.

Diversionary tactics aside—and he knew that was part of Marcy's heedless request—he needed to mesh mouths and tangle tongues with her. He unfolded his arms and disposed of the gap between them in a single stride. "Happy to oblige since you asked so nicely."

She grabbed his jacket collar and tugged. "You talk too much."

Jake lowered his head. Marcy's slim form pressed against him in a no-holds-barred embrace that belonged in the privacy of a bedroom.

Their shared bedroom. With sound-proof walls.

If only they had one.

Her tongue slid along his lips, inviting him out to play. If he'd thought their first encounter had been promising, this one delivered, with extras. Every sane thought fled as Marcy slid her arms around his neck and brushed her hips across his arousal.

Like he needed any more incentive. Marcy had taken charge and, as far as distractions went, he'd give her an Oscar for her performance.

Jake groaned with frustration at the layers of clothes separating them. The sight of her under the shower, bubbles sliding down her body, was imprinted forever on his memory. And the need to see all of her again, to take a leisurely tour all over her body, had nothing to do with his assignment.

His fingers touched a sliver of skin. Warm, silky skin. Marcy's shirt had pulled out of her trousers when she embraced him, offering limited access. He slipped one hand beneath the Gortex top, pressed his fingers into the indentation of her spine and deepened the kiss.

She moaned softly into his mouth and tunnelled her fingers through his hair, holding his head down.

Heat raced from pulse point to pulse point like summer wildfire. He no longer cared that she was trying to distract him. This trip was one he'd sign up for every day.

Her knee stroked up his thigh, leaving a trail of heat that fuelled his need.

Sliding his hand under her raised leg, he wrapped it around his hip. His other hand traced a path to her butt and lifted her into position above his straining cock.

She wriggled her hips and he groaned as her mouth found his again. Lips locked, he acknowledged the inevitability of this moment.

But he needed to regain a measure of control.

With self-discipline honed by years of undercover work, he forced himself to break contact and open his eyes. He looked down at her face and bit back an expletive. Marcy's lashes fanned her cheeks, and kiss-swollen lips parted on a soft sigh. As he watched, her eyelids rose, her gaze unfocussed and bedroom-sexy. She wasn't role-playing any more. This was real for her.

He clamped his hands on her hips and eased her to the ground. That kiss went well beyond what his assignment required. Whatever else he did in their relationship, in this he was honest. Marcy appealed to him in a way that shook him out of the grey funk he'd lived in for the past two months. Vibrant and sexy, sweet and defensive, she would get hurt when it ended if he didn't keep it casual.

A wolf whistle pierced the haze induced by Marcy's kisses. Jake blinked and turned his head. Two young men lounging against a wall gave him a thumbs-up and grinned. One slipped his phone into his jacket.

Shit. They were making out beside the main route to Everest. Marcy's expression and the uncomfortable bulge in his pants were as good as a neon advertisement for their encounter. Since when had he lost all sense of time and place?

Since little Marcy pulled out all stops to distract him.

Muttering an oath, he took her elbow and guided her inside the teahouse to the far corner of the common room. He dragged two stools together and, none too gently, pushed Marcy onto one. Their knees brushed as he sat and he moved out of touching distance.

Marcy's legs clamped together as though super-glued. Hands pressed to her flaming cheeks, she refused to meet his eyes.

"You're playing with fire, Marcy."

"I don't know what you mean."

"You give me kisses that demolish my ability to think straight then clam up tighter than a Sydney rock oyster."

Her gaze flicked up, glanced across his face and darted away. "You didn't like it?"

Uncertainty tinged her soft question and she bit her lip. Difficult as it was to believe, Marcy seemed unsure of her effect on him, even after rubbing against what he considered a pretty substantial demonstration on his part. His little doctor needed more research but, willing as he was, offering to be her test subject for more than the time it took to establish which twin she was, wasn't on the cards.

He stroked a finger down her cheek. Taking a light hold of her chin, he tilted her face up until she met his gaze. Marcy needed to read his sincerity. "I liked it all right. More than all right. But, sweetheart, we were the R rated main feature playing out there. I think those guys filmed us—"

Her eyes widened and she gasped before a hand shot up and covered her mouth. "I did not just do that. Please tell me we're not suddenly going to trend on Twitter or appear on YouTube?"

Shit and double shit. He hadn't even thought of that. Nicholls would be pissed with him for attracting any sort of attention. But worse than that, he'd turned the spotlight onto Marcy. Alerting the drug cartel to her presence here with him if she was an innocent caught up in their web was a rookie mistake. Immediate damage control was essential. "Be right back. Stay here."

He bolted outside hoping the trekkers hadn't uploaded their footage.

# #

Marcy logged onto the Internet. What did one search for—'Hot Kisses in the Himalayas'? 'Trekking Tramp'? How could she have been so stupid? Tam needed her to be discreet, and careful, and she had tried to throw Jake off the line of questioning that threatened to reveal Tam's existence. But in her lust for him, she had probably found the one sure way to gain net notoriety. Extroverted Tamsin at her most flamboyant hadn't achieved that level of fame. Not even her LBD at the launch—

Frantically Marcy searched for her photo of Tamsin. She couldn't remember with certainty but the sinking feeling in the pit of her stomach suggested the worst. At last the car manufacturer's site loaded and she downloaded images from the launch. The photo she desperately needed to check unfolded in slow motion chunks on the expanse of blank white screen.

Paul and the Asian guy appeared at the top of the image followed by Tamsin's curls—her beautiful face—neck—cleavage—

The rest of the image didn't matter. Men's eyes zeroed in on her sister's chest and the funky heart shaped mark had provided an opening gambit to many of Tam's romantic conversations. But the birthmark on her sister's left breast branded Marcy a liar.

Marcy pulled her jacket zipper higher and hunched her

shoulders. The photo sounded the death knell to her hopes of a *romantic adventure*. If Jake had seen the photo, he'd have taken in the details and a birthmark couldn't be expunged or explained away like a sudden haircut or a temporary tattoo.

After that sizzling kiss, her libido was screaming to finish what she had begun. But Tam's email made nonsense of Marcy's procrastination over a holiday affair with Jake.

It can't happen. He'll work out that Tam and I are—.

"All sorted." Jake appeared beside her and dropped onto the stool.

Lost in her pity party, Marcy jumped, blinked rapidly, and scrambled to recall the topic of their conversation. "What's sorted?"

"Our would-be filmmakers."

"Oh, of course they videoed us. Everyone and everything seems to be fair game these days."

"They deleted it when I asked."

"Honestly? I'm surprised they hadn't already uploaded it. Thank you."

Jake smiled grimly. "I didn't appreciate them making a soft porn vid out of our encounter." He turned his attention to the photo, which had finished downloading. Leaning closer, he tapped the screen over Tam's birthmark. "I'm looking forward to seeing this little beauty."

So he hadn't seen *everything* in the shower. She shivered. Every fibre of her being wanted more of Jake. His touch had awakened the wanton in her. Perhaps she wasn't so different from her sister after all. If only she could take her courage in both hands and go after what she wanted as Tam did.

If only she had been born with that birthmark, she would lead him to her tiny bed this very minute and finish what they'd begun outside. She glanced at the photo and bit her lip to stop the invitation spilling from her lips.

Whatever danger Tam was in trumped her own physical needs. Marcy had a role to play and a sister to protect.

"I'm going out for a walk."

"I'll come with you." Jake barely lifted his backside off the chair before she threw up a hand to ward him off.

"No." She pressed her lips together and backed away. "I just need some time alone. See you at dinner." Shoulders hunched, she scurried out the door.

Featuring opposite Jake as the star attraction in her dreams was one thing, but to have it buzzing around on the net was far beyond her comfort zone. Marcy preferred to be behind the camera rather than steaming up the lens, and Tam needed her to keep a low profile. Had Jake contained the video in time? She could only hope and pray so.

Marcy pushed herself to walk until the heat of exercise replaced the heat of embarrassment in her face. How should she handle this attraction to Jake while keeping Tam's secret? Working on the assumption Jake had stopped the video from being uploaded, she began compiling a plan of action. If she could keep their sizzle on simmer, surely whatever was going on in Tam's life would be resolved within a day or two. For once in her life, Marcy wanted to be the bad girl.

With Jake, she wanted to be very, very bad.

#

Prickles of unease ran down Jake's spine as he made the scheduled call to Nicholls. Marcy hadn't returned and dinner would be served by the time he finished his briefing. Part of him wanted to shove protocol and head out to find her. But he'd already broken enough rules today without missing his contact.

Two clicks sounded and Nicholls' voice echoed down the satellite connection. "I'll have your balls for this lapse in protocol. What the hell do you think you're playing at, Harris?"

"What are you talking about—?"

"You are supposed to observe your assignment, not take personal inventory for the whole world to see."

Shit. The video.

"I thought I'd contained the situation. I was trying to find out why she won't talk about her sister. You said she's vanished and Dr. Westcott doesn't acknowledge her existence."

"And you thought you'd find the sister with your tongue down Dr. Westcott's throat, did you?"

Jake bit back a retort. "Our encounter didn't go as planned. It won't happen again."

"We have removed the clip but the damned thing may have been seen in the interim. You're supposed to be a top operator,

Harris. See that you fix this." Nicholls terminated the call.

Jake tossed the phone onto the spare bunk and leaned against the wall, arms folded behind his head. "Shit."

Never get involved. The agency's number one rule and he'd screwed up in the most damaging and public way. Worst-case scenario, the Chans had connections that could identify him. Facial recognition software available to the Bureau would have picked him up, and he had to assume Paul was keeping tabs on Marcy. If Paul was now working for the Chans, they would know Marcy had been compromised. If she was working for them, they would question her loyalty and probably try to take her out. But if her sister was being used to leverage Marcy's cooperation, the danger could be greater. Instinctively, he knew Marcy would risk everything to save her sister.

Damn it, where was Marcy?

He pushed off the bed and strode through the teahouse, scanning the growing dinner crowd. Why wasn't she back from her walk? Had there been enough time since the video was uploaded for the Chans to put a man in place? If they had someone in Kathmandu, Jake had a day at best to relocate Marcy. He needed to find her and convince her to talk. And hope that the agency had removed the video before it caused serious damage.

Colour leached from the sky as night closed in. Figuring Marcy would seek solitude rather than company, Jake headed for the quietest part of the village. On the outskirts around the first bend in the path, he could just make out a figure huddled on top of a rock. The reflective strip on her Gortex vest glowed in the fading light.

Quiet as he was, she half turned her head at his approach.

He wished he could make out more than her shape but moonrise was still half an hour away. "Dinner is served. Come back and we can talk later."

He heard her sniff and imagined how sadly her eyes would look at him now. Like twin silver pools of regret. Was she upset because she was attracted to him?

It was all very well to say it took two to tango. He was the one who had broken the rules of his assignment. Who knew what the game was. For all her doctorate and education, he sensed Marcy had acted innocently, guided by no more than instinct to protect her sister. Had he endangered her by allowing that kiss on the track?

Wrenching his thoughts away from the taste of Marcy's lips, he hunkered down beside her. "I'm sorry, Marcy. I should never have let that kiss happen."

She cleared her throat and he heard her swallow. "Jake, it's not your fault. I started it. You just accepted the offer. Forget it."

"We need to talk. About several things, but first, you need to eat." He reached for her hand and drew her to her feet. "Come on."

In strained silence they walked until rectangular patches of light brightened the street in front of their teahouse. As he pushed open the door she gripped his upper arm.

"Are you sure you got to those boys in time?"

Whatever the stakes were, secrecy was important to her. If he wanted to convince her to talk, she needed to know the truth. "Probably not."

"Oh God." Anguish filled her eyes, and her voice was no more than a whisper.

"Food first, then you talk to me and we'll make a plan." His appetite had disappeared but he forced himself to consume a plate of rice and lentils and a cup of tea.

Marcy toyed with her helping then dropped her fork into the mess and pushed her plate away. She picked up her cup and stared over the rim into the darkness beyond the window.

"You won't get far if you don't eat, Marcy. Your body needs fuel to finish this walk under your own steam."

"You don't understand. That video—" She pressed her lips together and turned her head.

"Might be embarrassing but it's not like it's life or death." He hoped to God it wasn't that bad.

She lowered her cup and dropped her hands into her lap. Her next breath was ragged as she faced him. "It might be."

Chapter Ten

Outside, beyond closed doors that muffled the sounds of laughter and singing within the teahouse, they sat on red plastic chairs in the darkness. Marcy tugged the hood of her jacket over her head against the chilly night air.

Jake's voice pitched soft and low. "I doubt we'll be disturbed out here. It's time to 'fess up, Marcy. I don't think you're the type to dramatize so . . . what makes an admittedly embarrassing video clip dangerous?"

She shook her head and stared at the ground. "I don't know. I wish I did but even if I knew, I couldn't tell you. It's not my secret to share."

"Whose is it?"

"I can't say." Her voice cracked. She wrapped her arms across her stomach, wishing she could do something to help Tam, knowing there was nothing to be done this far from home.

Jake moved his chair and leaned close. A faint scent of sandalwood carried on the breeze. She would always associate that smell with Jake—spicy, dangerous . . . reassuring.

An edgy awareness of him was growing that she couldn't

entirely put down to lust. Somehow he made her feel—safe.

Could she trust him with Tam's safety?

He scanned the area and turned back to her. "No more secrets, Marcy. Tell me the truth. If it's not your secret, is it your sister's?"

Her head snapped up. "How do you—?"

He tapped the spot on her thigh where Tam's tattoo would be. "Hair can be cut, wigs can be worn, but showers reveal all. You haven't got a snake tattoo."

"Gecko." The correction dropped from her lips before she could stop it. She clamped her lips together. "It was a—a temporary tattoo. To see if I liked it."

"So you didn't keep the tattoo."

"I don't really like them."

"And the birthmark on your left breast?"

She clutched her jacket high under her chin.

He looked pointedly at her hands. "I'm willing to bet you don't have one. Tell me, is your sister the events coordinator?"

Heart thudding louder than a freight train during banana harvest and dizzy with despair, she felt herself falling. The darkness of the night seeped in, claiming her. She'd failed her twin. She'd failed Tam.

Jake's hand gripped her shoulder, his fingers digging in, pulling her back to the present. "Breathe, Marcy."

She drew a ragged breath that sounded loud in her ears, and nodded slowly. "How did you know?"

He shrugged. "It wasn't hard to guess."

"Please, you can't tell anyone about her. I don't know why, only that you can't." Gripping his arm, she willed him to listen. She couldn't bear it if her pathetic attempts to pass herself off as Tam put her sister in jeopardy.

Jake covered her death grip on his arm. Her fingers were icicles beneath the heat of his hand. Gently, he squeezed until she eased her hold then enclosed her hand between the warmth of both of his.

"Do you think she's in danger?" His calm voice anchored her, kept her fear at bay.

"I know she's in trouble, threatened somehow."

What did she really know? Had she allowed distance and heightened emotions to overwhelm her common sense? "I've had this bad feeling for the past few days."

"Wouldn't she tell you if she was in trouble? Email her and ask."

"I did but she only asked me to keep a low profile. And not to return home. I'd already spun you that cock-and-bull story about being her—I mean, being an events coordinator. Then you nosed around and found that photo."

And frustratingly little else.

Jake suppressed a sigh. How could there be nothing on her sister? "You didn't do anything wrong."

"Aside from lying to you. Lies always come back to bite me on the backside."

He couldn't suppress his grin. To think he'd imagined she was a consummate actress when they'd first met. "You couldn't lie to save yourself."

"Twice in my life I've caused trouble for Tam. I'm the older sister; it's my job to protect her but I let her down. This time, I'm really worried she's involved in something bad."

Knowing what that something was, his grin disappeared. Getting the dirt on the Chans and putting a stop to their operation was the most important job he'd undertaken. It might take down Marcy's sister too but collateral damage meant little if he achieved vengeance for Pete. "What is Tamsin's connection with the Chan family?"

He watched for the almost imperceptible tells that she recognised the surname.

Marcy shook her head. "I've never heard of them. Are they clients of hers?"

"It's possible."

"I don't recall her mentioning them but we haven't talked as often as usual. She's busy planning a wedding. Hers."

His subconscious latched onto that morsel and filed it away. The lead might give Nicholls something more to use in the search for the missing woman.

Marcy's eyes widened. "Oh, no. I wonder—" She slapped her hand over her mouth.

"Have you remembered something? No matter how small, the answer is often in the fine details."

"Promise you won't say anything, Jake."

"Why?"

"Because I won't say any more if you don't."

If what she said related to the case, he would use it and live with the lie. He nodded. "What have you remembered?"

She folded her hands together as though praying. Even in the fading light he could see her white knuckles and the tense line of her shoulders. "Tam's fiancé, Paul Rimmer, disappeared."

Paul's missing? He's her sister's fiancé?

Both facts registered but his former partner's disappearance caused less surprise than his impending marriage.

Hair rose on the back of Jake's neck. This assignment was throwing up more twists than the Everest track. His mate was missing, Marcy's sister had disappeared and Marcy was involved in unknown *research*.

The back door opened spilling light on the fear in her eyes. Two trekkers stepped out and wandered around the corner, laughing loudly. She leaned closer, her voice little more than a whisper. "It's impossible. Paul's her fiancé. He wouldn't do anything to her, would he? But why else would she not want her whereabouts known?"

If Paul had gone undercover and Tamsin Westcott was his suspect, Jake could think of one very good reason. If her twin was the Chan connection Paul had flagged, he may have already dealt with her.

Jake could see it now—twin shots to her head and heart,

red blooms growing, the life snuffed out of silver grey eyes. Marcy's eyes.

Jake looked at Marcy's face, pale in the glow of the rising moon, and his gut twisted.

He should never have kissed her. Never got close.

Now she was under his skin and in his head.

He released her hand and took a turn around the rocky yard, putting a check on his emotions. Emotions that were forbidden in his work.

He shoved his hands in his pockets and stopped in front of her. "What do you mean by disappeared?"

Marcy shook her head. "He's a personal trainer. I can't imagine why he'd suddenly leave his fiancée."

Paul's new cover was a personal trainer?

"Cold feet before the wedding?"

"No. I'm sure he loves Tam too much to do that to her." Certainty dissolved in the space of a single sentence. From vehement denial, her voice changed back to a whisper. "He wouldn't, would he?"

Jake squatted in front of her and wrapped his hands around her clenched fists. "I don't know, Marcy. I just threw the idea out there without thinking. I didn't mean to upset you."

She sucked in an audible breath and shook her head. "He's an honourable man. He wouldn't do that to her. And Tamsin would have heard from the police if Paul had been in an accident."

"What do you know about him?" He leaned forward on one

knee, invading her space.

The scent of coconut drifted from her hair as she shuffled back on her chair. Her eyes widened and her gaze stayed riveted on his face. "He loves my sister."

"What about other stuff? Work? Friends? Anyone doesn't like him?"

Pale faced, Marcy tugged her hands from his grasp. She stood abruptly, her chair fell and she edged towards the back door.

He should be relieved from duty. Hell, he should back off now but he couldn't let go. Not when the first break in ages to take down the cartel was so close. So temptingly near he could taste it. Not when the chance to avenge his little brother might rest with Marcy.

He breathed deeply, trying to calm the turmoil he couldn't afford to overwhelm him. "I'm sorry."

Marcy moistened her lips and eyed him warily. "Who are you, Jake?"

Chapter Eleven

"Or should that be what are you? What's with the third degree interrogation?" Poised to flee, Marcy flicked a glance left then right. Had she made a monumental mistake confiding in Jake?

He rose slowly, stooped and picked up her fallen seat. He set it on its legs between them, as though sensing she needed distance from him. "Occupational hazard. I'm used to being in charge." Steely determination and something dark, dangerous, simmered beneath his offhand response. Somehow she knew that what Jake wanted, he would pursue until he succeeded.

She shivered. "It's more than that. It's like—I think you see things in black and white and there aren't any shades in between. Some things aren't that clear-cut."

"Look, I'm sorry if I appeared to pry. You're worried about your sister, and you're far from home. Maybe my company can help you contact her." His hands spread wide like he had nothing to hide, but his smile didn't reach his eyes.

"Maybe. But I prefer to deal with my own problems, thanks all the same. I'm going to bed."

"Marcy, I can help."

She shook her head. "Goodnight."

She could feel the weight of his gaze on her back, sense his displeasure as she walked away without giving him answers. Jake had control issues if he couldn't accept that. Hot as he was, she wouldn't accept another controlling man in her life, even for an affair. Absent for weeks at a time for work and a control freak, like her father. It was the worst possible combination.

Sabita, their host's daughter was wiping down tables. She glanced up and smiled shyly as Marcy leaned against the wall. "You like tea?"

Marcy tossed a glance over her shoulder. What were the chances of Jake pursuing her inside, with witnesses all around? "If there's any left in the pot. Please don't make it fresh just for me."

Sabita returned, carrying a teapot and two earthen mugs. "Is okay to join you? We talk?"

Mind swirling with too many questions about Jake, Marcy sat and patted the space next to her. "I'd love to talk. You're Chewang's girlfriend? Do you see much of him during tourist season?"

"He busy. Saving for us to marry. I see him when he walk track, then nothing for days. Is hard. Miss Doctor, I want to go to university in Kathmandu. I want to be nurse. But—" Sabita dropped her gaze.

There was no doubting the longing in the young woman's voice. Keeping her voice gentle, Marcy asked, "But what?"

"I miss Chewang but it will be worse if I go to city.

Months, not days before I see him. But I want so much to be useful. You are doctor. You spend long time studying. My father say I am greedy to want more education. He say my husband want wife, not woman who is never home. What do you think, Miss Doctor?"

Shades of heated arguments with her own father flashed through her memory. Despite his frequent absences from home, he expected his family to be there whenever he returned from his travels.

You're trying to break up this family, Marcia. You don't need to go to university. Why do you want to be a doctor? Stay and look after your mother and sister.

"If it's the right thing for you, go for it. If you want to return here to work, think what you can contribute to your community. Nursing is a noble profession and your country needs more like you."

"What about Chewang?"

"Wouldn't he be proud of your achievement?"

"He has encouraged me, but my father—"

"Don't let others tell you what to do." She swallowed the last of her tea and smiled at Sabita. "Follow your heart. Good night, Sabita."

In the quiet of her room, Marcy dragged off her boots and flopped onto her hard bunk. Worries about her sister rushed back. What had Tam got into? Did it have anything to do with Paul's disappearance?

And who was Jake?

His questions assumed a menacing quality she hoped would vanish with daylight. She'd never forgive herself if she'd put Tam in more danger. Why had she put her trust in a man she barely knew?

Except that his kisses sent longing for more of his touch coursing through her body. She closed her eyes and prayed for sleep.

What had she got herself into?

Chapter Twelve

Sydney, Australia

John Chan's phone buzzed as he sat alone at the dining table in his apartment. A bowl of shark-fin soup steamed beside a plate of beef noodles. Placing his chopsticks on the ceramic rest, he checked the caller ID and accepted the connection.

His informant wasted no words. "Lucky break. We've found her."

"Where is she?" Luck had nothing to do with it. Obscene amounts of money changing hands could buy anything.

"She's on the Everest track. Do you have a contact in Kathmandu?"

"No. I can get a man there by tomorrow evening. How did you find her?"

"Chance. She was all but fucking some guy in public and got caught on video. It came through the Bureau's feed. Facial recognition software picked up the man first and the Bureau removed the clip immediately."

"Why?"

"He's one of their agents. Check it out,"—a sneering chuckle interrupted his report. "The guys tagged it: 'Tip #1 on

How to Stay Warm in the Snow'. I've sent the link to your computer."

Chan pulled his laptop closer and accessed the link. Handheld amateur filming captured simmering public sex. He watched the woman climbing a tall guy's body and wrapping her legs around him. Soft porn didn't do it for him. Usually. But seeing the woman he'd been grooming to be his mistress demonstrating how hot a fuck she was made him hard. And more angry than ever that she'd withheld her lush body from him.

"She's cut her hair but there's no doubt it's her. Do you need anything more from me?" Background sounds of boozy voices and glasses clinking gave Chan a fair idea of his informant's whereabouts and he grimaced. Only necessity would make him deal with a man like this.

"Not for the moment." Chan ended the call and stared through the picture window onto the Harbour. His body clamoured for relief. Pushing away from the table, he thumbed another number on his phone.

"What do you require, sir?"

"Young, light-skinned, long, dark curls. Expendable."

His frustration needed the ultimate release.

Chapter Thirteen

Marcy sat on the bunk with her camera and flicked through images of her trek. "Scenery, more scenery," she muttered.

She slowed when Jake's shots at the *stupa* appeared. Well composed and with good contrast, he'd captured a sense of place. She clicked on the next one.

Her.

He'd caught her in an unguarded moment that both disturbed and riveted her.

Zooming in, she stared at the face of a woman she barely recognised. Lips parted, faraway gaze, there was something sensual, more like Tamsin than her. Was that what a woman who'd been made love to by Jake looked like?

Where were the photos of Jake?

Scrolling back, it struck her as odd she had none of Jake. How could he have erupted into her world and she had nothing to show for the impact? Not quite true. There could be a very revealing video flying around the Internet of the two of them. She thumped her head against the wall and groaned.

A knock sounded and Jake stood in her doorway. Rumpled clothes, bed hair, everything looked sexy on him. Or nothing at all—

He stepped into her room and tipped his head, waiting for an answer. Her answer. "Do you?"

She cleared her throat. "Sorry, what did you say?"

"I'm going to the street market. Do you want anything?"

Certain his wicked grin meant he knew where her thoughts roamed, she fiddled with her camera. Unsettled after last night's discussion, the less time she spent alone with him, the better. "No, thanks. I want to take some photos at the monastery."

"No sweat. See you later." Jake pulled the door shut behind him.

She listened to his footsteps and the sound of the front door closing before packing up her camera and water and heading out. Morning light was perfect for the shots she wanted. Maybe the monks' chanting would stop her obsessing over things she couldn't control.

As she strolled the short distance to the Buddhist monastery, she planned the shots she wanted to capture. She positioned the camera on the monastery wall, set the timer, and raced to take up a pose for a long-shot selfie. Tam would get a giggle out of it.

The camera clicked and she strolled back to review the image. Two male trekkers joined her, cameras in hand.

"Hi there. All by yourself today?" The men leaned against the stone entry blocking the gateway. And her retreat.

Disquiet skittered down her spine like fingernails on a

blackboard.

Vendors' cries floated around the corner from the market. Inside the monastery, monks chanted *"Om Mani Padme Om"*, interspersed with the sound of a single gong. She glanced around. It was a rare, quiet moment on the Everest track.

The dark-haired man in his early twenties looked her up and down like she was on the menu in King's Cross at midnight. "You're the girl on my mate's video. Some bastard blocked it from the net, but he sent it to me. It's you, isn't it?"

"No, not me. Excuse me please." She aimed to slip through the narrow gap between the men's bodies.

The second man, face red with acne scars, grabbed her upper arm. "What's your hurry, babe? Wanna share some of that sugar you were dishing on the vid? I'd sure like to taste that mouth of yours." His Southern drawl carried predatory intent.

"Yeah. You can put your mouth on parts of me anytime." Dark Hair stepped across, trapping her between him and his friend.

Adrenaline rushed through her body and the back of her neck tingled. How unlucky to encounter this pair of ass-holes. How unlucky they'd seen the video clip.

Her self-defence classes hadn't equipped her for multiple attackers. Mind racing through the list of attack points, she shifted her weight onto the balls of her feet.

Scarface grabbed her upper arms and Dark Hair held her face. His open mouth descended like a gaping black hole intent on devouring her.

She jerked her knee up as hard as she could and was rewarded by a howl of pain.

Scarface tightened his grip and lifted her off the ground.

She kicked backwards but only scraped the outside of his leg. Excited at getting rid of one attacker, she threw her head back and heard a satisfying *thunk*.

Her second assailant hung on. "You bitch. Like it rough, do you?"

Hot breath crawled across her neck. He spun her round and shoved her against the pillar. Rough-dressed stone scraped her back and beer breath assailed her nose. A hand grabbed her breast, squeezed.

She turned her head away and pushed ineffectually against the dark jacket. Her hips were pinned. There was no room to knee him in the groin, but she worked one arm free and lashed out at his face. Her fingers found an eye socket and her thumb landed in his nostril. She dug in.

"Marcy!" Jake's voice registered before Scarface's body and hers parted company.

Jake hauled her attacker away and dealt him two swift, thudding body blows followed by an uppercut. Her assailant face-planted and lay groaning into the stones.

Dark Hair launched himself at Jake's unsuspecting back.

"Behind you!"

Jake spun, threw the man over his shoulder, dropped to one knee and held him in a throat lock. Eyes wide, face brick red, Dark

Hair's hands scrabbled to free himself.

Jake flicked a glance her way. "You okay?"

She breathed hard and nodded. "Thank goodness you came along."

"Even though you don't like interfering males?"

"I do when my back is to the wall—" Strength ebbed with the loss of adrenaline and she sagged against the pillar, grateful for its solidity.

A shrill whistle sounded and two policemen pounded up the incline to the monastery gate. Jake stood back from the prone figures and addressed the officers in the local language. He indicated the two men, then her. Truncheons and voices raised, the police hauled her attackers to their feet and led them away.

A sigh of relief slipped out and she rested her head on the stone. "I hope they have a very uncomfortable night."

Jake stood in front of her and brushed her hair off her forehead. His gaze assessed even while his voice reassured her. "Let's get you a coffee and a seat away from here." His hand enveloped her fist and his thumb caressed her knuckles.

She uncurled her fingers and intertwined them with his as they headed towards the markets. His hand was warm and reassuring.

Safe.

"I'm grateful for the rescue, but I have to work out how to deal with others who see me as an easy lay." Her heart still hammered and her skin crawled at the memory of being pinned against the wall.

Jake led the way to a corner table in a café. "Those were good moves you used against your attackers." He held out a chair for her then slid along the bench opposite.

"I took self defence classes at uni. But when both of them surrounded me—" Chills crawled across her skin. Damn that video. "I'm going to spend the rest of my trek looking over my shoulder."

Jake covered her hand with his. "Marcy, open your eyes and look at me."

Her face felt tight and she realised she'd scrunched her eyes shut and gritted her teeth. Consciously relaxing, she met his gaze. "My problem. I'll deal with it. But thanks again for the rescue. You've got some cool moves. Scary, but cool."

"I can teach you moves against an attacker who's twice your size."

Independence meant not relying on someone else to rescue her, things her father had derided her for wanting. Jake's offer meant more than she could tell him. "I'd appreciate that."

A waiter took their order and quickly returned with two mugs and a coffee pot.

"Where did you train? You took those guys down like Jack Reacher."

"What, not James Bond?"

"I didn't figure you for a ladies' man. You're definitely a man's man. And you're trying to misdirect me again. Why?"

"The less you know—"

"Jake, I'm feeling pretty pissed at the world right now so how about you cheer me up and tell me the truth? You asked that of me. Now I ask you for the same."

He picked up his coffee. "It's not mine to share." Raising his mug in silent toast, he drank.

"You're not going to tell me." She gripped her mug with both hands and sipped. Through the steam, she met his hooded gaze. "Guess I'll have to settle for you being my mystery spy."

Jake's eyes narrowed. His gaze slipped away and he scanned the café.

Was he offended by her throwaway line? Why couldn't she think before she spoke? They drank in silence until the tension lay thick around them.

She set her mug on the table with a thump that drew his attention. "So, Yoda, where can we have my lesson?"

"Now I'm a green midget?"

"Warrior teacher. Come on."

He pushed up from the bench, took her hand and led her through the market square and out to a flattish patch of ground on the road out of Namche.

"A common attack method is the back choke hold. As soon as you feel an arm around your neck like this"—he stepped in behind her and applied a light pressure—"lower your chin." At the edge of her vision, Jake's bicep curved up as he gently tightened his hold.

She gagged as pressure mounted on her throat. Panic welled and cold sweat trickled down her spine. Her lungs couldn't drag in enough air. She stretched her neck up and banged her head against his shoulder.

Jake's arm loosened. "Put your chin *down*, Marcy. Make space to move."

"I don't know if I—"

"You can. Again."

She dragged in a big breath and slowly released it, then nodded that she was ready.

His arm closed around her neck and she concentrated on following his instructions.

"Now, grab my wrist and arm, step to the outside and aim a blow to the groin with your fist. As I bend forward, jab up into my face with your elbow."

Suddenly a sense of control, missing since the attack, returned. Air filled her lungs.

She could do this.

"Again. Show me again."

Patiently, Jake ran her through the simple steps. "That's it. You've got it. Well done."

She knew she was grinning like a loony, but nothing could quench her elation at Jake's words. "What if an attacker lifts me off my feet and I can't step to the side? Like—today."

"Kick back into his groin. You had the right idea earlier but you used your outside foot. If you'd kicked with the inside one, he'd have been in plenty of pain."

"You saw that?"

"I saw brave resistance. With a little practice, your moves will be very effective. Marcy, you got rid of one assailant by your quick thinking. With a little more knowledge and practice, you could have dealt with the other as well."

Jake's praise was unexpected. Her father had laughed at her when she admitted to enrolling in self-defence classes.

Really, Marcy, women are misguided if they think they can do things as well as a man. Find yourself a local man to marry and take care of you.

But Jake encouraged her to do it for herself. He believed in her. She blinked away moisture that threatened to undo her rediscovered sense of self-worth.

"So, if your back is to the wall, use it." Hands on her shoulders, he backed her against a boulder.

"Keep your bottom against the wall, keep your arm straight and dig your fingers into this soft spot in the throat and hook downwards." He placed her hand against his sternum and guided her fingers to the soft depression at the base of his throat. "Push in and down."

She pressed. Soft, warm skin moved beneath her fingers as he swallowed. A look of discomfort flickered across his face and he eased back.

She snatched her hand away. "I don't want to hurt you."

He replaced her hand on his chest and laughed, the sound vibrating beneath her palm. "It takes more than that to put me out of action but it's effective on most people. Do it again."

Only Jake wasn't most people. He'd breached her defences by not treating her like a porcelain doll. His respect and praise filled a yawning gap she hadn't even realised existed until now. And no matter what happened, she'd be grateful to him for that gift.

They repeated the defensive back-to-the-wall moves until he was satisfied she could hit the spot every time. "Remember, no holds barred if someone attacks you. Let's try one more. Do whatever you can to stop me." He stepped behind her.

Ears straining to hear, she sensed rather than heard him move.

Arms lifting to protect her upper body, she started to turn.

Jake caught her arms and wrapped his around her. Plastered against his front, her bottom brushed his groin and her Jake fantasies flooded back. Enveloped by his lean, hard body, she breathed in his scent.

Eau de Mountain Man. God, she'd make a fortune if she bottled it but no way was she sharing Jake.

His voice rumbled through her, his breath warm on her bare neck.

Goosebumps raced down her body. She had no idea what he said, but pressed against him. His arousal pressed back. Satisfaction zinged through her as he eased away. She pressed again and wriggled her hips.

"Marcy!" Her name snapped out, low and growly, with a note of warning that sent a thrill to her womb. Had she hit on the perfect revenge for her frustrated libido?

"Am I doing it wrong?" The sugar-sweet tone was borrowed straight from her sister's repertoire. "You said *do whatever I can* to stop you."

"Move the *other* way."

Like twin steel bands, his arms held her. Briefly, she considered staying there all afternoon.

Jake's voice prompted her back to her lesson. "Step to the side, backstop my knee with your left leg—that knocks me off balance—bring your left elbow up towards my face and jab hard."

She completed the manoeuvre to his satisfaction and stepped back. Shaking out her arm muscles, a buzz of excitement went through her. "I'm amazed I can stop you like that."

He grinned. "It's just about knowing where and when to exert pressure."

Like rubbing against his arousal. She'd affected him, aroused him, and the thrill of knowing she'd got under his skin gave her a high she wanted again.

Tilting her head to meet his eye, she stepped into his space. "But what if I'm in a bear hug facing you?" She closed the gap and rested her hand on his chest. Close quarters action of a different sort enticed her to push Jake. Would he cave and give her more hot kisses?

His body stiffened. "We've done enough for today." He stepped back.

She followed. "What's up, Jake. Afraid I'll beat you?"

She rubbed the spot over his left breast. Beneath her stroking fingers, his heart beat a little faster.

"Not a hope, little one."

"But my education is missing something." Closing the last inch of space between them, she tilted her hips and brushed against him.

Behind his zipper, his cock twitched. "You really want me to supply the missing piece?"

Hell yeah. Even though she couldn't reveal her missing birthmark, she wanted whatever Jake could give. If that meant more self-defence lessons to stay close to him, so be it. Nerdy Marcy was responsible for his current physical state.

Heady with the power of her effect on him, she nodded. Balanced on the balls of her feet, she wriggled against him. "What do I do in this position?"

His eyes narrowed and he captured her in his arms. "Surprise me."

She reached up on tiptoe and brushed her mouth across his. When his lips parted she traced their outline with her tongue.

His grip loosened.

Swift as a taipan, she grabbed his neck, pulled his head down and raised her knee, stopping short of inflicting damage. "Will that do?"

"Clever move." Doubled over, his voice sounded strained.

Congratulating herself, she stepped back.

Lightning fast, he grabbed her legs out from under her and she landed on her back.

Triumph gleamed in his eyes. The almost-grin should have annoyed her but his body covered hers, pressing her into the ground.

Delicious heat surrounded her like a blanket. "Now what will you do, Marcy?"

She ran her tongue slowly across her upper lip as she'd seen Tam do and held his gaze.

His eyes tracked the movement. Against her mound, his cock was rock hard.

"Submit."

Jake groaned. "You don't play fair."

"You talk too much."

His mouth crushed hers, the kiss savage with need. She opened to him and his tongue invaded her mouth, stroking, almost devouring her in his need to be inside her.

She wriggled an arm free, flung it around his neck and held him tightly.

Jake wrenched his mouth from Marcy's, his breathing ragged. Lilting Nepalese voices heralded the approach of a group along the track. He jumped to his feet, pulling her with him, and stalked to the big boulder where he'd had her back to the wall.

What was wrong with him? They'd almost been caught making out in a public place. Again.

"Jake?" The hitch in her soft voice tore at his self-control. What was it about Marcy that made him break every rule of his training?

"I'm sorry. I'd say it won't happen again but I don't even believe myself."

"Hey, I was with you all the way there."

"Yeah, but—" Damn it, why couldn't he remember the reason he had to keep his hands off her? Despite everything, she was involved with the Chans through her sister. But as soon as he touched Marcy, none of that mattered.

"There's no but about it. You said it last time—we have chemistry."

Light as her touch on his shoulder was, it ignited his need for her. His brief was to observe Marcy. Not to touch her, or succumb to her innocent sexiness.

And not to get involved with her.

More than his job would be at stake if he took that path. "Chemistry which we don't need to demonstrate to every trekker and string of yaks. Marcy—"

Hurt darkened her eyes and she dropped her hand as though burnt. "Don't say you're sorry. You told me to do whatever I could to—"

Right and wrong didn't matter. Ridiculous as it was, he felt proprietorial about Marcy and the thought of her kissing another man twisted his guts. "Don't you dare use that tactic on anyone else."

"What tactic?"

"Seduction."

Eyes wide, her lips parted and she whispered, "Or what?"

"I may have to hurt them."

Chapter Fourteen

The first sight of the river failed to divert Marcy's dark thoughts and she pushed ahead. Jake had kept his distance after her lesson, and joined the all-male group heading into town for what sounded like a beery boys' night out. Uninvited and the lone female at the teahouse, she'd claimed a headache and gone to bed early.

Over breakfast this morning, Jake's gaze had scorched her but his frown failed to lift.

Had she misread his attraction to her?

Embarrassed and uncertain, she kept quiet. If her presence annoyed him, why didn't he leave her to finish her trek alone? She picked up her pace, but couldn't outrun her angry thoughts.

Chewang stopped at the side of the path. "Doctor, steep ahead. We stop for tea now?"

She pulled up, her breath coming hard and loud. "Let's push on, Chewang. I'd like to get to Lukla as soon as possible. We could make it by tonight if we keep moving."

Jake stopped beside her, looking as cool as if he were out for a stroll. "It's one more day's walk after this." His first comment since they'd left reminded her how much she needed to distance herself from him.

"But it's doable."

"You'll miss Tengbouche."

"I've had enough of the track. An extra night or two of comfort in Kathmandu would be welcome." Striding ahead, she eyed the narrow, steep descent. One of the few such stretches, it needed a little more concentration and a lot less conversation with Jake. She hitched her backpack and set off.

Behind her, Jake set loose a flurry of small stones that rolled past her and *plinked* over the edge. Ahead, the path narrowed to single file. She moved closer to the carved out rock, away from the drop.

A cowbell tinkled beyond the bend and she pulled up short. Where she stood was probably the narrowest part of the path. How close was the yak?

Her fingers trembled on the rock face as she dithered. Retreat or hurry around the bend and hope she didn't come face to face with four hundred pounds of bovine?

Wiping her sweaty palm on her pants, she dragged in a deep breath and headed downhill.

A string of shaggy beasts plodded up the hill. Laden with brightly coloured plastic ware on top of multiple bulging sacks, the lead beast filled the space. By virtue of size alone, it had right of way.

She backed up and looked for somewhere to climb off the path before the beast knocked her off or squashed her.

"Marcy, come back." Jake beckoned from the bend. "There's a spot back here where we can get out of the way. It's small but we'll both fit."

Up close and personal with Jake wasn't in her plans. After yesterday's brush off, it wouldn't feature ever again. She waved him away. "You take it."

"Don't be silly. There's nowhere to go down there."

"I'm fine here." She eyed the shallow depression with distaste. Eating dirt was the least of her worries. And the worst?

She turned to check the yaks' progress.

The lead yak scrambled up the rocky path with an agility she envied.

A little way in front of the string of yaks, a Nepalese man carrying a stick saw her and approached. "Are you the doctor lady?"

Taken aback, Marcy nodded. "I'm not a medical doctor though, if that's what you need."

"From Australia? Dr. Westcott?"

"That's me."

"I have something for you." He reached into his jacket.

Behind him, the lead animal jumped a gully across the track, looming large as it neared. There was no room to pass, no room for the man, the yak, and her.

As the animal drew level, instinct forced her back.

Her boot slipped and the weight of her backpack dragged her over the edge of the path. She twisted and fell on her back.

Grey rocks skittered past as she hurtled down the steep slope. Bottom and backpack took the brunt of her slide. Frantically, she scrabbled for a handhold and missed.

Dust flew up around her. Blinded, she tried to dig her heels into the slope. Rocks dislodged and raced her down the slope.

Suddenly, she flew through the air.

With a thump that knocked the wind out of her, she landed. Her tailbone ached, dust filled her nose and eyes and she was certain she'd landed in something soft and smelly. But her slide from hell was over.

A shower of small stones rained down on her. She lifted an arm to protect her head before Jake skidded into view.

He threw off his backpack, and knelt beside her. His gaze raked her face. "Are you hurt? Any bones broken?"

She shook her head and spat out a mouthful of dust. "I don't think so."

"Wiggle your fingers. Can you move your feet?"

"I came down on my backpack."

"Humour me. I need to see for myself." Rough tones tinged his voice.

Before she could think logically and tell him she was a doctor and could self assess for injury, his hands were feeling along her left leg.

"I told you, I'm fine."

"Good. I'm just checking." He ran his hands down her right leg.

"I told you I'm—ow!"

Jake unclipped her boot. His hands parted the sides and he held her calf firmly as he eased her boot off. Strong fingers gently probed.

She bit her lip as a shaft of pain like a red-hot poker speared up her leg. How had she missed that?

"Your ankle is swelling. Probably sprained." He unzipped a side pocket of his backpack and opened a first aid kit that rivalled hers in size. Easing her foot onto his thigh, he wrapped her ankle in a wide bandage, making a neat figure-of-eight pattern that could have earned him a position in a hospital.

"You've done that before." She winced as he lowered her heel onto his thigh and clipped the bandage.

"I've done a lot of things but that's the first yak attack I've dealt with." He pulled her spare water bottle from the side of her pack and opened it. His gaze caught and held hers as he offered the bottle and a painkiller. "Like a slug of water to sluice out that half the mountain you swallowed?"

Now the shock of her rapid descent had faded, Marcy became aware of how dry and gritty her mouth was. With a nod of thanks, she took the bottle and swallowed several mouthfuls before taking the tablet. "Better."

"Want to tell me what happened?" He zipped his pack closed and sat back on his heels.

"There wasn't room on the path for three of us. I gave way to heavy traffic." She sipped more water.

"Three of you? What do you mean?" His voice had the sharp edge of a snapped-out order. It made her stomach clench. Was he about to go all macho control freak again?

Keeping a light tone, she looked back up the slope she'd descended. From where she sat, the path and the animals weren't visible. "The yak, the man who stopped to talk—he might have been the herder—and me."

"What man? What did he say?" Jake's gaze roamed the slope above and flicked back to the track they should have walked.

"Not much. He asked if I was the doctor. I figured he was looking for medical help and I told him I wasn't a medical doctor. That's it. The yak got too close, I panicked and took a step back."

"Was there anything else? Anything at all?"

Annoyance vied with the sharp pain in her ankle and she was grateful for the distraction. "No. I have what might be a tiny, tiny phobia about cattle. Can we move now? I think I landed in something."

"If you're sure there wasn't anything else." His steely gaze bored into her and she wondered again about the abrupt transition from guide to interrogator.

"I told you." She'd had it with his questions. Keeping quiet about the man's strange final comment, she drank the last of the water, wiped her mouth with the back of her hand and grimaced at the dirty streak she created. "I must look a sight."

Jake helped her to stand. "You're going to want another shower when we get to Tengbouche. Let me know if you need help." He released her and picked up his pack, then added hers on his front.

Putting weight on her foot was painful. She hissed as she drew breath and tried to balance on her good leg.

"Lean on me." Jake dropped both packs and kneeled beside his. He pulled a trekking pole from his pack, extended it to suit her height, and offered it to her. "Use this."

# #

The village came into view across the drop-away side of the mountain. If only she was a bird and could fly straight across. Marcy eyed the winding track, a fifteen-minute walk under normal circumstances. She gritted her teeth at the ache in her ankle.

"How are you holding up?" Jake stopped beside her and lowered the two packs. Sweat sheened his brow but his breathing seemed even for a man who had carried a double load.

"Just wonderful." She leaned against the rocky cutting and lifted her chin in the direction of the village. "Not far now."

Jake tipped her chin until she saw the concern in his eyes. "It's aching, isn't it?"

She considered denying the pain and pushing on, but she'd had enough of lies. "A bit."

"Chewang, can you take Marcy's pack for me?" The guide nodded and slung it over his small, personal pack.

"I can take it. I'm fine." Becoming reliant on Jake just because she was injured wasn't going to happen.

"That's not what I meant." Hands on her waist, he picked

her up and lifted her onto a low rock, slung his pack across his chest and turned his back. "Here, climb aboard the Everest Express."

Thoughts of climbing all over Jake had filled several of her nights, but not like this. "You can't carry me all that way."

"It's not far. Besides, this is the way everything gets to its destination on the track. Unless you prefer being slung over my shoulder?" One eyebrow quirked and devilment gleamed in his eyes.

She wouldn't put it past him to use his superior size to force her agreement. "Bossy boots. On your own head be it then."

Shuffling forward, she gripped his shoulders.

He leaned forward, arms clamped around her thighs, and adjusted her position. "On my back, actually. All set?"

She crossed her arms and gripped her elbows each side of his throat, trying not to choke him. "Ready. All aboard."

Jake's hands gripped her calves and he settled into a comfortable rhythm. His long stride ate up the distance while his breath huffed out more audibly than before.

Hugging his back, she forgot the ache in her ankle. Thighs tightened around his hips as a new ache settled between her legs. She wriggled, the distraction from her injured ankle both a blessing and a curse. Leaning forward, she put her mouth close to his ear. "Thanks for the ride, Jake."

He turned his head, his sideways gaze wicked. "I imagined a variation on this position, but glad to be your—ride."

Her heart skipped a beat. She forgot about his take-charge attitude, forgot the yak encounter. She hadn't made a mistake.

If she could convince him to leave the lights off, maybe they still had time to explore the attraction zapping between them.

"We should talk about these visions you're having."

He didn't answer straightaway, but his pace seemed to increase the closer they came to the village. "We need to talk, Marcy. But it can wait until you've rested."

"Why wait? Talking won't hurt my ankle."

"No, but you'll probably be glad to elevate and ice it. I've more painkillers in my pack if you need them."

Okay, fine. He didn't want to talk about them now. But later . . .

Lukla would have to wait a day while she rested her ankle. A lot could happen in one day—and the intervening night.

\# #

Jake deposited her carefully on the padded bench by the teahouse window and swung a stool across to rest her leg on. He was right. Despite being carried on his back, she felt exhausted. Now she wasn't bouncing along the track with his body as distraction, her ankle was killing her.

"I'll register both of us and then scare up a pot of tea."

"Could you see if they can scare up ice too, please?"

"Sure." Jake slipped through the doorway to the tiny foyer. The murmur of voices rose and fell.

Tipping her head back against the window, she closed her

eyes. Jake's take-charge attitude rubbed her up the wrong way. He could be arrogant and bossy, but she was grateful he'd carried her the last stretch.

Jake returned and scooped her into his arms. Her head lolled onto his shoulder and she struggled to open her eyes as the owner led the way to a standard, cubby-sized room.

"Let's get you more comfortable before Madhev comes back with ice." Jake unzipped her jacket and slipped it off then turned his attention to her remaining boot.

"I'm not a child."

Jaw muscles tight, Jake paused in the act of untying her boot. He looked at her, his gaze hungry. "Believe me, I know."

"Then why won't you—?"

"Do you want to get out of the rest of your clothes and sleep for a while?"

Only the first part of his statement registered. In the back of her mind, a faint alarm sounded, but she couldn't remember why. Hadn't she wanted them to shed their clothes earlier? But she was tired. So tired.

# #

Marcy curled onto her side and mumbled, "Later."

Jake covered her with a blanket and went in search of ice. The memory of her falling off the path and disappearing in a cloud of dust replayed in his mind and a lead weight settled in his stomach. Instinct had spurred him into a hair-raising chase as she slid towards the edge of the mountain, while his mind refused to believe he could lose her.

She was his link to the Chans. There was no other reason. There couldn't be.

He stood in the kitchen doorway and rubbed the back of his neck. Marcy was his assignment, his job. And she had lied about almost everything. Maybe she was protecting her sister the only way she could.

By putting herself on the line.

Like he would have done to protect Pete.

He shook his head. Getting involved had distracted him to the point he'd made a rookie mistake. One he hoped he wouldn't pay for by losing the connection to the Chans. If he couldn't keep his head screwed on properly, he should ask to be pulled from the assignment. But he refused to lose the chance to shut down Pete's suppliers. Torn between avenging his brother and not losing his first real link to the cartel, Jake stalked back to Marcy's room. Ice water dripped down his shirt from the bag of ice cubes.

He expected her to sleep after the pain medication he'd given her. Not bothering to knock, he opened her door. Her bandaged foot poked out from the blanket. Carefully, he wrapped the ice around her ankle. She didn't stir.

Finished with first aid duties, he rocked back on his heels, edged up the narrow space between the beds and sat opposite her.

Marcy lay as he'd left her, one hand tucked beneath her cheek. Dirt streaks led from the corner of her mouth to her ear and dust coated her clothes. Spikes of hair stuck out and a bruise shadowed her chin.

With one finger he traced the line of her jaw to the bruise. By tomorrow she'd have trouble tucking her chin in for the self-defence moves he'd shown her. But he knew she would try.

He left her in a deep drug-induced sleep and stowed his gear. Glancing at his watch, he was surprised to see it was almost time to phone Nicholls. He gathered the satellite phone and a bottle of water and retreated to a quiet spot some distance from the teahouse.

"Any news, Harris?"

"Dr. Westcott had an unusual accident today. She—fell off the track. Sprained ankle. Claimed a yak startled her."

"Is there something that makes you think it wasn't an accident?"

"Nothing concrete." Nothing but the feeling Marcy hadn't shared everything about the encounter with the herder. "Call it intuition. Do you have people keeping an eye on the airport?"

"Of course. Both regular and private flights are being monitored. Do you expect trouble before your return to the city?"

"It's possible. I don't think Dr. Westcott is the woman in your photo, but the link to her sister could endanger her."

"Stay with her. Report again same time tomorrow." The connection was cut.

Jake leaned against a wall and slipped the phone into his jacket.

Trouble with a capital T; that was Marcy.

Practising basic self-defence moves had been fun until her slim curves overwhelmed his good sense and he'd grabbed her. She was so determined to be self-reliant.

But who looked out for her?

He shouldn't be feeling protective towards her. He had to maintain his distance and objectivity. Besides, Marcy wouldn't thank him for treating her as less than capable of defending herself.

And if Marcy wasn't part of the cartel's plans but her sister was?

Jake rested his elbows on his knees and looked out into the gathering dusk.

If Marcy's little sister was involved with the cartel, he'd take the sister down too.

He had no choice.

Chapter Fifteen

"This is my trek and my guide and my decision and I say we go today." Marcy glared up at Jake from the window seat of the teahouse and curled her hands into the blanket.

He grinned. "I didn't appreciate how much you enjoyed riding me."

She flicked an embarrassed look at Chewang and prayed his English didn't include idiom. "What do you mean?"

"The only way you'll reach Lukla today is on my back. Not that I'm averse to the idea but you may wear me out for—anything more." He winked at her.

"You've got tickets on yourself if you think—"

He stepped into her personal space, and placed a hand on the window either side of her shoulders. "Forget the insults and consider the facts. Rest, ice, and elevation are the best cure for that sprain. Your best chance of rapid recovery is to follow the doctor's orders."

Boxed in on the bench and at a height disadvantage, she raised her chin. "The doctor thinks it would be better to get back to Lukla."

"The *doctor* is the one with most experience in the situation. Me."

There it was again. Chest-thumping, know-it-all, take over the little woman's plans, arrogant bastard. Damn him, why did the men in her life think they knew better than her?

"I'm the one who studied anatomy. It's my body and I know what I can push it to do."

Jake's nostrils flared. He leaned in, his mouth close to her ear. "So do I, Marcy."

Trapped beneath his dark gaze like a pinned butterfly, she wrestled the urge to place her mouth on his and damn the consequences. He was dictatorial and arrogant and she longed to slap him down to size.

She also longed to kiss him until she forgot her own name.

She fisted her hands beside her thighs. That *chemistry* between them urged her to plaster herself to his chest and test both their limits.

Clinging to Jake's back yesterday, not even the pain of her ankle had countered the desire thrumming through her body. Climbing aboard today was a no-brainer. Thighs clamped around his hips, she wouldn't last the first hundred metres, let alone the morning.

Chewang cleared his throat, reminding them of his presence.

"What do you think, Chewang? Is it better to push on or stay another night?"

"Mr. Harris has it right. Rest."

# #

But the extra night in Tengbouche allowed her to walk the final leg to Lukla, albeit slowly, under her own steam.

Jake insisted on carrying her pack. "It will balance out our walking speeds."

She bit back the retort that sprang to her lips and tried to accept with good grace, secretly applauding his perseverance in the face of her grumpy mood. Sometimes self-reliance was overrated.

And there were advantages to slow walking.

He climbed the hotel stairs ahead of her, his backpack failing to hide the view of his taut butt.

Pushing open the door to her hotel room, he lowered her pack to the floor at the end of her bed. "I'll dump my gear in my room then we can get some lunch. Unless you want to put your leg up and rest for a while?"

"Food please. I had enough of being good and resting in Tengbouche."

"Back in five then." He dropped her key in her palm and pulled the door closed behind him.

The room was marginally bigger than those in the teahouses but, after the freedom of walking the track, Marcy needed air. She opened the window and stuck her head out.

Beyond the wire fence, a Yeti Airlines plane taxied to the upper end of the steep runway, its tail pointed at solid rock, its nose aiming for the not-so-distant drop-off. Engines revving to maximum, it rolled swiftly down the slope and lunged off the end of the tarmac into thin air. The plane dipped, found its balance and curved away towards Kathmandu.

Marcy released her breath and backed into Jake's chest. Her heart skipped a beat. "You gave me a fright. How do you move so quietly?"

"You were intent on watching the take-off. It still amazes me, no matter how many times I watch them land or leave."

"Yeah, that drop at the bottom of the runway is scarily fascinating. Give me a minute to wash my face and hands and I'm ready."

#

An hour later, Jake pushed his chair back and patted his flat stomach. "Best pasta I've eaten in ages." I don't think I could eat another thing."

"What, no dessert? I'm treating myself to dessert tonight." She tossed her serviette on the table.

"Aren't you having withdrawal symptoms from *dahl baht*?"

"As if. This body needs something sweet put into it. Don't you long for something sweet, Jake?"

Jake's gaze locked on her mouth. He shook his head, although she'd said nothing for him to disagree with. Abruptly, he stood and pushed his chair under the table. "I have to check in with work. I'll pay on the way out. See you later."

"But—okay."

He strode away before he said something he'd regret.

One night, Harris. One sweet night with Marcy is all you're allowed. Tomorrow you'll hand her over to Nicholls and keep looking for that link to the Chans.

The bell on the door dinged as a new patron entered. Jake flicked a glance up and groaned. He should have known she'd make straight for the Internet café after lunch.

Sweet? Hell, it wasn't her fault he made more of her innocent comments than she intended. Since his uninvited view of her shower and their first ball-breaking kiss, his one-track mind was fixated on Marcy's luscious body. But while a question hung over her link to the Chans, he couldn't afford to lose himself in her sweetness. One night was all they had.

He knew it wouldn't be enough.

Nicholls' latest message appeared on his screen. Jake read the first paragraph twice then sat back.

Marcy's research was legitimate. A big pharmaceutical company had funded her research trip to Dolpa. Details were sketchy but her work was *bona fide*.

It looked like his gut instinct had proven correct. With half the Westcott women's mysteries solved, he looked up as she moved to the only free booth—beside him. He tapped the mouse to close his email.

"Hi again. I won't bother you but there's nowhere else free." Her gaze skimmed the top of his head as though determined not to intrude.

"No bother." At least, none he would share in the middle of a busy café.

She slid onto the stool beside him. The slowly oscillating corner fan wafted the scent of her coconut shampoo to him. He closed his eyes and breathed deeply. Opening them again, he met her gaze. "Whenever I smell coconut, I'll think of you, Marcy."

"I'm glad you'll remember me. I just wish—" She cleared her throat, turned to her screen and logged on.

"Me, too. There's still tonight."

Her hand stilled on the mouse. She lowered her chin and tilted her head to look up at him. "Don't make promises you don't intend to keep."

"I don't."

"All right then."

He couldn't promise what tomorrow might bring. He may have to go after her sister and that would hurt Marcy. But tonight, they both had an itch to scratch.

"Meet you back at the hotel for dinner?" He needed a different sort of protection before tonight.

# #

Jake knocked on Marcy's door and waited then knocked again.

"Sir, Missy downstairs in bar." The maid folded a fresh towel over her arm and collected a small bar of soap from her basket.

"Thanks." He headed downstairs. Not a good start to the

evening.

Marcy was seated in the far corner of the bar where the lights were low. As he approached, he saw she was still wearing her trekking outfit and the table in front of her held two cans of pre-mixed rum and Coke. One lay crumpled on its side; the second sat in a pool of condensation. She clung to a half-empty glass tumbler.

"Marcy, what's up?" He slid onto the opposite bench.

Red-rimmed eyes blinked and she raised her tumbler in a mock toast. "Here's to me stuffing up." She sipped her drink and banged the tumbler on the table. Anger rolled off her in palpable waves.

Anger he could deal with. "What's happened?"

"Damn, I want to wring their necks."

Not his neck then. "Whose?"

She drew in a deep breath and slowly released it. "I guess it doesn't matter if I tell you. Not now. I won a research grant and was supposed to be heading to Dolpa after my trek to Base Camp but my funding has been withdrawn. You'll never guess why."

His stomach clenched. "Don't tell me, the video?"

She clicked her tongue. "Clever boy. I'm not, to quote my former funder, *the right face for their family focussed company.* Unquote."

"You mean they've pulled out solely on the basis of one kiss? How the hell did they get hold of the video? I thought it had been pulled down?"

She dragged her finger through the puddle of water left by her glass. "Apparently someone sent them a copy, even though it had been blocked. I was to write a travel research blog from Dolpa with photos etcetera. Not the secret stuff, of course. Apparently, they had a promotional package planned around me. Seems my *notorious behaviour*—their words, not mine—doesn't meet the company image."

"I'm really sorry, Marcy." Blindly, he recognised his loss of control had created a ripple effect. Major companies had far-reaching power when it came to protecting their reputations. They wouldn't think twice about offering up Marcy's career to save their public image. But Nicholls had said the Bureau had blocked the video quickly, as soon as their software picked up his face. There had been no chance for it to go viral. So who had leaked the video to the pharmaceutical company, and why? Steamy as the footage might have been, the youngsters who'd filmed them hadn't been so close that Marcy would be easily identifiable, unless someone was already looking for her in that area. Was there a hidden agenda he wasn't privy to? Was the Bureau involved in the leak?

"Not your problem. We were both right into that kiss. At least I'll be able to head home sooner and find out what's going on with my sister. It worries me not being there for her."

He shook his head, frustrated as questions compounded around Marcy. "You sound like you've had experience of being disappointed."

She ran a finger around the rim of her glass then pushed it

away. "You could say that. My father—let's just say there was always another mountain for him to climb. Tam and I had each other but it was tough on our mum to be alone so much."

Her father again. Every reference to the man featured him as a distant figure more than a family man. Was that why she insisted on doing everything for herself?

"You said your sister is younger. I thought you were twins? Does she still live with your mum?"

"We are twins. I'm the elder by eighteen minutes and no, we shared a tiny flat in Sydney while I was studying. When she got the event co-ordinator's job, she moved closer to the CBD. It made more sense with all the evening events she organises and I worry less about her travelling on late night trains."

"You're very protective of your sister. Tell me, what's she working on now?"

"Her wedding. At least—" Marcy's calm dissolved.

Her guard was down and he pressed for more information. Covering her hand with his, he squeezed gently. "Have you heard any more about her fiancé? Has he turned up?"

"Not a word. And now it's like she's disappeared off the face of the earth too."

"Both of them are missing?" This assignment attracted bad juju like horseflies to a cowpat. His brain clicked through possibilities, none of them any good. "Would they have eloped?"

"I'd have considered that if I didn't know her so well. Small white wedding on a boat on Sydney Harbour, that's what she's planned. Once Tam's made up her mind, it would take a meteor hitting Earth to change her plans. Maybe not even then." A tiny smile quirked up one corner of her mouth, disappearing as quickly.

"My offer to help through my company still stands. We have an office in Sydney—"

"Jake, it's a thoughtful offer. But I'll be back in Sydney within a couple of days. I'm sure she'll contact me then. Since there's not a thing I can do about it tonight, can we stop talking about Tam, work and all the crap that's happened and just eat?" Her eyes were sad, her spark, dimmed.

Her attempt to soldier on touched something inside him. Respecting her need, he nodded. "Fine. Do you want to go out for dinner or shall we grab a bite here?"

"Can your stomach wait fifteen minutes while I get respectable? We can try that Moroccan restaurant you pointed out, if you like?"

"Sure. I'll grab a beer while you change."

#

Dessert arrived, and it seemed to Jake that Marcy's mood lightened.

Sliding her finger through the powdered sugar dusting her plate, she traced random lines. "Did I mention I love sweet things?" She raised her finger and turned it to catch the light.

His gaze locked on her fingertip.

She slipped her finger between pink lips, and sucked. Her

finger emerged along with a soft, satisfied sigh. "Do you want a taste of mine? Bet it fills your need for something sweet."

In the days since they'd met, Marcy had become more confident and assertive. Jake didn't care how that played out in bed, so long as he sank into her body before he exploded. All he wanted was to set loose the woman who'd shaken him out of his depression and enjoy the ride.

"No, thanks. But I know what will." He reached across the table and took hold of her chin. Brushing his thumb across her bottom lip, he listened as her breath hitched, watched as her breasts rose and fell. That soft gasp was all the answer he needed.

She was very good at making him feel like being very bad.

He picked up the last square of Turkish Delight and offered it to her.

Leaning forward, she bit the piece in two, grazing her lower lip against his fingers. That plump, moist lip he needed to nibble on.

Slowly, she poked out just the tip of her tongue and licked stray smudges of powdered sugar from her lips.

Two could play that game. He slid the remaining half into his mouth and, holding her gaze, licked his thumb.

Her lips parted and she edged forward. "Have you had enough?" Husky-voiced, her invitation was clear.

"Yes."

"Thank goodness. Let's go."

He pulled her chair out, grabbed her hand and headed to the

door. Releasing his hold long enough to pay the cashier, he added, "Keep the change."

Mist, poor street lighting, and Marcy's injured ankle slowed their pace. The caveman part of his brain considered throwing her over his shoulder and jogging home. Regretfully, he suppressed the idea. The last thing they needed was any more publicity.

Her hand gripped his arm tighter and he slowed his pace more. This time, they'd make it to bed. This time, they would not be interrupted. He hoped bedding Marcy would get her out of his system.

Yeah, right. Like kissing her had stopped him thinking about her?

Finally, the hotel appeared through the mist. He turned to climb the steps.

Marcy's hold was wrenched from his arm at the same time as the sound of two bodies colliding.

Jake spun on his heel, aware of a dark-clad figure merging into the misty night. He wrapped an arm around Marcy and pulled her close. "Are you okay?" He searched the shadows but the person had vanished.

She nodded and caught her breath. "Someone ran into me."

"Probably too drunk to realise." Jake scanned the area again. If the man had been drunk he'd have been sprawled on the ground at her feet. Sharing that seemed less than helpful. Instead, he stroked her cheek. "My fault for hurrying you along. I should have slung you over my shoulder."

She rested her hand on his chest and leaned in. His arousal brushed her stomach, reminding him of the urgent need to reach their destination. "I want you naked beneath me within two minutes or we're going to cut another indecent news flash on these steps. Coming?"

"Your place or mine?"

"Who's closest?" He held the front door open and led her towards the stairs. "On second thoughts, come here." With a move she didn't see coming, he scooped her up in his arms and took the stairs two at a time.

Arms wrapped around his neck, her breath fanned his cheek. She nuzzled his ear then nipped his earlobe.

The dart of pain sent blood pulsing south. At the top landing, he lowered her to the floor outside her door.

Her ankle gave way and she fell against him with a soft curse. "Damned weak ankle."

He cradled her hips and pulled her butt against his throbbing cock. "It won't be a problem once we're inside and horizontal."

The first time he took her was going to be hard and fast and out here on the landing if she didn't hurry. "Come on, Marcy."

She slipped her hand into her pocket. Dismay coloured her tone as her fingers poked through a hole in the fabric. "I've lost my key."

Physical need overthrew chivalry.

"We'll get you a new one in the morning." He grabbed her hand and pulled her down the narrow corridor, slid his key into the lock and, within a heartbeat, pulled her into his room. He shut the door and pressed her back against it.

Lost key forgotten, she slid her arms around his waist. "You were saying something about getting—"

"Naked, yeah."

He dragged her jacket down her arms and pulled her shirt out of her trousers.

She tugged his shirt and T-shirt loose. Lowering his head he took a step backwards so Marcy could pull both off in one movement. As he stepped back her hands reached for his trousers.

"Boots first." He tipped her onto the bed and made short work of unlacing first her boots, then his. "Now, Dr. Westcott, let's get to that exploratory."

# #

Jake stripped his shirt so fast Marcy had no time to appreciate the view. In the dim light, she ran both palms over his chest. A light covering of hair tickled the tips of her fingers around the flat disks of his nipples. Raising her head, she licked the nearest one and blew gently across it. Beneath her hands, his pectoral muscle twitched. "First lesson in anatomy . . . "

"Peel back extraneous covering." Smoothly, he took back control, sliding her trousers and underwear off before shucking his. He laid her on his bed.

Her breath caught in her throat. Naked and standing proud,

his gaze devoured her sprawled body. Jake was magnificent. Muscles like tempered steel, broad shoulders, lean hips and an erection she needed to taste. Like a panther stalking prey, he padded up the bed and covered her body with his.

Trapped within the cage of his arms and long, muscular thighs, she slipped her hands across the bulge of shoulder muscle and into his hair. Street lighting filtered through the open curtains, and her skin glowed pale against his tanned body. Dark and intense, his gaze pierced her as firmly as his hips pinned her to the bed.

Quick little pants of longing for Jake's body and hers to get on with merging filled the silence. She needed the connection more than she needed air. Tipping her head in invitation, she boldly met his eyes.

He lowered his head. Her eyelids fluttered down and she simply—felt. Skin seared by her all-male, full-body-blanket, the weight of his hips, the impression of his thickening arousal on her belly. Oh God, the heat of his mouth!

In a tangle of tongues, his mouth plundered hers. Swift nips on her lips, along her jaw sent a surge of lust coursing through her.

He moved lower, hands and mouth licking, kneading, sucking her breasts and stoking a furnace in her belly. His fully aroused cock stroked her thigh.

Darts of pleasure-pain shafted through her. She wriggled her hips, needing to feel him deep within her. "Jake. Please. Now."

"Thank God."

He rolled to the side. Foil crinkled then he covered her body with his. Leaning on his forearms, he captured her gaze. "Ready?"

"Yes."

Like a heat-seeking missile, he entered her in one swift, deep stroke.

Her body welcomed him, muscles rippling around his length. Legs wrapped around his waist.

He pushed deeper, pulled most of the way out then thrust again. His long frame quivered, his breath grated harshly in her ears. "I don't think I can take it slow this time."

"Slow is overrated."

Groaning, he thrust faster, the tempo keeping pace with her thudding heart.

Tight lines of pleasure centred on their joining, built until she shattered like crystal against a mountain of rock. Her scream of release was overtaken by Jake's shout.

Head thrown back, he pumped into her one last time before his body relaxed.

Forehead resting on hers, their panting breaths mingled. Her body shivered with aftershocks of pleasure.

Jake rolled onto his back, taking her with him.

Sprawled across his chest, their legs tangled. She traced his jaw and dropped two light kisses there before lethargy claimed her. Outside, it could be a snowstorm for all she knew. In this room, in Jake's arms, his hard strength enfolded her. She felt safe.

Snuggling into his shoulder, she closed her eyes.

Chapter Sixteen

Promoting his dick to decision-maker was the stupidest career move ever. Jake rolled onto his back, one butt cheek finding only air. He edged his behind across the sheet and his hip was surrounded by heat.

Marcy.

In one hot encounter he'd broken every rule on personal engagement. Forget reprimands. Nicholls would have more than his balls if he found out. He'd be off the Chan case for good. Great way to avenge Pete.

Pins and needles tingled in the hand curled around Marcy's hip.

Distance. He needed to get up and away from the temptation of her silky curves and honeyed musk. He flexed his fingers and tried to ease his arm out from under her body. His chest brushed her breast as he manoeuvred a silent retreat.

She sighed, her breath soft and warm against his neck. Her knee skimmed his thigh and rose towards his groin.

And he wanted to do it all over again.

Resting his head on his bent arm, his gaze roamed across

her face. How had she slipped beneath his defences? When had sweetly determined replaced *know-the-score-let's-party* women for a one-night stand?

Butterfly-light, he traced a path across her stomach and over her ribs to her breast.

And stopped.

There's no birthmark.

Hell, he'd been so engrossed in making love to Marcy he'd forgotten to check. Temporary tatts might be all the rage but that missing birthmark was proof. Not that he needed further evidence.

Was the uncanny likeness between the sisters common knowledge? More importantly, who knew? If the Chans were responsible for the disappearance of Marcy's sister, was there a chance they knew about Marcy? Was there any reason they would come after her?

Was Marcy a pawn in a bigger game that he was still working out the rules of?

Bile rose in his throat. She'd hate the thought of being used, of losing control. Already she'd lost so much; her father, her funding. What if her sister was caught up in the drug web?

Like Candace. Best not think of the woman who had used her relationship with Peter to seduce his young brother into trying party drugs.

Mind racing, he started building alternate plans. Marcy might need protection from shadowy figures out to get her or her sister. If they believed Marcy was Tam, was the danger greater?

Absentmindedly, his palm brushed her nipple. She arched into his touch.

His cock stirred, brushing across her mound. What an idiot to think one night with her would be enough to scratch the itch. Lowering his head, he nipped the sensitive spot where her neck and shoulder met. Beneath his mouth, she shivered.

"Like that?"

"Uh huh."

He cupped her breast and teased the tip with his tongue. Nip—lick—blow. Beneath his sensual assault, her nipples pebbled.

Half-awake, she ran her toe along his calf.

He slipped his knee between her thighs. This time he was determined to take it slowly.

Chapter Seventeen

Sydney, Australia

John Chan buckled his belt and adjusted his trousers. The young whore's naked body sprawled across the bed. Blood trickled from wrists manacled to brass railings. Legs spread-eagled and tied to the lower bedposts gave him an unimpeded view of her glistening pink flower. Like a lotus on the water.

He finished buttoning his shirt and spared a glance at her face. Dark curls half-hid the still pink cheeks beneath the plastic bag. Sex was much more pleasurable when they struggled. When they fought and he subdued them. A moment of regret passed through him. This one had given him much pleasure. Under other circumstances he would have reserved her to his exclusive use, but until the woman was brought back from Nepal, his appetite could only be met by complete surrender.

He unlocked the door and stepped into the corridor. Two burly guards waited, their faces showing no expression.

"Dispose of the body then pick me up at the office after lunch."

The encounter had taken the edge off his frustration. For

now.

Madame Wu approached and bowed, her blood-red fingernails a stark contrast to her pale cheeks. "Sir is satisfied?"

"You chose well, Madame Wu. But next time a woman will be delivered to you. See that she is prepared to my requirements." The madam bowed low as he walked to the reinforced steel door and turned. She looked up and her breath hitched softly. Fear flashed through her dark eyes before she lowered her lashes, and a sense of his world righting itself speared through Chan. Just so would the woman look at him as he described in stunning detail what she would experience at his hands. Every exquisite pain he would inflict. "And Madame Wu, has the Wheel been delivered?"

She rose and her lips pressed together briefly. "Yes, sir."

"Have it installed and fully set up before my next visit."

Madame Wu inclined her head and bowed again. His bodyguard opened the door and held it as Chan stepped into the private underground car park. He pressed speed dial and his contact picked up on the fourth ring. "Yes, boss?"

"What news? Where is she?"

"She's reached Lukla, but she's with an agent from the Bureau."

"Eliminate him when you take her. I expect your next call to be the news that you have her." He severed the connection. The woman he wanted would soon be in his reach. The man—the one who had dared take what Chan desired of the woman—would be dead.

Both results would suffice.

Chapter Eighteen

"How can I lose anything in a room this small?" Marcy scrabbled through their combined clothing, tossing items onto the bed. Knickers didn't just disappear into thin air.

"Is this what you're looking for?" From his forefinger dangled her practical boy-leg trekking knickers.

Why couldn't they have been her black lacy pair? She grabbed the underwear and turned her back, hopping between the bunks in her haste to dress. Hauling up her trousers she prayed for better coordination in her next life. "Can you pass me my shirt please?"

Their hasty strip of last night had sent clothing in every direction. Her shirt decorated the wall light.

"I didn't realise you'd hung anything." Jake's lips twitched as he handed over her top before pulling up the zipper on his trousers. In the corner, her jacket lay in a crumpled heap.

As he bent to retrieve it, she tilted her head for a better angle. Low-slung and fitted, Jake's trousers covered the best butt she'd seen. And groped.

Before she could drag her eyes off his behind, he caught

her perving and grinned. "Like what you see?"

"A fine view from where I'm standing." What did one say after the night they'd shared? She cleared her throat. "Thanks for last night. It was great."

"I aim to please. Want your jacket?"

"Thanks. Meet you downstairs for breakfast." She grabbed the last of her clothing and hugged it to her chest as she walked to the communal bathroom.

In typical rotten Marcy timing, she'd be flying out today after the best night of her life and probably never see Jake again.

Half an hour later, she pushed her plate of half finished food to the side. "About last night—"

Across the table, Jake mopped up the last of his egg with toast. His smile dimmed. "It's a one-off, Marcy."

"Of course. I know that." Goodbyes were never easy. If only she had been more like Tam, grabbing life by the horns and digging in the spurs. Lost nights in his arms would haunt her when she returned home.

She pressed her lips together to prevent the words escaping. *Stay with me. Make love to me one more time.*

"Tell me about your sister."

Her stomach clenched. She picked up a piece of toast and crumbled it onto her plate. Why should she trust him? Sleeping together didn't change her issues, especially with domineering men who wanted things all their own way.

"There's not much to tell. We grew up together and we had

each other's backs. I'm sure you and your sister were the same. Siblings look out for one another."

"True. Why didn't you mention you're twins?"

"How did you—?"

He tapped her chest. "No birthmark." His touch lingered on her skin like a phantom presence long after he lowered his hand.

"I knew you were too observant to miss that. That's why I couldn't sleep with you, not until—"

"You knew your sister was safe?"

"I still don't know if she is. But now I'm going home, I'll find her." Without achieving her research. A small part of her ached for the lost chance. It wouldn't come her way again.

"You know what I was going to do in Dolpa?"

"Research. Into what baffles me though."

"The Yarsagumbu beetle. Heard of it?"

# #

"I saw the stampede to collect it first-hand. Never again." City crowds were bad enough but thousands of people swarming over usually deserted slopes was Jake's definition of hell. "What do you want with it?"

"It's coveted as an aphrodisiac. Chinese merchants pay big money for even half a kilogram." Marcy ripped pieces off her serviette and dropped them like confetti onto her plate.

Another blasted Chinese connection. Jake's gut clenched at another tenuous link.

Even though Nicholls had validated her research, the

coincidence struck him as odd. In his bones, he felt Marcy was innocent, but was that because he'd allowed himself to fall under her spell? Giving in to physical impulses had been stupid on so many levels.

But I'd do the same again, just without the video.

When he returned to Kathmandu, he would apply for leave to go home. If the Chans were in Sydney where both Paul, and Marcy's sister had disappeared, there had to be some link.

And Marcy works there.

So what? His brain snarled a warning at him. *Stay the hell away from her.*

Marcy offered a tight little smile that failed to reach her eyes. "Sometimes scientists are on the right track, just with the wrong goal. I doubt the use of the fungus helps men's vigour in bed but it has potential in other areas of medicine. At least, the company who was backing my research had faith in my proposal for a real drug. Of course, it's all academic now they've rescinded my funding."

Because he'd compromised her. If he'd remained in control, none of this would have happened. But so far, only her reputation had taken a hit. He prayed that was the worst thing that happened.

"What will you do?"

She shrugged and scrunched the remains of her serviette. "Look for more funding. Get a job in a lab helping someone else achieve their research goal. After losing my backing, I doubt anyone else will be willing to give me a go. In the scientific world, it's like you're blacklisted once a grant is pulled."

"It's a pity. I rather like the idea of hunting aphrodisiacs." She didn't need to know he'd already found his. In her.

"What about you? Will you be leading another trek?"

"Maybe. I'd thought of offering my services for your Dolpa trip."

Her forehead creased in a frown before she took a deep breath and met his eyes. "Did you think the aphrodisiac properties of the beetle might help you?"

Recognising her nonsense as the diversion it was, he silently applauded. If it helped her deal with the pain of her lost dream, he'd play along. "Help me? Are you saying you weren't completely satisfied with my performance?"

Marcy threw him the ghost of a cheeky grin. "There might be certain refinements of technique you could try if—"

"If you live long enough to experience them." *Shit. I don't mean* if *she lives.*

"Oh-ho, fighting words, is it?"

He checked his watch as a matter of course. "I'd love to stay and cross swords with you, Marcy, but if we don't get down to the booking office soon, you won't be catching a flight until late afternoon." He reached for her jacket and held it while she pushed her arms into the sleeves. Gripping the bottom edges, he slipped the metal ends of the zipper together and drew it up to her throat.

"Still not a child, Jake. Learned to do my own zippers

when I was four." She thrust her hands into her pockets. "Damn." Her fingers poked out the slit her key must have slipped through last night.

He sat on his chair, pulled her closer and examined the rip in her pocket.

"What are you doing, Jake?"

He fingered the edges of the slit. "This was cut by a knife."

"No. It can't be. That man last night—" Colour drained from her cheeks and she sank onto her chair.

Memory unfurled like a slow-motion film—him impatiently turning into the hotel and tugging Marcy up the stairs, her off balance, two bodies thudding together.

Her key had been in that pocket. Jake had watched her zip it in as they headed out to dinner. Had the accident been no more than an attempt to rob her? Or was he projecting danger because of the Chan connection?

He surged to his feet. "Let's get our ride off this mountain organised now."

"Our? I thought you were going back to work."

"I am. I'm heading back to Kathmandu with you. Can't let my favourite doctor finish her trek alone. Come on."

Chewang approached their table, a frown marring his usually serene expression. "Doctor, sir, there will be no flights off the mountain today."

##

"You're staying with me tonight." Jake opened the door to

his room and ushered her in ahead of him.

Marcy shrugged out of her jacket and dropped it on the bed, distaste clear in her expression. She raised one eyebrow. "One date and we're moving in together? You're a slick mover, Jake."

"We've got the day to fill. Have a look at that." He handed her a tourist brochure before dumping his pack on the second bed. "Are you saying you didn't enjoy last night?"

Turning his back on Marcy, he dug deep.

"You made it quite clear last night was a one-off affair—I mean, not an affair but—"

"Afraid another night will tie us together for life?" His fingers wrapped around the handle of his gun. Keeping it hidden from Marcy, he tucked it into the back of his trousers and adjusted his jacket over it.

"Don't flatter yourself. Besides—" She looked up and he raised a hand to cut off the rest of the sentence.

"You mentioned something about refining my technique. You can't make a statement like that then back out on me."

Not when someone had used a knife on her jacket and run off into the night. And not when the chance to lose himself in her once more was tantalisingly possible thanks to heavy fog closing down the airstrip. Who was he to ignore a gift from the gods of the mountains?

Besides, he considered staying close to her after last night's incident part of his job. He was ramping up his brief—from observation to protection.

"Come on. Let's go find a tailor to mend your jacket. Unless you'd prefer to buy a new one?"

"I'd like to burn this one, but it's brand new." She shrugged into the jacket, thrust her hand into the intact pocket and threw him a look filled with frustration. "It's not like I've got job security and money to spare now."

"There's a tailor near the Moroccan restaurant. Shout you a Starbucks coffee while he repairs it."

An hour, two coffees and one repaired jacket later, they walked back to the hotel.

Dense fog blanketed the town, hiding the airstrip from view and turning the midday light into dusk. As they walked into reception, a wall of noise hit them. The bar was filled with trekkers delayed by bad weather. Chances of getting a flight out tomorrow decreased when someone mentioned the forecast was for continued fog.

"And a possible unseasonable fall of snow," added a dour voice. "I'll miss my connection to Bangkok."

Jake found space at the bench looking over the street and nudged Marcy onto the single remaining bar stool. "Stay here and mind the space. I'll grab a couple of beers."

"Yes, sir." She threw him a mock salute. "Yours to command, sir."

"Remember that." He tapped her nose and shouldered his way back to the bar.

Marcy's independent streak was going to make his next move problematic. Should he rely on charm to convince her staying with him was her safest move, or tell her the truth?

What was the truth? Were the Chans after her, or her sister? Was Marcy in danger?

Options at zero, Marcy was glued to his side until Nicholls and the department found her sister, or Paul resurfaced to explain the connections. Protection was his new brief, but from whom he had no idea.

A lick of pleasure caught him unawares. Adrenaline mixed with lust in his belly, the combination potent. But while another night of losing himself in Marcy was damned appealing, there would be no more dick-decisions.

He pushed through the throng and handed her a bottle of beer. "You can move your gear into my room when we've had a drink."

"Has anyone ever told you to mind your own business?"

"It's a sensible option."

"I'm a big girl now. I can take care of myself." She turned away and tipped the bottle to her mouth.

"I'll move my gear into your room then."

She turned back and glared at him. "Oh, for heaven's sake—can't you invite a girl nicely?"

"Marcy, please join me this evening for fun and games in my room. Or yours, if you prefer. We can explore how well your aphrodisiac works."

"Jake—" Annoyance tinged her voice but bright eyes gave the lie to her mock censure.

"Teasing aside, there's no more room at the inn. Some of these guys will spend the night on the floor down here and, while it's not a hardship, there are a couple of young women over there who would appreciate a room." He swung the arm holding the beer and indicated two female trekkers at the bar. Raising it in a silent toast to them, he smiled and nodded. They waved back, giving him a thumbs up.

Marcy couldn't hang onto a room for two under these circumstances. "I should have thought of that. I'll clear my gear out now."

He peered out the window, assessing the chances of a break in the fog blanketing the village. "Take your time. No one is going far today."

Including Marcy's assailant.

"When I've moved my things, I'll go to the Internet café and see if there's any word from Tam."

"I'll come with you. I need to check in with work. Do you want help changing your flights?" Until he knew what threatened her, he was her shadow.

"I'm sure I can manage, but thanks for the offer." She finished the last of her drink. "Can I borrow your key?"

"I'll come—"

Her hand rose between them in the gesture he was coming to recognise. Marcy didn't like to be told anything.

Giving her space challenged his need to provide round-the-clock protection. Sitting on the stool she'd just vacated, he pushed aside the niggling desire to tuck her under his arm and handed over his room key. "I'll wait here."

Relief shone in the smile she threw over her shoulder. "Back in five. My shout then."

Jake leaned an elbow on the counter and cast an eye over the assembly of trekkers and guides. If the whiteout continued for a few days, frustration levels would be as high as the body count sleeping in the bar room.

It galled him that he'd been unable to catch the guy who'd ripped off Marcy's key last night. Was he one of the crowd here or an opportunistic thief?

His gaze narrowed on a lone male propping up the bar. The guy held a bottle of beer. Eyes fixed on the door through which Marcy had passed, he hadn't raised his hand to his mouth until Marcy left.

What if the Chans were after her? Had they activated a kill order on her or was last night just coincidence? Damn it, he shouldn't have allowed Marcy to go up alone. Every second out of his sight dragged like an hour.

He surged to his feet and pushed through the bodies blocking the entrance. If only to set his mind at rest, he had to check on her.

His foot hit the bottom tread as his name was screamed from above.

He pounded up the stairs. From her room, the sound of scuffling bodies was just discernible above the dull roar below.

He stood to one side and flung her door wide.

Two figures locked together blocked the narrow space between the bunks. As he charged into the room, Marcy side-stepped and elbowed the face of her doubled-over assailant. Bone crunched before Jake grabbed her arm and hauled her away from her attacker. Her knee came up in a reflexive movement Jake was proud of, even as he dealt with her attacker.

Blood spurted from the Nepalese man's nose; his eyes blinked rapidly. He swiped an arm across his face. Light from the hallway glinted on metal in his other hand.

Jake grabbed his wrist and twisted. The knife clattered to the floor and the attacker cried out, pain etched on his bloodied face.

Jake grabbed a fistful of the man's shirt and hauled him upright. "Who sent you? Why did you attack her?" Jake questioned in the local language. Smashing a fist into the guy's face for daring to attack Marcy might make Jake feel better but unconscious prisoners didn't talk.

The man held out his hands and shook his head. He looked past Jake's shoulder and his eyes widened.

Jake dived to the side as two shots rang out and the man slumped to the floor.

Jake pushed to his feet, pulled his gun, and swept the corridor and stairs. He spared a glance for Marcy, huddled in the corner, white knuckles pressed to her mouth. Blood streaked her sleeve.

"Stay down."

He took the stairs in two bounds, spinning around the tiny mid-point landing in time to see the front door close. He wrenched it open, jumped down the steps and rolled into a crouch, scanning the street.

A subtle shift in the fog at the far end of the building gave him his direction. He ran, staying low, and peered around the corner.

Muffled footsteps thudded and a dark shape disappeared into the shadows of a laneway. Fog reduced vision to a few metres, compounding his dilemma. He glanced back at the hotel entrance. Was this a decoy to lure him away from Marcy?

Shit.

Both choices were problematic. The attack on Marcy and the shooting of her assailant made his position clear.

She was now a target.

While his quarry escaped, Jake doubted he would have got the answers he needed. Flicking on the safety catch, he tucked his gun into the back of his trousers and jogged back. Marcy's protection was priority number one.

Uproar greeted him inside the door and the stairs were blocked. He shouldered through the crowd of anxious trekkers to Marcy's door.

Pale and shaken, she sat on the end of one of the beds. Her

gaze darted to the body and she covered her mouth and nose.

"Come with me, Marcy." He held out his hand.

The manager tried to step between them. "Sir, please leave."

"She doesn't need to be in the same room as the body." He took her cold hand and drew her to her feet.

The manager stood in the doorway. "Sir, I don't think—"

"We're travelling together. I'm taking her just down the hall to my room. Number eight. I'll give the police my statement when they arrive." Arm tight around Marcy's shoulders, he eased her past the manager.

Putting the local police offside wasn't a good idea, but he'd be damned if he'd allow her to remain with a corpse.

Shutting his door muted the hubbub. He encouraged Marcy to sit on the bed and stood.

She grabbed his shirt. "Don't leave me. Jake, I don't want to be alone. Not yet."

"It's okay, Marcy. I'm not going anywhere." He sat beside her and took her hands between his.

Cold as ice.

Damning the faceless people responsible for her attack, he hauled her onto his lap and cradled her like a child. Rubbing one hand up and down her arm, he rocked and murmured nonsense phrases.

She burrowed into his shoulder. Slowly, the tension drained from her muscles and her death grip relaxed. Her hand crept around his neck.

Was her skin a little warmer? A shot of brandy might do her good.

Warm breath grazed his neck. Cool lips whispered against exposed skin in the open vee of his shirt.

His groin twitched and he suppressed a groan. Now wasn't the time to think of her body moving under and over his. It was a terrible time to remember the slide of her mouth on his cock but her lips were sinfully soft.

His hand trailed off her arm and along the length of thigh resting across his legs. Through the material, he felt the flex of her muscles before she wriggled her bottom against his belly and his rapidly hardening arousal.

Gritting his teeth, he raised his head and prepared to lift her from his lap. "I'll get you a brandy for the shock."

"No. That's not what I need."

Husky and soft, her voice left him in no doubt of her intention. Lithe and light as a cat, she slipped off his lap and wrapped her legs around his hips. Her core pressed against his arousal. Operating with a mind of its own, it hardened beneath her touch.

Eyes the colour of a stormy sky pleaded with him. She drew a jagged breath. "Make love to me, Jake. Make me forget." Trembling lips sought his mouth and her hands tunneled into his hair.

A heartbeat passed. He sucked in a breath.

Scent of Marcy filled his nostrils and he fell into her desperate kiss.

Shudders racked her body, ripples of need to blot out the last few minutes. Wild kisses, crazy, hard kisses conveyed her need for oblivion in his arms.

With his body, he could make her forget the terror and the lifeless man in her room. He could give her today.

# #

A dull headache thudded and Marcy frowned, unwilling to open her eyes. There were things she didn't want to look at, to think about. Not yet.

Warm, solid male wrapped around her, his scent musky and uniquely Jake. Beneath her cheek, his heart *ka-thumped* in a steady, reassuring beat. Snuggling into his shoulder, she smoothed her hand over the contours of his chest. His nipple peaked under her touch and, further south, his cock stirred against her hip.

Stubble scraped her cheek, he kissed her forehead then his fingers traced a soft path down her jaw. His thumb rested tantalisingly close to her mouth.

She turned her head and nipped delicately.

"Hi, sleepyhead."

Outside, night pressed against the windowpane. Beneath the door, a sliver of light illuminated vague outlines within the room. With her sight reduced to shadowy blurs, she brushed her nose against his neck, concentrating only on the scent of Jake.

And sex.

In her mind, the two were one and the same. "What time is it?"

He stopped stroking her hip and raised his arm. A soft light lit the watch face. "Six thirty. Are you hungry?"

She shook her head. "Not really, but I'd love a cup of coffee."

He slid out of bed and felt around on the floor for his trousers. The bed dipped as he sat on the edge and she rolled against his butt.

An ache only Jake's body could assuage blossomed low in her belly. She caught her breath and traced the line of his spine to where it dipped below his trousers and wished he'd turn around.

"You'll never get that coffee if you keep doing that."

"Maybe I've changed my mind. Maybe—"

A flurry of short, sharp knocks on the door cut off her fantasy.

Jake stiffened, grabbed his shirt and hauled it over his head. "Just a minute." Turning to Marcy, he pulled the blanket up to her chin. "Stay there."

Unerringly, he found and flicked on the light switch.

Even the low wattage of a single dim bulb burned her eyeballs. Without Jake's body for distraction, her headache throbbed back to life. She groaned softly. Jake opened the door just enough to see their visitor yet keep her hidden from view.

Unfamiliar words couldn't disguise the authority behind the unseen speaker's voice.

They're here. They'll want me to give them details. To remember.

Her breath caught on a lump the size of a boulder in her throat. Her stomach ached with the need to throw up.

If only Jake would come back to bed. If only he would hold her and keep the nightmare at bay with his body. She closed her eyes and turned her head into the pillow, desperate for his scent as a promise he would be back.

"Yes, officer. I'll bring her down to the station as soon as she wakes." Jake closed the door and a moment later, the wood squeaked as he sat on the spare bed.

How had her dream holiday descended into the realm of nightmare? She massaged her chest above uncooperative lungs with a fist and dug deep for her courage. She could do it, she really could. She just needed a few more minutes alone with Jake. Reluctantly, she opened her eyes and peered over the edge of the blanket. "I have to talk to the police, don't I?"

His gaze roamed her face while a muscle ticked in his jaw. He nodded. "Are you up to it?"

She sat up, pulled her knees to her chest and tucked the blanket under her arms. "A man murdered in my room, my sister and her fiancé both missing, and our make-out session available—briefly—on YouTube—what makes you think a little visit to the police station would faze me?"

"'Atta girl. Want some company?" His expression was sombre but a gleam of what looked like appreciation softened his gaze.

Her heart flipped at the small sign of praise. At times, Jake could be downright pleasant. When he wasn't being domineering. Or sexy as all hell.

She moistened her lips. Independence be damned. The way her heart pounded, she'd have begged for his company if he hadn't offered. But she didn't want to sound needy. Aiming for casual, she shrugged. "If you like."

Jake crossed the gap between the beds and his gaze roamed her face. A frown created a small indentation between his brows but his expression remained enigmatic. Was he wondering what more could go wrong on their trek?

There was no point second-guessing him. She tugged the blanket higher. "I'm sorry for all the trouble I've caused you since we met. You must regret hooking up with me."

A fierce light lit his eyes. "Never. You've made me laugh more in the past few days than I have since—" He snapped off the end of the sentence and shut his eyes for a moment.

Not wanting to break the sense of connection between them, she kept her voice soft and low. "Since what, Jake?"

His jaw hardened and his eyes flicked open. Pain and loss flashed through them before he moved to the door. His back to her, he reached for the handle. "Since a long time. I'll let you get dressed while I check out the weather forecast for tomorrow."

"I'll buy you a coffee after—the interview."

He nodded and pulled the door closed behind him.

Moving automatically, she dragged on the clothes she'd worn earlier. One elbow of her shirt felt stiff. She glanced down.

Bile rose in her throat. With an incoherent cry she wrenched off the bloodied garment and threw it in the corner. No amount of washing would remove the memory of the attack. Or the violence of that death.

A sob broke from her throat. She gulped a lungful of air, held her breath then swallowed. Disgust at her weakness made her stiffen her knees. Breaking down was not an option.

She pushed the heels of both hands against her eyes and counted to ten as she breathed in, then reversed the process. Marginally calmer, she moistened her dry lips and heaved her pack onto the spare bed.

Shaking fingers made opening the stiff zipper of her pack more challenging than the climb up Kala Patthar. Finally, she dragged it open and dumped a pile of clothes on the bed. Grabbing the first shirt she found, she slipped it on and wished Jake was there to hold her.

Stupid. Where's your backbone?

Being dependent on a man was lunacy, especially a man like Jake. He spent weeks away guiding trekking groups into remote terrain, and once she returned home, an ocean would separate them. Why was she even thinking of him in terms of *being there?*

Sleeping with him had been for fun. For the hell of an adventure.

For comfort.

But the hint of vulnerability she'd glimpsed made her pause. What had happened in his life to shake him so badly that her silly banter was important to him?

The mystery stopped her dwelling on her own horror and she made it down to the bar in one piece. Between moving bodies, she spotted Jake in the corner, his gaze scanning the crowd.

Whispered comments—*that's her*—followed as she pushed through the crowd.

"You okay, love?" a grizzled Englishman asked as she squeezed past.

She nodded, unwilling to make eye contact and headed towards Jake. Maybe she would have a medicinal brandy before the interview with the police.

#

Her red plastic chair was the only spot of colour in the tiny, utilitarian police office. Dark walls seemed to close in and her chest tightened. She gripped the edge of her seat and stiffened her spine.

The senior officer leaned across the desk and offered her a photo. "This is the man who attacked you?"

Unclenching her death grip on the chair to take the photo, her stomach did somersaults while her heart rate kicked up to ridiculous. Was this the same man? "I barely saw him before he grabbed me. I—I think so."

Jake moved from his position at the door and stood behind

her. His hands rested on her shoulders, his touch reassuring and calming. Leaning closer, he took the photo. "That's him."

"There is a reward for his capture. Who will be claiming it, sir? You, or madam?"

A strangled cry escaped her throat. "He's dead. Isn't that enough?"

Jake's grip tightened, grounding her.

She forced herself to breathe in and out slowly. "It's okay. I know where the money can do some good. Sabita. Unless you—"

"Good idea," he whispered close to her ear. In Nepalese, he spoke to the officer.

Marcy's mind wandered and she looked without seeing through the window in the opposite wall. Fog pressed more thickly than before and their chances of flying out in the morning decreased with each passing hour.

Jake finished speaking, took her hand and tugged her towards the door. Turning to the policeman, he added, "Thanks for your help."

"You are most welcome, sir, madam. Good night."

Before stepping through the front door of the police station, Jake scanned the area beyond the glass. More than ever, his movements reminded her of a big cat hunting. Without a word, he ushered her to the right and down a laneway then into the deepest shadows of an unlit alley.

"What are you doing? Are you mad? The hotel's back the other way."

"Sshh, Marcy. If ever you're going to learn to do what you're told, now is the time."

"You're scaring me—"

"Just listen. The man who attacked you worked for a group who the police suspect has drug links to Australia. I recognised the group's tattoo in the police photo."

"Drugs? What does that have to do with us?"

"It means they think you are your sister. You're now a target."

Chapter Nineteen

"I don't understand. For God's sake, tell me what you mean." Marcy's fingers dug into his arm like talons. Whether through shock or finally understanding their danger, she whispered.

"Whoever's after you has already tried twice so the hotel's a no-go zone. We've got to find a safe place for the night. I've got a friend who lives nearby. Stick to me like my shadow and not a word till we're there."

Jake took several detours to throw any tail off their trail. Satisfied at last, he turned into a lane not far from the police station.

The police photo of the dead man had confirmed his worst fears. He knew the neck tattoo well. Marcy's attacker and probably his killer were linked to the Chan cartel, and Marcy was in danger.

He had to get her off the mountain and into the relative safety of the embassy in Kathmandu. Once there, and with more resources, they could work out a better plan.

Fog trailed cold fingers across his skin as he knocked softly on his friend's door.

It cracked open. A face peered through a narrow slit then

the door opened wide. "Jake Harris, come in."

Jake led Marcy through and softly shut the door behind him. Raj's family chattered in the common area beyond a closed door. Jake jerked a thumb in their direction. "Don't tell them we're here. Can we talk upstairs?"

Raj glanced at Marcy. "Of course. Please, follow me."

He led the way up narrow stairs, opened the second door and ushered them into a bedroom before quietly closing the door. Several sleeping mats were stacked in the corner and a small set of shelves held neatly folded clothes for each of Raj's three young sons. "How can I be of service, Mr Harris?"

"We're fogged in. There won't be any flights out tomorrow and we can't go back to the hotel. Can you organise two packs with enough food and water to walk down the mountain? No-one must know."

Raj had helped him out a time or two before and Jake was confident of his silence. "No problem. No one would expect you to try that. Would you like dinner before you go?"

"If you can, but don't involve your family. The fewer people who know we're here, the better." Raj had the right of it. Watching eyes wouldn't expect them to risk the mountain in these conditions. Fog and the night would hide their departure.

"I will arrange it quietly."

As soon as the door closed behind Raj, Marcy pinned Jake with a fierce look. "Now talk. Why do you think my sister would have anything to do with a drug family and why is she a target?"

"She's not, you are."

Marcy's lips parted and her tongue swept over her top lip. He watched as she gathered her courage around her like a coat. Straightening her shoulders, she snapped her mouth shut and breathed deeply.

God, she had courage by the bucket load.

"Stop splitting hairs. What did the policeman tell you?"

Jake leaned against the door and folded his arms. "How well do you know your sister, Marcy? I mean, really know her?"

"As well as I know myself."

"How can that be? You can't know what she does now you don't live together."

She crossed her arms and glared at him. "I know her."

At last the feisty woman he'd come to know and respect was back from the shadow land of shock. A wave of relief rushed through him. Marcy was a survivor and she was going to need every shred of courage for their escape. And for the news about her sister.

"We're twins, Jake. Identical."

He eyed her speculatively, his gaze flicking to her chest. "Not in everything."

Against the pallor of her skin, pink flared in her cheeks. "Aside from a birthmark. Now answer my question. Why do you think Tam is in danger from a drug family?"

"Your sister has connections to a Sydney cartel. The Chans are—"

"Chans?" She frowned and clasped her hands in front of her mouth.

"Do you know them?"

"I'm not sure. There was a Chinese guy talking to Tam during the car launch about an event at his mansion in Rose Bay. It was scheduled for the night I flew out. Tam couldn't take me to the airport for my midnight flight because she was working."

Had something gone down at the Chan's event? Was Tamsin involved? If she had somehow cheated the cartel and then her twin sister was seen boarding a late flight out of the country—

The timing fit. Marcy's twin must know something important for the video of Marcy and him to have caused such a swift reaction. Nicholls and the Australian authorities needed to know about Tam as soon as possible.

Jake's satellite phone was hidden in his hotel room. Risking Marcy's safety to communicate with Nicholls galled him, but every hour's delay put the cartel further out of reach.

"I have to fetch something from the hotel."

"I'll come with you."

"No."

She stood in front of the door, blocking his exit. Small as she was, in that moment she looked fully capable of taking him on. "Which is it, Jake? You've asked Raj for backpacks because it's dangerous for us to reclaim our gear, but you're going to fetch something. If you think it's dangerous, why are you taking the risk?"

"It's a question of priorities. There's a contract out on you so you have to stay hidden."

"While you do what?" Marcy relaxed her arms and shifted her weight, ready for whatever move he made.

Like she could stop him.

It was a novel experience having Marcy looking out for him. He shouldn't have enjoyed it as much as he did. He shouldn't wish for it to continue.

"I have to make contact with someone."

"Can't it wait?"

"I don't have time to explain. Just—trust me." He waited until her expression changed from suspicion to resigned agreement. Gently, he moved her aside, cracked open the door and peered down the short hallway.

"How is it, Jake, that you join me on my trek and bad things start to happen? You walk and talk and fend off bad guys like James Bond. You're like no tour guide I've ever seen. So what are you, really?"

"I'm the man who's going to get you safely to the capital." Smiling grimly, he slipped into the empty hallway and shut the door softly behind him.

Marcy was too intelligent not to work out at least some of what was happening. Could he keep her out of her sister's affairs? Unlikely, but he had to try. Hell, he wanted to make things better for her but that didn't extend to letting her sister walk free.

There was payment due for drug involvement. If that meant

hurting Marcy by taking down her sister, he'd live with it. Pete's death wouldn't allow him to do otherwise.

Following a circuitous route and a rooftop descent into his hotel room, Jake climbed in through the window. He retrieved the phone, a spare gun, ammunition, and packed a small daypack, all he could carry on the perilous return trip over the roof.

He dropped softly into the alley behind the hotel and tucked himself into a dark corner. Checking the time, he called Nicholls.

"Where the hell are you? What's going on up there?"

"We ran into trouble. Someone's after Dr. Westcott. We're fogged in at Lukla with a killer waiting to pounce. I'm going to bring her down on foot."

"Are you mad, Harris? Didn't you hear the weather warnings? Stay put. It's safer."

"Negative. Priority change to protection. We have to leave. No one will see us in this weather." Succinctly, he filled the commissioner in on what Marcy had revealed.

Over the line, he heard rustling as though Nicholls sifted through papers followed by a heavy sigh. "Okay. There's a hut about two hours walk down the track. Take her there for the night. If the weather turns nasty as they're forecasting, you'll have some protection. I'll arrange a vehicle to meet you at the end of the track around midday. And I'll contact your Sydney office and bring them up to speed."

"Affirmative. See you tomorrow night." He stuffed the phone down the side of the daypack and slid his arms through the loops. Staying in the shadows, he took a different route back to Raj's home.

By the time he returned, he half expected Marcy to have fallen asleep. Instead, she was pacing the floor in her socks. As he slipped into the room, she threw him an agitated gaze.

"Walk off the mountain? Won't that be more dangerous? Raj said there's a snowstorm coming."

"I won't lie to you. It's going to be a tough walk but we have to escape under cover of dark." Methodically, he packed the bare essentials into the larger backpack Raj had provided.

"I still don't understand why you think my sister is involved with a drug cartel."

"She's associating with a known drug family."

Marcy grabbed his arm and forced him to look at her. "For goodness sake, just because she has clients who might not be legitimate doesn't mean she's a criminal. If you knew my sister, you wouldn't believe such nonsense. She's a beautiful, warm-hearted, funny, intelligent woman."

Jake cupped Marcy's face and stepped into her space. "That sounds like you, Marcy."

Need drove him to taste her lips. Just one taste before they walked out into the cold and the dark.

She held back briefly before opening her mouth to his kiss. He wanted nothing more than to sink back into bed with her and forget the mess crashing around them. Forget the killer with the gun.

She pressed into his body and wrapped her arms around his neck. Her mouth was hot as she rubbed her belly across his aching groin.

He groaned.

Exhibiting a resolve he was far from feeling, he pulled away. "We have to get going. Put your boots on while I talk to Raj."

#

Sleet slashed Marcy's face. Shivering, she lowered her head and trudged on behind Jake, no more than a shadow in the gloom ahead. He'd set a slow, steady pace in deference to her injury, but her ankle throbbed.

"Shouldn't be much further." His voice was pitched low and soft, and sounded close.

She looked up to see if he'd stopped and her boot slipped on a slick patch. A rock skittered down the path, the sound of its passage muffled by the thick night. "Damn it."

Jake turned and grasped her arm, steadying her. "Let's approach the hut quietly, just to be on the safe side."

"Sorry.

"It's not far. You okay or do you need a rest?"

"When you say *not far*, what, exactly, do you mean?" Why wasn't he panting like she was? She heard rather than saw his smile.

"Another fifteen minutes more or less. Conditions have made our little jaunt slower than usual."

"Want a drink and half an energy bar?" She flicked on the flashlight Raj had given her and reached for the zipper on his daypack.

Jake's hand flashed out and covered the beam. "Don't use—"

Two shots rang out.

Arms tight around her, Jake pulled her down and rolled off the path. Fire burned in her upper arm with pain worse than the sharp rocks digging into her back.

Jake lay on top of her, his elbow pressing into her shoulder and she squealed with pain.

He clamped a hand over her mouth. "Sshhh." Above her head, something scraped over rock.

A soft snick sounded by her ear. Did Jake have a gun?

His weight shifted as he eased the pack off his back. She heard the slide of his hand against material then a soft click of metal on metal. Images of silencers and infra-red scopes played through her imagination.

He's a spy. I've landed in my own spy thriller and Jake is my personal James Bond.

Her spy moved his arm across her shoulder.

Pain flared brighter than before. She bit her lip and held her breath to contain the whimper rising within. Unable to reach between their bodies to apply pressure to her wound, she gritted her teeth.

Snowflakes floated across her face, settling on her

eyelashes and lips. When had it started snowing? A curious combination of heat and cold consumed her body. Was she going to pass out? Then what use would she be to Jake?

She blinked and peered into the darkness.

Warm breath teased her cheek followed by his lips, which trailed up to her ear. He whispered. "Don't move, don't make a sound. I'll be back." He eased off her and merged into the fog and the night.

Cold flooded her body where Jake had been, a cold so intense her teeth chattered. Sure the shooter would hear her, she clamped her jaw shut. Gingerly, she raised her right hand and explored her wound. Painful as it was, she knew the bullet had missed the artery but her freezing hand came away sticky with blood.

Grateful she couldn't see and give rein to her haemophobia, she eased her injured arm across her chest then reached into her jacket pocket. Clumsily, she grasped the pashmina scarf she'd purchased and tucked away only this morning.

Before the world went mad.

She cut off the useless thought and concentrated on the present. Easing the scarf beneath her arm, it took three attempts to get her uncooperative fingers to make a simple knot. Strength drained from her body as she raised her head and gripped one end between her teeth. She tightened her tourniquet, hoping it was enough until Jake returned.

Jake would deal with the shooter. Jake would come back

for her.

She closed her eyes and concentrated on listening for his return over the sound of her jerky breaths. Her greatest enemy now was the cold.

\# #

Jake manoeuvred uphill in a cautious circuit away from Marcy. The bullet had whizzed past him before winging her. That meant their attacker was ahead of them.

To his left, the softest of soft scrapes sounded. Metal on rock.

He'd bet his life on it.

Certain the shooter was on the far side, Jake crept around a boulder.

There.

A shadow darker than the gloomy night edged toward the spot where Marcy lay, injured and vulnerable.

Jake could just make out a rifle in the shooter's hands. If the hunter had night vision gear, even the partial protection afforded by Marcy's sheltered position wouldn't be enough to save her.

Tucking his gun into the back of his trousers he slid his hunting knife from its calf sheath. Below him, the shooter crept forward. Jake reversed his hold for a downward thrust and launched himself at the killer.

Some preternatural sense must have warned his quarry. At the last second, he spun and the butt of his rifle caught Jake's shoulder and skewed his aim. Instead of his arm circling the man's neck, Jake slipped. He hooked an arm around his assailant's legs and pulled him down. A shot ricocheted off a boulder.

The men grappled one another and rolled across the stony ground. Rocks dislodged beneath their heaving bodies set off a chain reaction. Jake slipped and landed heavily beneath the gunman. Winded, the length of the rifle pressed against his throat. He grabbed the weapon, kicked out and threw the man to the side. He kicked the rifle towards where Marcy lay.

Pushing up into a crouch he lunged and slashed upward, catching his opponent off-guard. Jake drove forward with an uppercut and heard the crunch of bones. His opponent's head snapped back. Staggering and clutching his stomach, the man fell to his knees.

Jake moved in. He pulled out his gun, cocked it and held it to the man's temple. "Who sent you? Who is your target?"

"Take woman"—he grunted and hunched further forward—"kill man. You won't live."

Both of them were on the hit list?

The man's breathing became rapid and ragged.

Jake needed answers. He pressed the gun against the man's temple. "Who sent you? Who gave these orders?"

"Kath—man—" The man gasped and toppled slowly onto his side. He lay unmoving.

Gun trained on his attacker, Jake squatted and felt for a pulse. The wound he'd inflicted wasn't a kill move.

Jake unzipped his jacket and retrieved a pencil flashlight. Shielding the light with his body, he checked the man's mouth. "Shit."

"Jake?" Marcy called, her voice no more than a breath wafting on the breeze.

He walked back to her side and set the rifle on the ground. Reaching down, he found her hand and squeezed it. "I'm here. You're safe, Marcy."

"What happened? Is he dead?" She sucked in a breath as she struggled to sit up.

"Yeah." Jake kneeled beside her and touched her cheek. Her skin was cold and her chattering teeth reminded him of the immediate need to reach shelter.

The pale blur of her face turned up to him. She took a long breath before she asked, "Did you kill him?"

Uncertainty lay beneath her question. One man killed in front of her this morning and another tonight was a lot to handle.

"The knife wound I gave him wasn't a killing wound. He took cyanide."

"Cyanide, killing wound? You talk like a spy."

He didn't want to have this discussion in the middle of a snowstorm. Not with the body of the man hired to kill them lying a few feet away. He didn't want to have the discussion, period.

But Marcy had a right to know. At least what he could tell her without compromising his work or tipping her off about his suspicions.

"Special agent. We've got to get away from here. We need shelter, fast. There's a snowstorm about to hit, and there could be others coming for us."

"Okay. But you're telling me everything when we find shelter."

"I'll tell you what I can, Marcy, but let's get moving. This track is too crowded for my liking."

He helped her to her feet then reached for Raj's backpack and slung it over his shoulders. "Take my hand. We keep moving, quiet as you can, and no more flash light. Can you walk for a bit longer?"

"I can walk."

Chapter Twenty

Snow had begun falling while she waited for Jake to return. Now, snowflakes clung to her eyelashes and her cheeks burned with cold as she trudged on leaden feet through the night. Her arm throbbed as though a hot poker had been thrust through it. Jake had said the shelter was nearby but each step sent arrows of fire up her arm. Gritting her teeth to stop them chattering and to hold in her moans, she plodded on.

One foot after the other.

One step at a time.

Head down, she cannoned into Jake. Pain shot through her arm and she bit off a swear word.

Blinking away snowflakes from her lashes, she peered through the gauzy curtain of snow. Just ahead, maybe a dozen metres away, she discerned the shape of a single dwelling. Jake could start a fire. Her numb fingers couldn't hold a matchbox let alone strike a match. Inside, they would be warm and dry.

"At last." She took a stumbling step towards shelter. Warmth. Sleep.

He put an arm across her chest, preventing her moving

ahead.

"Are you trying to make a snow woman out of me? Let's get inside." If her chattering teeth were anything to go by, she was halfway frozen already.

"Ssh." He pulled her behind a small cairn at the side of the track and helped her to sit.

"What are you doing? There's the hut. Can we go in?"

"The hit man came from this direction."

Marcy squeezed her eyes shut. Wasn't this hut their destination, the one Jake had held out as a promise of rest if she kept moving down the track? "Why is that important?"

"The shot came from behind me. Either the assassin followed us and managed to get ahead or he came up from the other end of the trail, which is more likely."

The cold had locked down her brain and Jake's words made little sense. She shook her head, but couldn't help the pleading tone that crept into her voice. "What are you saying?"

Jake eased off his backpack and felt around inside. He pulled out a miniature set of binoculars and scanned the area. "This is the building I was told to head to."

"And there it is. Why aren't we going inside?"

"I have a gut feeling about it. Something's not right." Clipped words, neutral tone. Jake was all business and focus, and dangerous.

"Are binoculars really helpful in the dark?"

"Night vision goggles."

"Of course. Silly me. Standard issue for trekking guides, right? Oh, I forgot, you're a spy."

"Special agent."

"With a license to kill. What's the difference?" Her words sounded fuzzy, like she was drunk, and her tongue felt too big for her mouth. Was it possible for a tongue to freeze?

"One day I'll explain it to you. Can you keep your voice down, Marcy?"

"If I talk, my teeth don't chatter so much. Which do you prefer?" She struggled to hang on to her snarkiness. Snarky was good. Snarky kept her angry and anger kept her warm.

"How many people knew we were heading down this way tonight, Jake?"

"Raj."

Jake's reply snapped back but she wasn't about to be quiet. If something about the building niggled at him, her concerns were as relevant. And damn it, he owed her an explanation. "No one else?"

He lowered the goggles and turned back to her. Puffs of white breath caressed her chilled skin, reminding her of his mouth on other parts of her body. Anger combined with hot memories was a better body warmer than snarky all by itself.

"One other person. He promised transport at the other end. Question is whether his phone or office might have been bugged."

"Who?"

"The commissioner in Kathmandu, Nicholls."

Surreal didn't begin to describe her feelings. Perhaps she was delusional. Maybe the whole weird trek was a nightmare and she'd wake in her apartment in Sydney. "Are you telling me you think a commissioner hired a hit man to kill me?"

"No. But if I had to choose between him and Raj, I'd pick him as the source of the hit man. I have what is supposed to be a secure phone line but it could have been compromised."

"Surely that's not possible. A commissioner? Why not the police in Lukla? Are they incorruptible?"

"I'm not saying it's Nicholls but his phone could have been tapped. And no, Marcy, no one is incorruptible."

\# \#

He thought about that statement. *No one* was a broad brush to apply. For God's sake, he even suspected his former partner, and Marcy's sister was top of his list.

And what about him? Where did sleeping with a suspect's sister leave him? His lapse left a bad taste in his mouth.

"You're right, Jake, so how do I know I can trust you?"

"You don't. But the hit man claimed we were both targets." No one should have known of his assignment, so why had he ended up as a hit? Simply the fact he was with Marcy? Or that he'd been recognised on the video?

"He's inconveniently dead and I didn't hear him."

"And I'm your only chance of getting out of this alive."

"So where does that leave us?"

"Out in the cold. Stay here. I'm going to check the hut."

He climbed the rocks behind Marcy's huddled figure and worked his way around to approach the building from the blind side. Snow fell more heavily with each passing minute. He'd rather take a chance on the hut than expose Marcy to a snowstorm at night. If they couldn't move, neither could anyone else.

Silently, he circled around and pressed his ear to the only door. Nudging it, he crouched and rolled through the opening. A quick sweep of the single room with his gun and pencil light revealed little trace of recent habitation.

The beam of light passed across the dirt floor, over a single, lopsided cupboard and a small pile of dried dung. Beside the fuel supply, a crumpled snack wrapper appeared to have been freshly dropped. Their attacker had probably stopped here on his way up to kill them.

Empty and dry, the hut would do for the night.

Jake loped back across the track to Marcy.

#

Hunched into a small ball of chattering teeth and frozen limbs, Marcy decided her life had turned into a Jack Reacher movie.

Aside from a price on her head and a would-be assassin killed in front of her, Jake had made her feel valued. And hot, heady sex with him was her idea of bliss. It didn't make him trustworthy as a romantic interest. He'd lied about who he was, but she trusted him with her life.

Stuck on a deserted track in the middle of a snowstorm

with assassins out to kill her, she'd choose Jake for protection every time.

Blurry white flakes drifted across her vision. Was the snowfall getting thicker? Heavy lidded, she lowered her chin onto her chest, and hugged her knees tighter. A delicious languor seeped through her body. It wouldn't hurt to close her eyes for a few minutes. What was there to see? Jake would come back soon—maybe—

"Marcy. Wake up." The speaker grabbed her shoulder and shook it.

She didn't want to wake. Why did he insist on dragging her away from her dream of a lazy summer day on the beach? "Go away." She pushed her face into the warmth of her arms.

"Come on. We're getting under shelter." Strong arms slipped behind her back and under her knees and raised her off the ground. Her head fell into a curve of neck and shoulder. There was something familiar about the puffs of warm breath that caressed her face.

A familiar scent.

The elusive memory slid away as she was set down and the warm body withdrew. She struggled to return to her dream. From a distance, she heard a scratching sound, then light flared. Fighting the red haze behind her eyelids, she forced them open. A blurry figure added fuel to a small fire, the source of her discomfort. Her eyelids fluttered down.

"Marcy, wake up. I need to get you warm."

Familiar and typically take-charge, at last she recognised the voice. "Jake? You came back."

"Of course I did. Now I'm going to warm you up."

Gently, he moved her closer to the welcome flames that danced and licked at the paper and dung fire. Her hand reached towards its warmth. Pain shot up and down her arm and she yelped. Bewildered, she focussed on the scrap of material knotted around her upper arm, and the red mark spreading beneath it.

"Oh, no." She slapped a hand over her mouth and nose and struggled not to breathe in the coppery tang.

"Does the sight of blood worry you, Marcy?"

She sucked in a mouthful of air and focussed on the flames. "You could say that."

"You did a great job on this tourniquet."

"I couldn't see it then. Could you—would you mind?" She held out her arm.

Jake squatted beside her and untied the scarf. She turned her head away from the sight of oozing blood and breathed through her mouth. He unzipped her jacket then eased it off, first her right shoulder followed by her injured arm.

She bit her lip and winced. "How bad is it?"

Jake extracted his first aid kit from the backpack and took out a pair of scissors. Gently, he cut away her sleeve and examined the wound. "Flesh wound. You'll have a small scar as a memento of this trip though."

"Great. I never did like bringing home the same tourist

stuff as other people."

One side of his mouth tipped up briefly. "I'm going to clean your wound and bind it. Here, have a swig of this first." He thrust a small bottle of whisky under her nose.

She swallowed a mouthful. Instant warmth followed the whisky down and she had a second drink before handing the bottle back to Jake. "Ready."

He dabbed around the wound. Sharp, biting pain made her jump. "Dammit, Jake." She gasped and bit back a worse imprecation.

"Sorry. Hold still." He padded the wound and she dared a peek at his work. Carefully, he wrapped a bandage around her arm and secured it with a clip.

The pain ebbed to a dull ache. "Thanks. Glad to have you and your kit on hand."

His smile was tight and gone faster than it came. "At your service. Now"—he packed the kit away and offered her a ration pack—"let's get you warm and fed."

Careful to avoid her injury, Jake lifted her across his lap and leaned back against the cupboard. One arm supported her and she wriggled a little closer. Her hard mountain man shouldn't have felt so good, so safe and reassuring. Not when she was uncertain of his motives. But two dead bodies and a midnight escape off the mountain bound her to him. For now.

She snuggled into his chest and took a bite of the protein bar. Beneath her cheek, his warm skin heated hers.

"Now we talk, Marcy. You were saying you don't trust me."

Chapter Twenty-One

Jake held Marcy close and rubbed her back and thigh in turn, encouraging the blood to circulate. Safe and reasonably warm inside the hut, cold fear ran through him. This was what it was like to care about someone again, to fear for their safety.

He didn't want to care.

Not about Marcy, not when there could be no more than these few hours between them.

To care and not be trusted. Shit, he'd hit the double with her.

Even if he convinced her to trust him—and there was no option if he wanted to get her safely down to Kathmandu—what would she think when he tracked down her sister?

But when she raised her head and looked him in the eye, he lost himself in her soft grey gaze.

"I trust you to keep me alive."

Relief coursed through him, but there was more she left unsaid. He couldn't pursue that line of thinking; of hoping. He had no hope left. "That's all I need to know."

"Trapped in a hut in a snowstorm doesn't leave many

options unless I disarm you and then manage to stay awake to keep a gun trained on you." She snuggled into his neck.

Snuggled? That level of intimacy left him tense and uncomfortable, but he couldn't release his hold on her. Not while shivers still ran through her body.

"You're capable of disarming most men." In every way.

"What about you, Jake? Can I disarm you?"

Hell yeah, but it was a weakness he couldn't afford to reveal. "Just don't—"

"Don't what? Seduce them? Why put restrictions on it? They make no sense—unless you care for me. Do you care, Jake? Even a little bit?" She raised her head, lips parted.

His gut clenched and his throat closed on words that would give her power. Caring meant opening up and letting Marcy in. It scared the shit out of him. And he had let her in further than anyone else. But it didn't mean he'd give her the power of knowing she'd succeeded. "What is this? We were talking about trust and now you're bringing emotions into it. Where has sensible scientist Marcy gone?"

She caught her breath.

That would snap her out of thinking of seduction.

If she hadn't been sitting on his lap, he might have missed the shadows that clouded her bright eyes. There was no missing the stiffening of her back, the widening gap between them. She struggled off his lap and moved to the far side of the fire.

"Sensible scientist Marcy is right where she should be.

Now. God, I'm so gullible, I even opened up to you about why I never tell a guy who I really am. Stupid of me to think you might be different. That you might understand. Of course you don't care. I'm just a job, aren't I?"

Just a job? That's all she should have been; what she had to be again.

He added another yak pat to the fire to avoid the accusation in her eyes. In his peripheral vision, he saw Marcy support her injured arm with her other hand and awkwardly sit as far away from him as the small space allowed.

"I meant that you're too intelligent to overlook facts for some quasi-emotional connection. I gave you the courtesy of respecting your analytical skills. Do you respect my ability to keep you alive?"

"Actually, I do. Not because you told me I should. Actions speak louder than words and now my brain has defrosted and re-engaged, I realise you've had more than a few opportunities if you wanted to knock me off. Therefore, by a scientific process of deduction that I think quite clear-sighted under the circumstances, I believe I can trust you. Is that scientific enough for you, Jake?"

His chest tightened as if he'd scaled a mountain and stood staring into a thousand-foot drop. What the hell else had he expected from her? "You give your trust easily."

"No. As you pointed out, I examined the facts and reached a sensible conclusion."

"So we no longer have an issue?"

"I trust that you'll get me to Kathmandu where I can find out what the hell is going on. As for trusting you with my emotions—"

"I wouldn't."

"I don't plan to."

They stared at one another through the haze above the flames. They might as well have been on opposite sides of a crevasse.

Smoke drifted lazily beneath the roof while outside, snow wrapped the hut in a shroud of white.

He indicated her injured arm. "I can put a sling on that if you like."

"No, thank you. I'll tuck my arm inside my jacket. It can do double duty and keep me warm as well."

"It's warmer this side of the fire. Two bodies make more heat you know." Inviting her to lie with him was flirting with disaster, but he couldn't pass up the last chance to hold her. Just once more couldn't hurt.

"Yeah, basic survival 101. I'll take my chances over here. Got any more of that whisky?"

"Here." He passed the bottle, careful to avoid touching her fingers. Hurting Marcy had never been his intention but he had failed her. One touch of her sweet mouth and he'd thrown caution to the winds and endangered her life. Her sweet body was the only one he wanted but the emotional cost to both of them was too high. No matter what, he had to let her go to keep her safe.

He leaned back and closed his eyes.

# #

Marcy welcomed the warm slide of whisky down her throat. It wouldn't give her the oblivion she craved but then, how could she forget when Jake feigned sleep across the hearth from her? She could have told him not to bother. It wasn't as if she was going to jump him. He'd made it perfectly clear tonight what he thought of her.

An inconvenient assignment with a willing body.

If only she could control her body's reaction to him. She swallowed a second mouthful then placed the bottle to one side and reached for her jacket. It was easy enough to slip her right arm into the sleeve and pull it around her left shoulder. But as she grabbed the empty sleeve, the sight and smell of blood made her gag. Stomach roiling, she turned away and breathed through her mouth.

"Here, Marcy. Take this."

She held her breath and turned back. Jake knelt beside her holding out a neatly folded thermal blanket.

"If this isn't enough to mask the smell, my offer to share body heat remains open."

She pushed the offending jacket off her shoulder and shivered. "I'll take the blanket."

"As you wish." Jake's mouth clamped shut. In silence, he opened the blanket and, careful not to touch her, draped it around her shoulders. He moved back and stretched out on his side of the fire, folded his arms and closed his eyes.

Marcy pulled the sides of the blanket together under her chin and allowed herself the small weakness of studying his features in the flickering firelight. Could she have got things more wrong with Jake?

A draft stirred the dust and firelight danced in shadowy patterns on the far wall. Cold seeped into her lungs with each breath. Jake's body would keep the cold at bay but that luxury was no longer hers to accept. Cuddling up as *an assignment* held no appeal.

She drew her knees up to her chest, rested her head on her good arm, and prayed the whisky would work its magic.

##

Marcy woke, stretched her legs and kicked something solid. The heat at her back moved, her grip loosened on the blanket and she tried to turn over.

Jake rose on one elbow, his gaze roaming her face. His lower body spooned hers and their legs intertwined. Tousle-haired and dark-eyed, he was the essence of every erotic dream she'd dared to dream. And now, all that she couldn't have.

"What are you doing here?"

"Good morning to you too. Your teeth were chattering so loud I had to do something."

"You're not responsible for me. I can look after myself." Spending the night unconscious in his arms didn't figure in her plans.

"Letting my assignment freeze didn't seem a clever move so I made an executive decision to join you since you were reluctant to join me. Breakfast?"

"Damn it. How can you be so blasé about sleeping together when there's nothing between us?"

"That's all it was. Sleep. Nothing happened." He pushed to his feet and strode to the door. Easing it ajar, he looked outside.

Freezing air whooshed through the crack and she pulled the thermal blanket under her chin. "Is it still snowing?"

"No, but the track is going to be hard going. We should get underway as soon as possible."

Keen to put this whole miserable episode behind her, Marcy sat up quickly. Pain arrowed through her arm and she bit her bottom lip. She looked up into Jake's concerned gaze.

"Is your wound caning you? I've got a couple more pain killers in my kit."

"Yes, please. I'd hate to slow you down any more than I already have." When had she turned into a bitch? Hating her loss of control, she moderated her tone. "How far do we have to walk?"

"A long way. It won't be easy, but this hut is not the place to be when whoever is after us realises their man failed last night."

She stood carefully and cradled her left elbow. Hunger fled and her stomach did a series of flips as the reality of their situation struck. "Do you think they'll send another man after us?"

"My guess is that we'll have a reception committee waiting at the bottom of the track."

"So—we head in a different direction? Don't all roads lead to Kathmandu?"

"There aren't that many roads to choose from and I can't risk using the phone to arrange a new rendezvous. We'll have to improvise."

He sighed and reached out as though to touch her cheek then shoved his hands in his pockets. "I'm sorry it's come to this, Marcy. If I hadn't let emotion cloud my better judgement, we wouldn't be in this situation. You were right all along. You can't trust me with emotional stuff. But I make you a promise now; I will get you to safety."

He turned away and reached into his backpack.

Marcy stared at his back. Mercurial man. Just when she finally disliked him, he went and said that. And why did that make her feel better?

She filed the thought and accepted the trail bar and water he offered. While she ate, Jake picked up her jacket, took out his knife and cut out the bloodied patch.

He tucked the rest of the sleeve inside and met her curious gaze. Holding it up for her to inspect, he said, "You can't walk and hold onto that blanket over rough terrain. Like this, your jacket won't turn your stomach and you'll be warm. Here." He stepped in behind and helped her don the jacket, easing it over her injury. She turned to face him.

"Don't think I'm treating you like a child." He fitted the zipper ends together and zipped it up then pulled the hood over her head and stepped back.

"I don't. Thanks."

Methodically he doused the embers of the fire and checked the hut. Satisfied, he repacked the backpack and slung it over his shoulder. "That's everything. Ready?"

She nodded and he cautioned her to wait. Gun in hand, he opened the door and scanned the area.

Jake's promise hung in the air between them. No matter what happened, she trusted him. With her life, but never with her heart.

Chapter Twenty-Two

Who knew we were coming this way?

Round and round in Jake's head, the security breach echoed in time with his steps. Snow lay in thick drifts as they slogged along the barely discernible path. One positive, *the only positive*, he grimaced; the track stretched ahead in pristine condition. Theirs were the first boots to pass since the storm ended sometime in the night.

Welcoming the bite of cold air, he checked his watch. Their pace was slower than he would have liked, but Marcy's pinched expression reminded him she was doing her best.

Grey rocks began to break up the unremitting line of white and his fingers closed over the handle of his gun. While there was any chance of a hostile encounter, Jake's attention had to be firmly on protecting her.

And afterward? What about when they were back in Kathmandu? When they were safe. What then?

Why did Marcy think her vibrant intelligence turned men off? She had dragged more genuine laughter from him in their days together than he could remember since he joined the Service.

Marcy confronted life head on with her quick mind and quirky humour. As far as he was concerned, a man should count himself lucky to connect with such a woman. Under other circumstances—

"Jake?"

He cast a quick glance ahead before turning around. Marcy leaned against a boulder, her face almost as white as their surroundings. A spurt of anger with himself and their situation flared as he hurried back. A protruding rock offered shelter and he helped her underneath the overhang. "You should have told me you wanted a rest."

Pushing to keep their noon rendezvous was ridiculous in light of Marcy's injuries. She needed rest and warmth. He ripped open his pack and dragged out the water bottle and another pain killer. "Here, take this."

Her fingers shook when she took the tablet from him and she tipped water down her chin as she drank. "Thanks. I—need a few minutes. Sorry."

"Not your fault, Marcy. At least we have shelter here."

Her eyelids fluttered closed and she sagged against him. Jake wrapped an arm around her body, and tucked her head into the curve of his shoulder. Chilled skin pressed against his.

He stroked her cheek and smoothed loose strands of hair behind her ear.

What was he missing in this damned mess? Nicholls' information suggested Marcy was involved in manufacturing drugs. Jake was convinced all she'd done was research the healing properties of the aphrodisiac. If he was wrong about her, he'd chuck in his job and head home. And that wasn't going to happen.

A distant, regular *whump-whump* impinged on his conscious mind. Marcy startled as the noise drew closer and sat up. "Is that a helicopter? Do you think your contact has sent one to pick us up?"

Jake peered around the overhanging rock. The chopper seemed to be following the track up the mountainside. "It might be our ride."

A sense of relief ran through him. Nicholls must have opted for the quick, if expensive, pick up. Marcy wouldn't have to slog on to the bottom of the mountain and then suffer bouncing in a vehicle for a further eight hours to the capital.

In the seconds it took him to close his pack and drag it onto his shoulders, the chopper passed overhead. Jake glanced up and his blood ran cold. Protruding through the open doors, two rifles pointed at each side of the track.

The logo of a private, foreign owned company flashed before his eyes as the chopper turned and hovered low barely a hundred metres from their shelter, then disappeared as it set down.

Marcy eased out from their shelter and peered up the track. "Should we go and meet them?"

"Stay there."

She took a couple of steps back the way they had come. "Did they see us?"

Jake grabbed her hand and pulled her off the path. "Not yet.

I want to check them out."

"Is that necessary? I mean—"

He spun her around and met her startled gaze. "You said you trusted me to get you to Kathmandu. Do you?"

"Y—yes. But—"

"Then let me do my job. It's a private company chopper and there were two high-powered rifles on board."

"Oh my God."

"My contact may have sent them—"

"Or whoever is trying to kill me." Her voice wobbled over the last two words and she bit her lip.

Jake's chest tightened. God, could he have messed up any more? He forced himself to look at her pale face. Uncertainty filled her gaze. She'd offered him her trust and he'd royally stuffed up.

He pressed the smaller of his two guns into her hand. "If I'm not back within five minutes—" *What? Shoot anything that moves? Make a run for it?*

Up the track, the noise of rotors turning faded to silence. Priority number one was Marcy. Self-recrimination could wait till later. "Stay here, out of sight. I'll be back."

#

Marcy's injured arm collided with a sharp rock edge as she wedged herself into the narrow space formed by two leaning rocks. She bit back a whimper. Between throbbing pain and the blood pounding in her ears, she could hear nothing after Jake departed.

Wind picked up grains of rock and dirt and flung them

against her bowed head. How had boring, nerdy Dr. Marcia Westcott got herself into this surreal nightmare?

But Tam might be in far greater danger than she was. Who was looking out for her twin? At least Marcy had Jake on her side. Stubbornly, she blinked away tears. Jake *was* on her side and he had promised to keep her safe. She clung to her belief in him.

"Marcy?" Jake was making no effort to keep his voice down. "Come on out, it's fine."

Crawling on her good hand and aching knees, she emerged from her hiding place. "Who is it in the chopper?"

She grabbed his arm with her good hand. Boots scraped on rock and she froze, gaze fixed on two figures that appeared behind Jake. A neatly dressed civilian male and a soldier carrying his gun at the ready approached.

Jake helped her to her feet. "Nothing to worry about, Marcy. This is Nicholls, my contact at the embassy."

Nicholls stepped forward. Urbane charm oozed from every pore as the commissioner offered a weak handshake. "How do you do, Dr. Westcott? You *have* got a lot of people looking for you."

Marcy shook her head. "I don't know why, Mr Nicholls. Are you taking us back to Kathmandu?"

"Yes, my dear. We have some questions we'd like your help answering, and then we'll get you back home as soon as we can."

Beneath her fingers, Jake's muscles tensed. He slipped his other arm around her waist. "Let's get Marcy into the chopper and back to Kathmandu. I'd like a doctor to check her arm."

"What happened?" Nicholls surveyed her mangled jacket. His tone conveyed concern but his eyes were a cold, pale blue.

Marcy recoiled into Jake's embrace. "Somebody shot at me. Last night on the track."

"How unfortunate." Nicholls' gaze flicked over Jake then slid away. "We shall radio ahead and have a doctor standing by as soon as we return to the embassy."

"It's okay. Jake took care of it."

Jake shortened his stride to match hers. "You should have it seen to by the doctor. There may be dirt in it. Conditions weren't good for treating it properly."

Thankful for Jake's support, she wrapped her good arm around him and pressed closer. Softly, she asked, "Jake? Do you trust him?"

Jake frowned. He looked from her to Nicholls but said nothing.

Nicholls was already at the helicopter, a hand held out to assist her to climb aboard. Reluctantly, she released her grip on Jake's jacket and took the Englishman's hand. Jake manoeuvred around the other man and sat beside her. "Let me buckle you in."

"Thanks."

The engine started, the rotors began to turn, and conversation became impossible.

Jake stretched his legs. One lean thigh nudged hers. His expression gave nothing away but his gaze swept the men in the cabin.

Marcy leaned back. Vibrations ran through her body as the chopper flew fast and low back to the capital.

To safety. And maybe answers to why people wanted to kill her.

So why did she feel as though her back was to the wall again?

Chapter Twenty-Three

As the helicopter came in to land at Tribhuvan Airport, Jake looked through the open door. The military presence seemed to have increased, but he couldn't see past the hangar to the main terminal building. Maybe what they were seeing was part of an army exercise.

And maybe he was overcautious. Safety lay within the embassy in Kathmandu, along with answers.

He and Marcy were hustled into an army SUV with dark tinted windows. Nicholls sat facing them, but each time Jake looked at the commissioner, the man's gaze slid away. They were back in the capital with an army escort. They should be safe, but tension coiled like a black snake in his belly, slithered through his brain, and kept the adrenaline pumping.

He'd take nothing for granted.

The heavy vehicle bounced along the main road, swerving occasionally around potholes. The stink of burning plastic filtered into the closed confines of the car as they drove through the outskirts. Marcy coughed and edged closer, not quite touching him.

Jake folded his arms and looked straight ahead. It wouldn't

do to show a personal connection to her. So far as Nicholls knew, she was Jake's assignment. Nothing more, in spite of that highly public kiss.

If the commissioner suspected an emotional attachment between them, Jake would be pulled from the case. If he lost access to Marcy he would be failing both her and Peter.

Especially Peter.

He stiffened his spine and clamped a lid on his memories.

The SUV turned off the main road into a driveway flanked by a high brick wall topped by razor wire. Heavy wooden gates opened and the SUV passed through, rolling to a stop beside a short flight of steps at the side of the building.

Jake took hold of Marcy's good arm and, under the guise of assisting her from the vehicle, swept a swift look around the compound. Guard numbers had doubled since his last visit. Was Nicholls expecting trouble? The hairs on the back of Jake's neck prickled.

Nicholls led the way upstairs and entered an ante-room, bare but for a desk and a single chair. The heavy metal-plated door swung closed behind them.

"Mr Harris, please deposit all weapons in the box." A young guard flipped open a security box and turned a weapons register around, ready for his signature.

Nicholls stood to one side, hands folded in front. "As you've probably noticed, we are on heightened security. When you're finished here, the corporal will bring you to my office for debriefing. In the meantime, I will escort Dr. Westcott to the surgery."

Beside him, Marcy hesitated. "Thank you, Mr Harris. I'm glad I trusted you."

"So am I, Dr. Westcott."

She followed Nicholls into a corridor and the door closed behind them.

Jake dropped the pen on the register and looked around. Four walls, closed doors, no window. He rubbed a hand over his chest, trying to ease the tightness that always came when he was inside.

And, for the first time in days, there was no Marcy to challenge him, or make him laugh with her dry wit and sharp intelligence. He shoved his hands into his pockets and waited while the corporal checked his weapons against the register then locked the box.

"Follow me, sir." The corporal led the way through a different door to the one taken by Marcy, and along a corridor. He opened a door to Nicholls' office. "In here, sir."

Jake entered and dropped into the same seat he'd occupied a little more than a week ago. He leaned an arm along the edge of the desk and tapped a rapid tattoo. Three folders were precisely placed in a neat pile in front of Nicholls' chair. The corner of a photo poked out of the top folder. Jake leaned forward and read the upside down label. *Dr. Marcia Jane Westcott.*

Did Nicholls still believe it had been Marcy who met John

Chan for dinner? Aware of subtle differences between Marcy and her twin, he thought he could convince Nicholls of Marcy's innocence. He'd mentioned his own connection to Paul Rimmer. But what of Tamsin? What had the commissioner learned about Marcy's sister? Had she been found?

Unsettled, he glanced at the antique clock on the side table. Fifteen minutes after the hour and they'd arrived just after noon. How long did it take to escort Marcy to the doctor's surgery? Certain the old clock was wrong, he pushed up his sleeve and checked his watch. It gave him the same time.

He pushed up off the chair and strode to the door. As he reached for the handle, the door opened and Nicholls stepped into the room. "Harris. Take a seat."

"How's Dr. Westcott?" Jake resumed his seat and rested his ankle across his knee.

"She's fine. She will, of course, remain here until we can arrange her safe return to Sydney. Now—" Nicholls tapped the top folder several times with his index finger without looking at Jake before taking out the photo. He studied the image for several seconds then met Jake's gaze. "Remind me, Harris. What was your original brief?"

"Observation and information gathering with the right to upgrade if the situation warranted it. Which happened."

Nicholls tapped a corner of the photo gently against his desk. "Tell me about that."

With clinical precision, Jake recounted the attacks on

Marcy, omitting only their sleeping together. Nicholls didn't need to know that.

"Why didn't you call for back up after the second attempt on her life? You still had the satellite phone, didn't you?"

"I believed there'd been a security breach, possibly on our secure line."

Nicholls' nostrils flared and he pinned Jake with a glacial look. "What makes you think that?"

"The shooter was waiting for us as we came down the track. Only two people knew our intended route. Me and—" He refused to bring his friend in Lukla to Nicholls' attention.

"Me. I see." The commissioner blinked several times then stared at the photo in his hand. Without looking up, he picked up the phone. "Send in the corporal."

Nicholls said nothing more.

Two precise knocks sounded.

Behind him, Jake heard the door open and the squeak of boot leather. The glass panel of the bookcase behind Nicholls reflected the young soldier, his hands grasping his rifle. He stood to one side of the open doorway and stared straight ahead.

Jake had three exit points and an escape route planned the moment the corporal entered the room. He edged his foot back ready to push forward.

Nicholls nodded at the guard before meeting Jake's eyes. "Harris, you are being stood down from this case pending a disciplinary hearing. You will leave on the first plane tomorrow and report to your headquarters in Sydney.”

“But Dr. Westcott—”

“Is no longer your responsibility.”

Jake’s jaw clenched and he took a deep breath. “I’d like to complete the assignment. There are a lot of connections that—”

“Rules are enforced for good reason. Your relationship with Dr. Westcott has compromised your ability to remain neutral. Your *assignment* is over.” He tossed the photo onto the desk in front of Jake and left the room.

Hands fisted in his lap, Jake looked down.

Shit.

Marcy’s legs were wrapped around his hips, his hands cupping her butt and their mouths meshed, taking close, personal inventory. It struck him that it looked so real because it was. He was into Marcy and she, God help her, was into him.

He was screwed.

##

“You’ll be right as rain after a good night’s sleep, Dr. Westcott.” The young male doctor withdrew the needle and covered the injection site with a sterile pad.

“Can I see Jake—Mr Harris, now?”

“No idea. I’ll just let Mr Nicholls know that you’re—”

Nicholls stepped into the room. “Dr Westcott, I timed that nicely. If you’re feeling better, we can have our little chat. Please come with me.”

Lying on a soft bed with no one shooting at her sounded

more appealing. Jake sharing said bed would be even better, but there was no chance of that now. Her brief affair was over the moment they boarded the chopper.

But Jake had told her to expect a debriefing session and it looked like it was happening now. Her stomach rumbled. They'd missed breakfast, and lunch seemed likely to go the same way.

Using her good hand to push up from the desk, Marcy rose. The room spun briefly before her vision cleared and settled on Nicholls' face.

"Luncheon is served. We can dine first, my dear." The commissioner offered his arm and Marcy needed no further prompting. Unwilling to risk spinning out again, she accepted his offer of support. Led by the aroma of curry, they entered the dining room. Two places were set at the far end of a dining table that would accommodate her extended family plus friends and not be a squeeze.

Nicholls pulled out a chair for her before seating himself at the head of the table. "Allow me, Dr Westcott. You must try some of these pickles with the curry." He served both of them, then picked up his fork.

"Will Jake be joining us for lunch?"

Nicholls paused with a loaded fork halfway to his mouth. He replaced it on the mound of rice and interlaced his fingers before meeting her gaze.

Marcy's appetite dissolved. His face wore *that* look, the same as her father's had when he was about to explain why something she would hate was *for her own good.*

"Harris's assignment ended when he delivered you safely to the embassy. He has gone on to his next job."

Nicholls' words shouldn't have hurt. After all, she'd posed the same question to Jake. Was that only last night? Raw uncertainty reopened the old wound.

Suddenly, Marcy felt more tired than she'd ever been. There had been an unspoken message in Jake's eyes—a promise or a plea, she couldn't tell—before she was whisked out of his sight.

Not saying goodbye felt—incomplete. Like music without a final chord. She had to know.

You need closure.

"Will it be possible for me to speak with him before he leaves?"

How had Jake known what she was seeking when she'd barely understood the driving need herself? Yet Jake got her. He'd made her feel safe and happy, and hot-in-lust for him.

But it was his gift of belief in her that was most precious.

"I'd like to thank him for his care of me."

"I would have thought you'd be angry. After all, his job was to keep you safe yet he almost got you killed." Nicholls' impeccable suit and tie, his polite charm should have reassured her, made her feel safe. His pale eyes shouldn't make her think of a bird of prey.

But his piercing gaze trapped her like a rabbit in headlights.

Food rolled off her trembling fork and she set it on her

plate. "His job was to observe me. As soon as my life was threatened, he did everything he could to protect me."

"He's a top operator, Dr Westcott, I'll give him that. But his methods leave something to be desired."

"Are you referring to that video? That was just—"

"Accidental? Unlucky?"

"Yes."

"And yet, it was precisely the thing that drew the attention of whoever is after you. Within hours, your room was broken into, you were attacked, and an assassin was sent to kill you. One event might be a coincidence, two are not."

Goosebumps raced up her spine. Nicholls didn't like Jake and the tension between the two had been thick on the helicopter ride. But it was difficult to argue with his reasoning.

"What are you suggesting?"

"Harris has been systematically tracking all links to a drug cartel operating in Sydney for the past year or more. You, my dear doctor, are his first new link in months. He wants the bad guys to come out and play."

"That's absurd. Jake didn't set me up. I kissed him. *I* kissed *him!*"

"And the young men who filmed you on their phones? I suppose you spoke to them afterward?"

"Jake did. He asked them not to upload the video, but he was too late. Just bad timing, that's all."

"I suppose it looks credible. It could almost have happened

as you say. But you were badly used by Harris."

Had Jake used her? She dragged a thin breath into resistant lungs.

"You make him sound cold-blooded." She'd trusted him with her life, not her heart, and she was sitting at the commissioner's dining table thanks to Jake's skills. He couldn't have set her up.

Could he?

Nicholls leaned forward, locking gazes. "You were the lure. When it comes to his work, nothing and no one will stop him getting what he wants."

Her stomach heaved at the implied betrayal. She gripped the edge of the table and swallowed—hard. "No. Jake wouldn't put me in danger. He got me safely here like he promised."

"After exposing you to an unknown enemy. You should not have been placed in such a position. On behalf of the authorities, I must apologise for that." Nicholls picked up his fork and began eating.

Marcy couldn't eat. Anger and an indefinable, ridiculous sense of loss merged, rose and threatened to choke her. She tried to swallow past the lump in her throat.

It didn't matter that she wanted to believe in Jake. In their connection. He'd done what he'd promised.

Nicholls neatly crossed his cutlery over his food and gestured at her full plate. "Would you prefer a less spicy dish, Dr Westcott? I can request a—"

"No. It's fine, thanks." Marcy picked up her fork and shoved a few grains of rice into her mouth. She forced herself to swallow, and scoop up another small forkful.

Nicholls topped up her water and pressed her to try a little of various dishes. He chatted about innocuous topics while they dined, keeping up a polite farce of one-sided conversation. Nearby, a clock chimed the hour.

Jake wasn't coming back and she was a fool to hope for anything more. She sat up straighter.

Why was she surprised? When had a man truly been there for her?

Jake was when I really needed him.

She would have been a basket case after the shooting in her hotel room but Jake had got her away from prying eyes. In his room, he had soothed her with his body.

Surprised to find her plate half-empty, Marcy lowered her fork and clenched her hands in her lap.

"If you've had sufficient nourishment, Dr Westcott, shall we adjourn to my office?"

"Thank you, yes. I would like to be finished with this whole episode." Nicholls helped her from her chair before leading the way into his office.

Elegant but dated, Nicholls' office was caught in a time warp. Colonial period furniture held modern conveniences, while the range of alcohol on the drinks table came straight from a 1950's movie set.

The commissioner held out a chair for her and moved around to sit on the opposite side of the desk. "So, Dr Westcott, we now need to debrief. Why did you leave Sydney on the night of the twenty-fifth?"

"That was when my flight was booked. What on earth does that have to do with the attempts on my life?"

"Please bear with me. When was the original booking made?"

"Five or six months earlier. When my research trip was given the green light, I booked the Dolpa work section."

"But you brought forward your departure date three weeks ago. Why?"

"All along I wanted to visit the Everest region but my grant could only be used for my actual research. I recently found someone to sublet my apartment to, which meant I had enough money to add on a short, private side trip. I was lucky to get the flight."

Tam hadn't understood Marcy's need to visit their father's resting place. It was the only thing they'd disagreed on. Tam had poured two large glasses of wine and sat beside her. "Don't change your departure date, sis. I'm working that night and I won't be able to take you to the airport."

But Marcy had held firm. Regardless of the danger she'd encountered, she would never regret the closure she'd found on this trek. Jake had been right about that.

"Who knew of your change of plan?" Nicholls' question

interrupted her meandering thoughts. Resenting his poking into her personal life was ridiculous. Two attempts on her life made every detail important.

Folding her hands in her lap, she sat straight and met the commissioner's gaze. "Friends, my employer, anyone in the same division at the pharmaceutical company. There was no secret about it, other than what my research actually entailed. I didn't breach any confidentiality clauses if that's what you're implying."

"Not at all. Tell me about your research, doctor."

"I'm not at liberty to discuss it with you." Telling Jake had been a different matter. He'd caught her at her most vulnerable moment and offered a sympathetic ear. And he was the other half of the video that started it all.

"Despite losing your grant?"

"How did you—?"

Jake. He must have reported everything about her.

But had he? Had Jake revealed everything, or was seduction a standard tool for spies and special operatives? Knowing she was just a job with fringe benefits didn't mean she'd accepted it. His love-making had felt real and wonderful and—

"When did you meet John Chan?"

That name again.

She stared at Nicholls and shook her head. "I'm sure you have all these details in Mr Harris' report about me."

Nicholls' gaze narrowed briefly before he leaned back in his chair. The lampshade cut the light and cast his face in shadow while daylight through the window added to her blindness.

"And now I would like to hear your answers from you."

Polite tones and pleasant phrasing no longer hid the menace beneath his words. She longed for the certainty of Jake, for her trust in his ability to keep her safe.

Unlike Nicholls who played his cards close to his chest.

"I have been told we were both at a launch event on the same night. Other than that, I don't know the man. Why?"

"I was hoping for more from you, Dr Westcott, since it appears the Chan family may be behind the attacks on your life."

"But why? It makes no sense."

"Tell me about the night you flew out. What did you do, where did you go?"

She thought about the rush from work, the excitement of the trip ahead, and the last minute detour. "I finished packing and checked my equipment, handed over the keys to my apartment and caught a taxi to the airport."

"No friends—family—to drive you? How strange."

"Not strange. Saturday nights are busy for most people. Why interrupt someone's evening when I'm perfectly capable of looking after myself?" Clenching her hands in her lap, she prayed her face wouldn't give away her lie.

"And yet you made a detour on the way to the airport. You told me you don't know John Chan so why did you stop at the Chan mansion?"

Mouth drier than the summer desert, Marcy struggled to

form words that wouldn't implicate her sister. Rose Bay and the Chan residence were hardly on her route to catch a flight. What possible reason could she give for being where she had no reason to be?

Nicholls reached back and grasped a folder on a side table. He tapped the closed cover on which a smattering of blue dots and her full name and title marked the otherwise pristine surface. "Please don't tell me you weren't there. Film footage—and taxi company records verify this—shows you stopped at the Chan home for several minutes. There was a party at the residence that evening, and a great deal of activity was logged by surveillance teams.

"Your taxi driver was directed to a side street where he pulled over near a locked side gate. A package was handed to you by an unknown person who returned to the mansion after the transaction. You proceeded to the airport.

"So, Dr Westcott, once again I ask you, why were you at the Chan mansion on the night of your departure for Nepal?"

Regretting every stupid aspect of that night's decision, Marcy considered why she hadn't listened to her twin. Tam had tried to convince her to stay away. "You don't need Dad's diary. With your memory, you must know it off by heart anyway."

Would a partial truth save her sister?

"A—friend was working at the party and wanted to farewell me and return a book she had borrowed."

"You're a poor liar, doctor. No book is that important that

one detours so far out of one's way on the night one is leaving to go overseas. What it the name of this friend?"

"The book was my father's diary from his last trip to Nepal. I wanted to retrace his steps, which is why I made time to pick it up. As for my friend, I won't make trouble for them by telling you their name." She sat back. A headache started thumping behind her left eye and she frowned as the pain grew sharper.

"It doesn't matter for the moment. The Federal authorities in your country will be speaking with you at greater length when you arrive back in Sydney."

She pressed her fingers against her temple. "Are you suggesting I've done something wrong, Mr Nicholls?"

"It's not for me to make that assessment. But your passport will be held by an agent who will accompany you to Australia."

Her stomach lurched, clenched, and threatened to hurl her lunch back onto the plate. "You can't be serious. Am I—am I under arrest?"

"Not arrest, doctor. Protective custody."

"But why? I've done nothing wrong."

"Perhaps not, but somebody wants you dead. That means they think you know something, or have something they want. We will keep you safe until your own authorities determine why."

"But—"

Nicholls raised a hand.

Realising the futility of further protests, Marcy gritted her teeth.

"I'll escort you to your room now. I regret the necessity of locking you in, but there will be a guard on your door. Should you require anything, simply knock and ask him."

Nicholls rose and she followed suit.

"As soon as can be arranged, your gear will be retrieved from Lukla. We have already secured your equipment boxes from your hotel here in the city."

Marcy cast a glance along the hallway. The shadow of a guard filled the opaque glass to her right. To her left, an unsmiling soldier held his gun across his chest.

Nicholls gestured to the central staircase ahead of them.

With no choice but to comply for now, she gripped the wooden railing and hauled her aching body one step after another. Her arm throbbed in time with her headache and sleep seemed unlikely, but rest would be welcome.

She was shown into a bedroom with a tiny en suite. Dark, carved wooden beams spanned the room and a double bed draped in mosquito netting filled the central area. An armchair was pulled up beside the single window.

"I hope you'll be comfortable here. A tray will be brought up to you this evening. I advise you to rest and—reflect. Perhaps you'll remember more tomorrow. Good afternoon, doctor."

The door shut, followed by the distinctive *snick* of a key turning in the lock.

Marcy tiptoed to the door. Pressing her palm against the wooden panel, she tested the handle. Locked, as Nicholls had said.

She rested her head on her hand and listened. On the other side of the door, booted feet approached and stopped on the polished wood directly outside.

Not that she'd expected Nicholls would lie about the guard.

Hope might be useless, but it didn't stop her from walking back to the window. Three floors below, the gnarled roots of an old fig tree had pushed through concrete. Craning her head as far as possible, she sought out the line of the branches. Nothing was close enough to grab, even if she'd had two good arms.

Deflated, she struggled to remove her boots and jacket, and then pulled back the bedcover. She flopped onto the softest mattress she'd had in weeks, wincing a little as she eased her arm across her chest and made herself comfortable.

Her last conversation with Tam had been about collecting their father's diary before she flew out. Only in passing had her twin mentioned organising a function at the mansion. She'd given up the address only after Marcy threatened to go to Tam's employer in order to track her down.

Was Tam connected to the Chans by more than client-customer status and, if so, how? More to the point, was Tam in danger from those clients?

Marcy thumped the bed and exhaled in frustration.

Locked within the depths of the embassy, what could she do to help? Nicholls' talk of protection and keeping her safe meant nothing. A guard at her door kept her prisoner.

She didn't trust this place and she didn't trust Nicholls.

The one person, the only person she'd felt safe with since this all began, was long gone. And her stupid, unreasonable heart thumped out a message of longing.

Where are you, Jake?

Chapter Twenty-Four

Jake stood motionless, his back pressed against the upper trunk of the fig tree. There were back ways into every building if one only had patience.

For two hours, he'd sussed out the embassy from a vantage point that should have been locked down, and watched staff and guests' comings and goings through the windows. Finally, he'd narrowed down Marcy's location to one of two rooms on the top level, both accessible via the massive Moreton Bay fig tree.

Marched out of the embassy under guard, and under threat of disciplinary action, he figured he might as well be hung for a sheep as a lamb. His dislike of the commissioner notwithstanding, he had no sensible reason for breaking in to check on Marcy except a gut feeling that all was not right.

And a need to say goodbye. Properly.

The last of the guests departed, the gates were locked behind them, and most internal lights were turned off, leaving only the perimeter security lights shining. Hidden within dense foliage,

Jake eased along a thick branch towards the nearest window and peered down into a dimly lit bedroom.

Light spilled from a lamp onto a rumpled bed, its covers in a heap on the floor. A sliver of light shone beneath what was probably an en suite. He waited for the occupant to emerge.

The bathroom door opened and the light was switched off before the occupant stepped into the room. Relief ran through Jake when the figure neared the bed.

Marcy cradled her left arm and wandered to the window. She pressed her forehead against the glass and closed her eyes.

He had needed to know Marcy was okay. Clearly, she was being treated as a guest so why wasn't he getting the hell out of there?

She opened her eyes and stared out into the night and the tree, right at the spot where he stood hidden behind a thin veil of leaves.

She was fine, safe and in good hands. Now he should leave her to get on with her life.

Except he couldn't.

Jake Harris, chief of operations, Asia region was going to put his career on the line because he couldn't let Marcy go. Perhaps Nicholls was right that he was crazy, but Jake needed to know if somewhere in the web of lies and deceit littering his relationship with Marcy, there was truth.

A connection he hadn't sought.

He glided along the branch, swung down onto the roof, and

lowered himself to the shutter beside Marcy's window.

He'd made no noise, but she raised her head and met his gaze. Smiled at him.

Thank God. Nicholls hadn't poisoned her mind with his version of events, or Jake's dismissal from the job.

She mimed that the window was locked.

He nodded, eased his penknife into position and jimmied the lock.

Gently, she eased the window open and stepped back.

He slipped over the sill into the room and stood, looking at her looking at him.

"Hi." She mouthed the word and touched a finger to his lips, flicked a glance at the door and whispered, "Guard."

He felt his smile disappear as he crossed to the door. Soft snores drifted in. Wood creaked and scraped followed by the sounds of a person settling against the wall. Why had Nicholls arrested Marcy? He walked softly back.

She moved into his arms and rested her head on his shoulder. Her hair was damp but her coconut shampoo filled his senses while she snuggled against him. Marcy was a snuggler. There was no other word for it. Her body pressed into his, familiar, arousing, breasts soft and—hell, she was braless and ready for bed.

He was simply ready. For her.

Easing away, he sat her on the edge of the bed, and sat on the edge of the armchair. They leaned towards one another. Voices soft, they sifted through the day.

"I'm glad you came. I didn't like not being able to say goodbye."

He took her hand in both of his. "Do you want it to be goodbye, Marcy?" A muscle ticked in his jaw.

She looked down at their joined hands, stroked her thumb over the back of his before raising her gaze. "There are things, lots of them, that I don't know about you, Jake. I'd like to. I've felt the safest I've ever been with you. I've felt things—"

Felt. That was it. Marcy made him feel alive again. It scared the shit out of him.

He wanted to feel like that all the time.

Wood scraped on wood outside Marcy's door. She sucked in a breath and looked over her shoulder.

Jake rose, poised to exit swiftly. "Has the guard done a random check yet?" Jake whispered.

"No. Just plenty of snoring."

They listened through several heartbeats until... *Snort.* Steady snoring filtered through the door.

Marcy dropped back onto the edge of the bed and gripped his hand. Her fingers were cool in his. She looked up and locked gazes. "Jake, I swear I don't know anything."

"It's not me you have to convince. Did Nicholls say why he's arrested you?"

Marcy grimaced. "He calls it *protective custody*. It's for my own good, so he says, but he's taken my passport. I'm to be accompanied back to Australia for further questioning. If only I knew why."

Guilt stabbed hard in Jake's stomach, turning like a knife, eviscerating him. If he hadn't stuffed up so publicly with Marcy, he would have been the one accompanying her home. She would be safe and he'd have had the chance to pursue the link between her twin and the cartel.

Instead, she would hate him when she worked out he was after her sister, not her. "What did you tell him?"

"How can I tell him what I don't know? And even if I did, I don't trust him."

Jake felt the same, but voicing his suspicion would only add to Marcy's worries. "Has he mentioned who he's protecting you from?"

"The same name you asked me about—the Chans. Who are these people?"

"Drug family, big in Sydney, but we haven't been able to pin anything on them yet."

Marcy shook her head. "What does Nicholls want with me? I've never met the Chans, and I'm sure Tam knows nothing other than organising a party for them."

"We took down their supplier in Afghanistan a few months back. Unfortunately, he died before we could interrogate him. We've been trying to find their link ever since."

"But if he was in Afghanistan, they're in Sydney and you're in Nepal, then how—why—?"

Her eyes narrowed and he could *see* her scientific brain

connecting the dots. Making the connections that were real and true and branded him as the bad guy.

"You—you're trying to establish a connection to them from here?" She slipped her hand out of his and edged away.

"Not establish, no. Follow leads."

With each attempt to reassure her he dug himself into a deeper hole.

Just shut the fuck up, Harris.

"Nicholls had a folder with my name on it. There was a photo poking out the side. Was that of me, Jake?"

He gritted his teeth. No more lies. He'd had a gut full where Marcy was concerned. From now on, no matter the cost, he'd tell her all he could without compromising her safety. "No."

"Then it was Tam, wasn't it?"

He didn't need to confirm it. Marcy knew; at least, she'd worked out the most damning connection. He waited for her to link the final piece.

"You thought it was me."

"Yes. I was sent in to check you out. The intelligence was faulty."

"Because we're twins. You think Tam has something to do with the Chans. Otherwise, why would you be after me?" Her voice rose and he shushed her.

He couldn't subdue her rising anger as easily. "You have to understand, the evidence is strong against your sister."

"You thought I was a link in a drug chain."

"I know *you* aren't." He'd stake his life on her innocence.

"Only a tattoo and a birthmark separate Tam and me. Is that why you slept with me, Jake? To find out if my body carried those marks?"

A murmur of voices outside Marcy's door drew her attention. She stood and stared as a key turned in the lock and Nicholls stepped into her room.

# #

"Good evening, Doctor."

A breeze cooled her back and she glanced at the window. Jake was gone.

Her stomach clenched and she gripped the windowsill. Nicholls' arrival might have interrupted her *tete-a-tete* with Jake but no answer was necessary. He was guilty as charged.

Swallowing the hurt that was her own fault, she strove for her snarky self. It was hanging by a thread.

"Mr Nicholls. To what do I owe the pleasure of this visit?"

He stood just inside the door, one hand resting on the handle. Was she so dangerous he was afraid to enter further? She caught a stupid grin before it escaped. Even with an injured arm her lessons with Jake gave her a sense of control, an edge Nicholls didn't know about.

"A car will be here early tomorrow morning. Your escort will take you to the airport and on to Sydney via Singapore."

"And you've come to wish me *bon voyage*?"

Nicholls slipped one hand into his pocket. "I'd like to

remind you we are on the same side. I realise you were aggrieved by my line of questioning at lunch."

"Curious, not aggrieved. Why didn't you want me to speak to Jake Harris?"

"I regret I'm not at liberty to tell you more."

"Was it because of the video incident?"

Nicholls' gaze slid away. He took his hand out of his pocket and adjusted his cuff link. "A word of advice; don't imagine any tender feelings for Harris."

"Why would you think that?"

"He may have saved your life, but consider what he set out to do."

"What's that?"

"Bring down a cartel. Aside from his one little slip-up with you he's a top operative. Don't take it personally, Dr Westcott. Harris is single-minded in pursuit of justice and drug dealers. You were a link in the chain."

The blunt reminder tore at her shredded emotions. That was the crux of her relationship with Jake. He'd warned her not to get emotionally involved, but she'd leapt into a holiday romance headfirst. But if she was nothing more than a job, why had he risked discovery and broken into her room?

Chapter Twenty-Five

Sydney, Australia

John Chan threw the porcelain vase against the wall, knocking the contemporary oil painting askew and drenching it in water that dripped into thick carpet.

"How can they have missed her? And he's supposed to be dead." Chan raked his hand through sharp white gravel topping an oversized pot plant. Blood streaked his fingers but the pain failed to distract him. The woman had survived two attempts to capture her. Sketchy information indicated the male companion had come to her aid and helped her reach the Nepalese capital.

So the bitch had hooked up with an agent. Yet she'd refused all Chan's overtures. Refused to share her body with him.

She hadn't held back with the guy on the video.

Each time Chan played the clip, he got the mother of all boners that not even Madam Wu's triple act would satisfy.

And now the bitch was being returned in protective custody to Australia.

To Sydney.

His nostrils flared and he dragged in a breath, releasing it slowly. When official interest in her relaxed, he would have her brought to the whorehouse.

Willing or not, she would be his.

Then she would die.

Chapter Twenty-Six

New South Wales, Australia

Jake drove his battered ute along the rutted lane and parked under the lean-to shed hanging off the side of his beach shack. Forty-eight hours since he'd left Marcy in Nicholl's care. He felt every hour and every mile between them like cuts from a knife, but his first objective was to find Paul Rimmer. So far, not one of his old connections was talking. Hesitance and vague replies told him his botch up in Nepal had left him out in the cold with the Bureau.

He grabbed his duffel bag off the back seat and turned to survey the building. Paint peeled off the façade and sand had banked up in front of the steps. He walked slowly across the patch of green that passed for lawn and onto the veranda he'd rebuilt from scratch with his brother the spring before Pete had—

Don't go there.

He dragged in a ragged breath. Pete had been his *gofer* man that uni break as they re-roofed with bull-nose iron and laid a new veranda floor.

His gaze was drawn to a darker patch where Pete had slopped decking oil in his eagerness to help. Just there in front of the door.

He lowered his duffel bag and reached for his gun. Sand had blown around the doorframe but it was the sharp ridge and bare patch where a passing foot had slipped that disturbed him.

He stood to one side, his back to the wall, and slowly turned the door handle.

Ears attuned to the slightest sound, he eased the door open, stepped into the entry and swept the hall with his gun. To his left, the bedroom door was wide open.

One more step brought him to the edge of the tiny, open-plan lounge-dining room. Gun first, he stepped into the doorway.

A man reclined on the two-seater, his gun pointed at Jake's chest. "I heard you coming a mile away. When are you going to replace that piece of shit you call a ute?"

"Hello, Paul. Nice to see you too." Jake had gambled his former partner would show up at the shack where they'd celebrated after their first shared mission. Innocence, or need, or both; their shared history gave them a strong bond.

"Yeah, figured you might eventually get the idea to come here in that tiny brain of yours. Have a seat."

Jake perched on the wide arm of an ancient armchair and kept his gun trained on Paul Rimmer. "So."

"Reckon you've got slow, old man. Once upon a time, you would have known you had an uninvited guest before you left the lean-to."

"And once upon a time you wouldn't have been so sloppy

as to leave a trail a blind man could see. Did your engagement make you soft?"

"How the hell did you know about that?" Paul's smile disappeared. He sat forward and Jake read the wary fatigue etched in his ex-partner's posture. Dark shadows underscored his eyes and he flicked glances towards the entry.

Questions about Paul's loyalty circled through Jake's brain. This whole mess just didn't add up.

Paul shook his head. "My trigger finger is itchy. Why don't we cut to the chase?"

Hope bubbled through Jake. "Tell me about your fiancée."

"What can I say? Gorgeous, with a rack you can—"

"I know what she looks like. What's the deal?"

"You never were long on words." Paul's voice grew husky and he cleared his throat. "Tam and I were working undercover, getting close to the Chans. The night of this big party at their mansion, someone gave us, or me—I don't know which—away. Could have been my partner."

"Tamsin was your partner?" In his wildest dreams, Jake hadn't envisaged this scenario. He'd tracked Marcy to find a link to the Chans and expected to snare her twin. But not like this. And not working with Paul.

But who was telling the truth?

I know Paul. I don't know Tamsin.

But you know Marcy and respect her judgment.

"Yeah. Our *engagement* was necessary after John Chan got

suspicious that I was hanging around Tam so much. That was sloppy on my part. I had to do that god-awful public going-down-on-one-knee and everything. But it bought us the extra time we needed. Tam was undercover as an event co-ordinator and she'd organized this big family gathering for Chan Senior's seventieth birthday party."

"And?"

"Nothing. We were supposed to use the event to infiltrate the home and gather evidence."

"What sort of evidence?"

"Computer. The cartel heads met under cover of the birthday. Tam was to slip into the main office. It was all supposed to be clear but there was a tip-off. I barely made it out alive."

"And Tamsin? Did she make it?" Undercover work was the most dangerous assignment, but he had no wish to try to explain that to Marcy if her twin was dead. His grip tightened on his gun.

Paul's gun wavered slightly. "No idea. I've had no contact with her or the Bureau since. I don't know who I can trust."

"Why did you come here?"

"I've asked myself that question each night while I waited for you." Paul blinked and steadied his gun. "Who shot Al-Kohari before he could be interrogated?"

"I'd like to know that too. But what's the shake down in Afghanistan got to do with now? That was months ago."

"Pretty convenient that the only link we had to the Chans was killed before he could put the finger on them."

"You don't seriously think I would—" A slow burn began in his gut and seared a path to his throat. Once upon a time, the idea of this conversation with Paul would have been laughable. Trust had become a precious commodity since the death of his brother.

"Like I said, I don't know who to trust."

"For fuck's sake, Paul. We're trying to nail the bastards responsible for the importation of bad drugs, the scum that killed my brother. Why would I let them get away?"

Paul stared at him, flicked on the safety catch and set his gun on the table beside him. He pressed the heels of his hands into his eyes. "You're right. Christ, I'm so tired, I'm even blaming you."

Jake thumbed his safety catch on and lowered his gun hand. "Have you any idea where Tamsin might have gone?"

"None. And I can't risk going into the Bureau until I know who ratted us out. It had to have come from central office. What I wouldn't give for access to our database." Paul stretched and leaned back. "I could murder a steak right about now."

"I get the hint. I'll ride back into town and get take out."

"Grab a six pack too, will you, mate? I'm drier than the Simpson Desert in summer."

Paul tipped his head back and closed his eyes.

# #

Jake cleared away the stubbies and packaging from their meal and carried them into the kitchen. Paul was sound asleep on the sofa, the grey pallor that tinged his skin less obvious after their meal.

Jake leaned against the counter and considered Paul's version of events. If what he said was true, Marcy's sister may have turned rogue.

Or she's hiding out too, and in danger.

Until they found Tamsin, and any evidence she had found before fleeing the mansion, their investigation was stalled. But how to get to her?

It wasn't like he could waltz into head office and calmly log onto a computer. His pending disciplinary action restrained him from accessing the Bureau's database and Paul couldn't risk contacting anyone. Matthew Danton, head of home branch, had been dismissive of Jake's request to complete his assignment. He had vetoed further access to information on penalty of dismissal for breaching confidentiality.

Jake would have done the same in his place.

He wandered down to the beach. Beneath his feet, the sand was cool and dry. He sat on a fallen tree trunk and looked out over the moonlit sea. Froth-edged waves crashed and ran up the gently sloping beach and salt-scented breeze cleared his mind.

In his bones, Jake knew the connection between Marcy and her twin was close and strong. While Tamsin might stay the hell away to protect her sister as fiercely as Marcy had done, he felt sure they would try to contact one another. He'd bet a year's wages Marcy had heard from her twin.

He pulled out his phone and searched for Marcy's address then walked into the shack to collect his car keys. Paul had thrown off the sheet and lay snoring on the sofa. Jake flicked off the light switch and checked the time. If he left now, he could be at Marcy's apartment in Sydney in three hours.

# #

Marcy tossed the bedcovers off and padded out to her tiny balcony. Clouds had built into towering pillars through the afternoon. Lightning flashed in the eastern sky and thunder rumbled beyond the Heads, over the ocean. Around her, darkness lay heavy and humid.

She ran her fingers through her hair and thought longingly of snow. Cold, wet snow and Jake to keep her warm.

Linking her fingers behind her neck she tipped her head when a faint breeze wafted by, carrying the smell of diesel and the *chug-chug* of a passing tinny. At the bottom of her street, the ferry pulled away from the terminal and headed back to Circular Quay. With a sigh, she stepped back into her bedroom.

"Hello, Marcy."

"Jake?" Her heart beat double time. Perhaps because she'd been thinking of him, she stepped towards him before it occurred to wonder how he'd got into her home.

Abruptly, she pulled up short. Heartache and the memory of their final encounter in Kathmandu roared back. Drawing a deep breath she folded her arms. "No point asking how the hell you got into my secure building, is there?"

Jake shook his head. "There's always a way in."

"Like in Kathmandu. And you didn't answer my question."

"We were interrupted or I would have told you then. I did not sleep with you to check out your tats and birthmark."

"How can I believe you?"

"You. Nearly naked. Shower. Do I need to go on?"

Naked? He'd seen her bikini-clad body, got the answers he needed, knew she was lying but let her. Then he'd teased her until their very public kiss.

He hadn't needed to sleep with her.

Heat exploded through Marcy's cheeks, between her thighs. Embarrassed as she'd been by that episode, Jake's heated gaze had been a turn-on.

The tipping point in their relationship.

She'd tried to convince herself the kiss that followed had been nothing more than an attempt to distract Jake from pursuing questions about Tam.

Some day, she'd stop lying to herself. "Okay. Good then. I just wanted to know."

Jake hooked his thumbs in his pockets and leaned against the door. "I would have seduced you if I had to, to find out, Marcy. I'm not Mister Nice Guy. But when we had sex, believe me, I wanted you. Still do."

For a man averse to conversation, his words packed a punch. A trickle of sweat ran between her breasts and she dug her fingernails into her arms to stop herself reaching for him. He sounded so damned believable. As much as she wanted to believe him, scientific Marcy demanded answers to the hard question.

"You wouldn't break in here just for a booty call so why have you crept in like a burglar?"

Sheet lightning streaked across the dark sky, revealing tension in his body, torment in his eyes. Did she really want to explode this precious moment of honest lust with unpalatable truth?

"Unfinished business. Have you heard from your sister?"

Like a bucket of iced water, his words reminded her they were on opposite sides of whatever was happening. Tam's email had been right.

Trust no one. Say nothing.

She'd be eternally grateful Jake had been at her side on the Everest track, but she'd been right not to trust him with her emotions. Jake didn't do emotions. He'd told her as much.

She clamped a lid on her lust, but fear for her twin vied with anger. "You thought I was my sister so you followed me in Nepal. Why would I tell you anything about Tam now?"

"It's important, Marcy, more than you can imagine. Have you heard from her?"

"I'd like you to leave now. Close the door behind you on your way out." She walked past him. At least, she tried to.

But Jake gripped her shoulders and swung her round to face him. In the low spill of street lighting, his gaze raked her face. "Your sister has disappeared; maybe she's hiding out. I don't know why or from whom but I can't help if I don't know where she is."

"Why would you help her? You think she's involved with a drug family that you're trying to catch. I can't give my sister up to you. I won't tell you anything."

His grip relaxed and he released an audible breath. "You just did."

"How did you—I mean, I didn't. There's nothing to tell." Frantically, she considered her words. What had she said? Had she really told him something, or was he playing her? Clearly she wasn't cut out for this cloak and dagger stuff.

"Really?" Jake's gaze searched hers, seeing deep inside to her secret fears. "If you knew nothing, you wouldn't have said you *won't tell* me."

Her heart hammered like a jackhammer digging up a road. How easily he'd winkled out the truth. Trusting Jake with her own safety was one thing, but not her sister's. He didn't know Tam like she did. She pressed her lips together. If she didn't speak, she couldn't betray Tam further. "Damn it, I don't need you hassling me on top of everything else."

"You mean the interview at the Bureau? Did they keep you talking for hours?"

"Your people don't stop at just talking. Those guys turfed out my sub-tenant then made a thorough job of pulling my apartment to pieces looking for heaven knows what."

"If the Bureau sent people in, you wouldn't have seen a trace of their visit. Shit." Without another word, he grabbed her overnight bag from beside the cupboard and tossed it on the bed.

"What are you doing? Stop, Jake." She made a grab for his arm as he strode towards her wardrobe.

He took her face between his hands, his eyes darker than she'd ever seen them. "Pack light and pack fast."

"Why?" Tired of being pushed around, first by Nicholls, then the men from the Bureau, she clung to his wrists, refusing to budge until Jake gave her something more than an order.

"I've got to get you out of here. That wasn't the Bureau that searched your apartment."

Nausea threatened and her stomach rebelled as his words hit home. Would it never be over? She clasped her hands tightly across her waist. "Who—"

He wrenched her cupboard door open and pulled out a T-shirt and jeans and thrust them at her. "Get dressed." Then he pulled open her top drawer, grabbed a couple more T-shirts and shoved them in the overnight bag.

"Maybe the cartel. Come on, Marcy. They're probably watching this place."

"But—"

She couldn't think, couldn't move. Flying out of Kathmandu, she'd thought she'd left the nightmare and danger behind. A lump the size of Everest blocked her throat. Her voice broke around her whispered, "Why?"

"Someone thinks you have whatever it is they're looking for. Twice you've been lucky not to be killed. Let's not give them a third chance." He strode into the bathroom and returned with her toiletry bag.

Gruff and bossy and downright annoying as Jake was at times, she longed for the luxury of being able to tell him to piss off and leave her and her sister alone.

But this was Jake doing what he did better than anyone.

Keeping her safe.

Keeping her alive.

He wrapped a hand around her arm and locked gazes. "Sweetheart, please. We can talk later but right now, I need to get you as far away from here as I can."

Galvanized by his touch, she dragged her jeans on and pulled the T-shirt over her sleep top. Fumbling with the laces, she slipped her joggers on.

Jake flattened against the wall beside her balcony door and scanned the street below.

Her stomach was doing flip-flops as she stood, grabbed her handbag and slipped the long strap over her head. "I'm ready."

He picked up her bag and led her into the tiny foyer. Pausing, he pressed his ear to the wood before easing the front door open and checking the approach. "Come on."

Heart in mouth, she followed him down the fire stairs to the basement car park. "Mine's the little blue car."

He paused for the briefest of moments and quirked an eyebrow at her. "A Beetle? I could have guessed. But we'll take mine. Follow me, and stick to the shadows." He slipped through a heavy exit door and set a fast pace, half-dragging her several blocks and doubling back as he had done in Lukla. Finally, he stopped beside a mud-splattered ute parked under the only broken street light on the block.

"*That's* our ride? My Beetle could outdrive this any day." Utterly out of place in trendy Balmain, Jake's ute dwarfed the string of Smart cars and two-doors lining the narrow street. He unlocked her door.

Metal creaked as he opened it.

Marcy cringed and looked over her shoulder. "I thought we were supposed to be unobtrusive." Fifty metres away something moved in the shadows beside stone steps leading to an alley. She hissed at Jake, "Over there. Who's that?"

He pushed her down behind him and drew his gun from a calf holster. Aiming at the shadow within shadows, he made his way between cars towards the threat.

Adrenaline rushed through Marcy's veins, blood pounded in her ears, deafening her to the sounds of the night. Crouched against the car she presented as small a target as possible. Her wounded arm pressed into the metal frame and she bit back a cry of pain. Fear stole her breath and she peered into the darkness. Where was Jake? Who was following them?

His voice came from behind her. "Just a stray dog."

She gasped and fell on her backside before Jake loomed beside her. Relief quickly replaced her fright and she took the hand he offered. "Well then, that's lucky." Her voice came out breathless, as though she'd run a sprint race.

"The sooner we get out of here, the better. Hop in."

Cradling her throbbing arm, she nodded and climbed into the passenger seat. Tugging her seatbelt across her lap, she tried to emulate Jake's cool control, but it took several attempts for her shaking hands to lock the seatbelt into the buckle.

Jake slipped into the driver's seat, reached behind her and pulled out a baseball cap. He passed it to her. "Put this on and keep your face turned away from CCTV cameras."

She settled the cap on her head before he turned the key in the ignition.

The engine roared to life and they headed onto the freeway and north out of the city. Outer suburbs flashed past before he broke the silence. "You won't tell me about your sister, yet despite all that happened, you trusted me enough to drop everything and bolt from the city. I'm glad you did. But why did you?"

She turned and stared at his face. In the headlights of passing cars, Jake's stern profile gave nothing away. How could he make her feel safe and yet be a threat to Tam at the same time? "I trust you with my life, Jake."

But I can't take a chance with my sister's.

"I will keep you safe, no matter what. That's a promise."

"I know."

And that was all he said until he turned into a busy service station and pulled up to a pump furthest from the highway. "Don't get out. I won't be long."

Scrunching down in the seat, she leaned back, angling her face away from the service centre.

Jake filled up the tank and strolled inside to pay.

A flashy sports job raced in off the service road, roared around the ute and pulled up in a parking bay behind her. Marcy tipped the rear vision mirror her way, looking for who knew what. Frayed nerves and fear had her jumping at shadows.

Two Italian studs jumped out of the low-slung car and sauntered into the café bar like young John Travoltas.

She peered into the service shop and willed Jake to hurry up.

He'd stopped in front of a display beside the automatic doors. With apparent unconcern, he lifted a pair of sunglasses from the stand and tried them on. He looked into the mirror, looked out towards the bowsers then flipped the glasses off and replaced them. Tossing a wave and good night to the attendant, Jake emerged with a cardboard tray of cups and a paper package. He opened his door and handed the bag to her.

The aroma of fresh coffee distracted her and she sat up. "You must have read my mind."

"Figured we could both use the caffeine." He handed her a cup from the tray and slipped his own into the cup holder on the dashboard. Without further conversation, he started the engine and pulled back onto the highway.

Marcy wrapped her hands around the coffee cup and sipped, welcoming the trickle of warmth in her stomach. Clouds scudded across the stormy sky, hiding the glimpse of moonlight. Cocooned in the dark cabin, it was easier to ask questions without Jake's intense gaze distracting her.

"Why do you think my sister knows any more than I do about the Chans and their drug trade?"

"I know she does." Jake took a slip road, then an overpass before turning east off the main highway onto a B road that eventually narrowed into a single strip of bitumen.

"How can you be certain?" Feigning unconcern, she opened the paper bag. He'd bought her favourite fast food. She bit into a sausage roll and prayed he would reveal more than he had in Nepal.

"Because your sister is working for the Bureau, like me. And like her *fiancé*."

Marcy paused, her mouth full of pastry and mince. *Tamsin is a secret agent?* Odd pauses in conversation, moments that only an identical twin would notice, flashed through her memory. Quickly, she chewed, swallowed and turned.

The dashboard light revealed Jake's mouth set in a grim line.

"You're not joking, are you?"

"No. Your sister is leading a double life as an undercover agent. Paul played her fiancé as part of her cover story."

"Impossible. I know her. She loves high fashion and six inch heels. A broken nail is a tragedy and her hairdresser is her best friend." Had Marcy really been so distracted finishing her thesis that she could have failed to notice such a major change in her sister?

Another thought hit, hurtful and inconceivable. How could Tam have kept something like that from her twin?

"Then Tamsin must be damned good at her role if she's convinced you too. For the past year, she's been working undercover with Paul. Since she disappeared, you're the only person she's contacted."

Mollified by that crumb of acknowledgement, Marcy wondered aloud. "Not even the Bureau?"

"No. Paul and your sister were tasked with gathering vital evidence the night of the party at the Chan mansion. Something went wrong."

Wrong? Her stomach roiled at the word. At the implication behind what might go wrong when drugs and criminals were involved. A chill gripped her heart.

He couldn't mean—*that*.

"Do you mean that Tam is—that she—"

She couldn't say the word. Saying it might make it true. Instead she sucked in a breath and held it.

"Dead? I don't know." Jake didn't sugar-coat his response, but his voice was gentle. He reached over and covered her hand as it rested on her thigh. "I'm sorry I don't have more information to share. That's why I hoped you had heard something from her. Have you?"

Tam can't be dead. Not vibrant, fun-loving, wilful little sis.

Staring blindly through the side window, Marcy blinked back tears and bit her lip.

Finally, her brain started functioning again. Jake's timing was out. Tam's communications in Nepal had arrived days after the Chan event. And then when she got home—

"I got another email . . ."

"And?"

Lightning flashed in the sky. In the split second of illumination, Marcy saw the ocean beyond low sand hills. Trying to sort out her chaotic emotions, she stalled. "It was in my inbox when I got home from the interview. Where are we going?"

"My beach house. Paul showed up this afternoon. He pulled a gun on me."

"What? But didn't you say you and he and—and Tam are on the same side?"

"Technically, yes. Someone blew their cover. Paul doesn't know who."

Her mind reeled as she struggled to make sense of Jake's revelations. Friends pulling guns on each other, maybe on her sister. Drug families trying to kill her—the world had gone to hell in a hand basket and she was trapped on its high-octane, triple loop rollercoaster ride.

She dug her nails into her seat, desperate to wake from the nightmare. "He suspected you?"

"I'd have done the same."

Trust no one.

Tam's fears were shared by Jake. And by Paul. What kind of dark world was her twin caught up in?

The ute bumped along a drive that was no more than dual dirt tracks and pulled up under a wonky, corrugated roof.

"By the way, Paul's probably still inside."

"Whoa! Why?"

"Together, we might be able to work out where your sister is."

"Then what? You said Paul pulled a gun on you. What if you do find Tam and he does the same to her?"

Jake turned off the engine. Waves crashed nearby, filling the silence. He took her hand and stroked his thumb across her knuckles. "We'll work it out as we go, but, Marcy—what if she did set him up?"

Chapter Twenty-Seven

Jake felt Marcy stiffen and pull away from him. Of course the idea that anyone might think badly of her sister was repugnant. Siblings defended each other. Hell, once upon a time, he'd punched a guy in a pub for looking cross-eyed at his younger sister.

But he had to consider the possibility that Tamsin wasn't like her twin. Enough money could turn anyone's head and the Chans had plenty to splash about.

Marcy jerked her door open and almost fell out of the ute before stalking into the gloom. He'd give her a few minutes to cool off and think before going after her. Her overnight bag was light as he hauled it off the cab floor and slung it over his shoulder.

He slammed his fist on the roof of the cab. Damn it. He needed the email from Tamsin plus a friend inside the Bureau to give him deep computer access. Even if Tamsin had changed SIM cards, she couldn't have disappeared so completely that she left no digital footprint.

He walked slowly up the stairs and pushed open the front door, dropped Marcy's bag in the bedroom and wandered back to the lounge. Paul was sitting on the edge of the sofa rubbing his hands over his face. "That death trap of yours is loud enough to wake the dead."

"It worked on you. Coffee?"

"Yeah, ta. Find what you wanted?"

"Not quite. I've brought Tamsin's sister back with me." He filled the electric jug and switched on the power.

"Marcy? But she was going to Nepal."

"Long story. Contact has been made though."

"With Tam?" Paul's eyes brightened. He pushed off the sofa and joined Jake at the kitchen counter. "Where is she?"

"Don't know yet. I have to convince Marcy it's safe to share what she knows with us."

"She knows me. She'll tell me."

Jake pushed a mug across the counter. "Marcy's had a rough time and there's no love for the Bureau since they questioned her. She sees them—and me—as a threat to her sister. You—I don't know what she'll think about you now."

Floorboards creaked and Marcy entered the living area. Hands in her pockets, she eyed both men warily. "Hello, Paul."

"Hi, Marcy. Good to see you." He moved as though to hug her.

Jake's muscles bunched as a surge of jealousy ripped through him.

She jumped back, one hand raised to keep Paul away. "I know you're not about to become my brother-in-law, Paul. Let's keep it real here."

Paul snagged hold of a breakfast stool and sat. His smile faded. "Sorry. I'm used to playing the role. Look, Marcy, I don't know what happened to your sister. Tam and I were separated. I haven't seen her since she entered the mansion to look for—something."

Cool, grey eyes assessed Paul as Marcy folded her arms. "So you don't know if she found anything, you don't know if she got away with it if she did, and you've lost my sister. Does that cover it?"

Paul squirmed on his stool. Jake drank a mouthful of coffee and silently cheered Marcy. What reply could Paul make to her succinct summary of the situation?

"When you think of a good reason why I should trust you—either of you—let me know." Marcy looked around the living area and back to Jake. "Where's my bag? It's been kind of a shitty day and I'd like to go to bed before the sun comes up."

"Through here." Jake set his mug down and showed her to the bedroom. The only bedroom. Paul was welcome to the lumpy sofa. For himself, he'd as soon camp outside if the rain held off because he was damned sure Marcy wouldn't want him in her bed.

He leaned against the door frame.

She glanced at the queen-size wrought-iron bed, picked up her bag and dumped it on top of the doona. Hands thrust inside the bag, she paused and eye-balled him.

"Was there anything else, Jake? Because, as much as I trust you with my life, that's all I trust you with. I hate what you're trying to do to my sister."

Jake straightened and pointed at the other door beside Marcy. "It's a two-way bathroom. Knock before you go in." He closed the bedroom door behind him.

# #

Marcy groaned, and flung an arm across her eyes. Early morning sunlight streamed through the east-facing window onto her pillow. Her head ached from too little sleep and too much secret agent business.

Needing a shower and a coffee, in that order, she kicked off the sheet, stretched and stumbled to the bathroom. She opened the door and stepped in.

Jake stood beside the shower, a towel slung low on his hips, toothbrush in hand, and water droplets sliding down his chest. He raised an eyebrow. "Were you thinking of joining me?"

Her sleep-muddled mind tried to catch up with morning.

"I—um—ah, no. That is, sorry. I forgot the two-way thing." She turned to escape but he caught her hand and pulled her back. Fingers linked with hers, and his gaze roamed her face.

"You're right, Marcy. It is a two-way thing. I forgot that in my pursuit of the Chans. All this time I've demanded you go along with me, do what I told you to do without giving anything in return. I'm sorry."

"And here was me thinking you were all tall, blond-streaked silence because you were bound by some official Secrets Act."

"There are things I can't talk about, but you deserve to know what I can tell you. Perhaps then you'll understand how important it is to find your sister and deal with whatever she discovered."

He cupped her cheek, and held her for the space of several heartbeats. "Let's get dressed and walk on the beach. We can talk there." He picked up his clothes from the floor and shut the door behind him.

Great. Just when she decided she was strong enough to let Jake go, he changed tack. She leaned on the vanity unit. Steam misted the mirror in a light veil. She cleared a patch and stared at her blurred image. *Can I trust him?*

Gritty-eyed, she filled the sink and washed her face. Cold water sloshed over the edge and down her thighs. She looked down, realising too late that she was wearing a T-shirt, bikini undies and not much else.

He's seen more than that of me. She shrugged and dried her face before dressing quickly. Whatever Jake had to say, she would listen and decide. She shoved her mobile into the pocket of her shorts and tip-toed into the living room.

Paul sprawled on the sofa, sound asleep. In the kitchen, Jake raised two steaming mugs and indicated they should head outside. She opened the front door and led the way down the steps towards the beach.

A large piece of driftwood lay half buried near the rocky, curved end of the bay. She headed in that direction and sat on the lower end, lifting her face to the early morning sun. The sea was calm after last night's storm, but tide-wrack littered the sand like a border between land and sea.

Jake handed her a mug and sat beside her.

"Thanks. So—where do we go from here?"

"We attempt to find common ground where we share what we know, find your sister, and put a stop to the cartel."

"Just like that?"

"I hope so. You know what I want from you. What can I give you in exchange?"

She tipped her head back and considered all the questions she'd wanted him to answer. Cotton wool clouds sailed overhead and a balmy breeze caressed her bare skin. She slanted a sideways look at him. The Everest track seemed long ago. "I can ask anything and you'll answer?"

"All that I'm able to, yes. Fire away." He sipped his coffee and watched her over the top of his mug.

Marcy wriggled her toes into the sand. Everything hinged on finding Tam. But just say they found her and she had evidence to put away the cartel for good—what then? *Was this thing between Jake and her viable?*

"Tell me about your family."

# #

Jake's hand tightened around his mug. At the core of his dogged pursuit of the cartel was his need to avenge Pete's death. There was no way Marcy could have known, but she'd zeroed in on what drove him. Chance, or had he subconsciously given it away?

His gaze slid over the waves as they built higher, pushed onshore by an increasing south-easterly wind. Since Pete's death, Jake had held onto his anger and guilt. Each small triumph in his quest had renewed his promise to his little brother to bring down the drug traffickers. No family should suffer what his had suffered. No young lives should be lost in such a terrible way.

He sucked in a deep breath. Marcy deserved to know what drove him.

"I had a brother. Pete was clever, studying medicine at Sydney Uni and hoping one day to join the *Medecins Sans Frontiers*. I had reservations about his girlfriend and when he started goofing off with her instead of studying, we had a big row. I backed off. If I'd paid more attention I would have picked up she was dealing. She had Pete hooked."

Candace had disappeared the day Pete died and Jake had found no trace of her since.

Marcy reached out and touched his arm. "I'm sorry, Jake. I shouldn't have asked."

He shook his head and met her gaze. "I found him when I got home. He'd killed himself. I vowed on his grave to do all I could to stop the trade."

"That's a long road you're on."

"Maybe. But not long ago, we seriously upset the supply out of Asia. If your sister got away with what we hope she did, we could put the cartel out of business in Sydney."

Marcy looked off into the distance. Her body language still screamed disbelief, but if Tamsin was like her twin, she had courage to burn.

"Tam would never have sold out to the cartel. I know her, Jake. So if she escaped with evidence, she'll be waiting for a signal that it's safe to reappear with it and that won't happen until—unless I can make contact."

Until—unless? As he suspected, she had a means of contacting her twin. Undercurrents of tension ran between them, questions of trust and truth circling like hawks.

Marcy seemed to be holding some kind of internal debate while he held his breath. Just how far would her trust in him extend?

Keeping his tone gentle, he touched her hand. "Do you have any idea where she is?"

Her gaze snapped back and her frown disappeared. "It's a long shot—"

"Better than what I've got so far."

"I'll make a couple of calls." She stood decisively before looking down at him, concern etched in her face. "Promise me that you'll listen to Tam's side. I know Paul is your friend but Tam's my sister. I know she hasn't done anything wrong."

"I'll listen. You have my word, Marcy."

She nodded, took her phone from her pocket and wandered out of earshot to the end of the rocky groin.

Leaning back against the sloping driftwood, legs stretched out along the trunk, Jake watched and waited.

The rigid line of her back and one hand clutching a small outcrop of rock were the only signs of her tension. Gusting wind carried snatches of her voice to him. Not her words but the lilting rhythm stirred memories of her singing in the teahouse and on the trail. If only he'd met her under other circumstances.

His phone vibrated in his pocket. He slipped it out and thumbed the screen. Stark black letters spelled out a directive from the Bureau. "Enquiry moved to 11 A.M. today."

On whose orders?

He checked his watch and groaned. The timing couldn't have been worse. Marcy had finally decided to trust him with her twin's whereabouts; she might even now be collecting an address, or a phone number that would lead him to the elusive Tamsin.

But his job was on the line. If he was to make it to the interview, he had to leave right away.

"Marcy!"

She turned, phone in hand, and covered the mouthpiece.

He held up his phone and waved. "I've got to go. I'll be back tonight. Text me if you find out anything."

She waved and turned back to her call.

Preoccupied by the change in protocol, Jake climbed into his ute and reversed out of the lean-to. Through the kitchen window, he caught sight of Paul's surprised expression as he pulled away. If not for the urgency of the request from the Bureau, he'd have stopped to update Paul. As it was, he'd be lucky to make it on time.

Chapter Twenty-Eight

Marcy sent the text and switched off her phone. Of course it was low on battery and she'd forgotten the charger in their haste to get away last night. She tapped the case against her chin and watched a grey mass of cloud building far out to sea. There would be another storm before the day was over.

She picked her way over the rocks back towards Jake's shack. The lean-to hung drunkenly off the southern wall looking as though one good blow might rip it down. Normally, she loved storms but would the beach house hold up in the storm that was building out to sea?

Paul emerged from the house and stood for a moment leaning on the railing. Assured and easy-going, it had been easy to imagine having him as her brother-in-law. He spotted her, waved, and bounded down the stairs. He looked the same, sounded the same, as though nothing had changed.

But nothing was as it seemed.

Tam and Paul had convinced her they were in love while playing a deadly charade with the cartel, and yesterday, Paul had drawn a gun on Jake.

I know Tam. How could I not have seen through her deception, even if I don't know Paul so well? Pocketing her phone, she waited for Paul to reach her.

He smiled as he jumped from the grassy edge onto the sand beside her. "Hey, Marcy, where's Jake going like a bat out of hell?"

"No idea." How long would it take to get used to the idea he wasn't going to become her brother-in-law? He'd been so convincing in the role.

So was Tam. What did that say about Marcy's ability to read character?

"Secretive son of a bastard. You sure?"

Sand stung her calves as the wind gusted. Marcy wrapped her arms around her waist. "He just said he'd be back tonight. That's all."

"I don't suppose you've heard any more from Tam? Jake said she'd contacted you."

A queasy sensation settled in Marcy's stomach. Sharing that information with Jake, trusting him with her twin's safety had been a big step.

Jake trusted Paul, and Tam trusted Paul, but someone had given Tam away to the cartel and now her twin was in hiding. Who betrayed whom?

She met Paul's gaze.

He was smiling pleasantly but his eyes were devoid of emotion. They hadn't always been so cold.

Goosebumps rose on her arms and a sinking feeling threatened to eject the coffee she'd only half drunk. "Nothing useful, Paul. I'm sorry. All I know is she's alive but I've no idea where she is." Brushing past him, she tossed over her shoulder, "I'm making fresh coffee. Do you want some?"

She didn't want coffee. She didn't want to be stranded in the middle of nowhere with Paul pressing her for Tam's whereabouts. She didn't want to be in hiding because every time she turned around, someone wanted to kill her.

"Sure." Paul's voice was friendly, the tone reminiscent of lazy Sunday afternoons in her little apartment, all three of them watching football and sharing a six-pack of Coronas.

Forget his eyes. Her imagination was in overdrive and she was frustrated another conversation with Jake had been cut short. Digging deep for her confidence, she led the way into the kitchen.

Paul followed and settled in the opening between the counter and the fridge. "So, what did she say?"

"Like I said, nothing about her whereabouts. Sugar?"

"Black and one. Did she mention me?"

"Only that you were missing and she was worried. I wasn't in a position to help from Nepal, and then I arrived home to learn she's missing and you're here." Marcy stirred the coffee, tapped the spoon on the edge of the mug and slid it across the counter to Paul. "Why are you here, Paul?"

He didn't touch the mug. Just stood, legs wide and blocking her exit from the kitchen. He locked gazes with her. "To catch the bastard who gave me away. To find Tam."

Harsh lines etched his features and she recognized the same look Jake had worn when she first met him. Nothing and no one would come between Paul and his goal.

She should have been happy to hear Paul's vow. To know he was committed to finding her sister. But in the back of her mind, Paul's phrasing niggled. Was it possible he believed Tam had left him to the mercy of the cartel while she escaped? Swallowing a mouthful of coffee, Marcy put her mug on the counter top.

"We'd all like to find her. But I'm not sure we're looking for her for the same reasons. Excuse me, please." She tried to move around him.

Paul stood, immovable as Uluru, and held out his hand. "Give me your phone, Marcy."

Shit. Now what?

Jake would never have been caught like this. He planned an exit from wherever he was. Wondering how she could have allowed herself to be boxed in, her mind frantically raced through scenarios with Paul.

Surprise me. Jake's instruction in their last self defence lesson ghosted through her memory.

She took a deep breath and stepped up to Paul. Hands resting on his shoulders, she willed herself to meet his fierce gaze. "I'm scared, Paul. So scared. Will you help me find her?"

Beneath her palms, she sensed a slight relaxation of his

muscles. Before she allowed herself to think further, her foot swept around behind his knee as Jake had taught her.

Thrown off balance, Paul crashed into the counter.

Marcy brought her elbow up into his chin and jumped over the sprawl of his body as he fell. She raced through the doorway and headed for the beach. There was nowhere to go, nowhere to hide.

But she could put Tam out of his reach.

Panting with fear and adrenaline rush, she fumbled as she pulled her phone from her shorts. It fell into the sand.

Feet pounded down the steps and across the grass.

Scrabbling to grab her phone, she knew she was out of time. Her fingers clutched the case and she heaved it into the rocks. A crack was followed by a spray of glass.

She fell to her knees and lowered her head, gasping for air.

Let him try to get any information from it now.

Paul grabbed her elbow and hauled her to her feet. A satisfying trickle of blood ran from the corner of his mouth.

He swiped the back of his hand across his face, smearing blood over his cheek. "Thanks for clarifying whose side you're on. I suspected Jake at first, but you've confirmed that Tam's the traitor."

"She's no traitor. I'm just making sure she's out of your reach. You won't find her through me." .

Paul's grip on her arm tightened and he marched her across to the rocks. Sunlight glittered on shards of her smashed phone. He reached for the case and turned it over. The back had broken off and the SIM card was gone.

Frantically praying the card had slipped through a crack, she scanned the rocks where her phone had landed. If Paul found it—

Beside her left foot, a glint of coppery gold reflected the sun's rays. Paul reached for a piece of phone casing on the other side and his grip on her elbow relaxed.

She twisted her arm, forcing his hold to loosen, and dived for the card. Frantic fingers snagged it and she ran to the water. She raised her arm high. An iron grip covered her hand and a muscular arm closed around her waist, lifting her off her feet.

She kicked backwards, hard.

Paul grunted but his hold remained firm as he carried her from the sea. He lowered her onto the sand and covered her body with his. Leaning on his elbows, he used both hands to prise hers open. The SIM card dropped into his palm.

Instinctively, she raked his face with her free hand. "Give it back, you bastard."

"Fuck!" He grabbed her attacking hand and pinned both arms beside her head. Beads of blood marked his brow and one cheek and his eyes watered. He blinked and shook his head.

Marcy glared at him. "I'll do whatever I can to stop you."

"You put up a good fight, Marcy, but it's over now. I'm going to find your sister—"

"It's not over. Not while I have breath in my body."

"You two are so alike." A hint of admiration coloured his voice before the hardness crept back into his eyes.

Maintaining a tight hold on her arms, he hauled her to her feet and led her back to the shack. With ruthless efficiency, Paul bound her wrists behind her back and attached the long end of rope around the iron bars of the bed head. While he tested the knot, Marcy aimed her knee at his groin.

One large hand caught her knee in a vice-like grip. "You won't catch me out like that again." He moved out of reach of her legs and inspected the SIM card. He blew gently then wiped it on his shirt before carefully checking it again. Satisfied, he inserted it in his phone and scrolled through her information.

A muscle ticked in his jaw. "When I've dealt with your sister, I promise I'll come back and release you." He turned and headed for the door.

"If you harm Tam in any way, I'll kill you. That's my promise." Her voice echoed round the empty room.

# #

Marcy's shoulders and wrists ached as she struggled to escape. Sweat trickled into her eyes and she flopped back on the rumpled bed and contemplated the ceiling.

It was hopeless. If only Jake hadn't left so early. Had he received her text yet or was he still driving? She rolled onto her side to wipe her face on the pillow. The iron bedstead groaned and a metallic crack sounded loud in the quiet of the bedroom.

Marcy rolled over and struggled onto her knees. From her

awkward position, she examined the bed frame. One of the bars to which her rope was attached had broken away from the outer frame.

She shuffled around to face the foot of the bed. Bracing herself on her knees, she strained forward. Was there a little more give in the rope? She looked over her shoulder.

The broken bar now angled slightly toward her. She turned back, and manoeuvred into a squatting position to maximise her power. Taking a deep breath, she lunged forward.

Pain shot through her shoulders and back but she was rewarded with the sound of another cracking bar.

Panting, she repositioned herself, allowing the rope some slack before she launched herself.

Metal screeched, Marcy tumbled over the foot of the bed and landed on the wooden floor. Her left shoulder throbbed where it had taken the impact of her fall, and her whole body ached. She pushed herself into a sitting position. Behind her, the rope trailed over the bed end.

She rested her head against the bottom bars for a few seconds and silently blessed old iron beds and sea air. Drawing a deep breath, she stood and looked behind. Mangled bars stuck out at odd angles from the top frame.

Staggering into the kitchen, she tugged open the top drawer, trying to remember where she'd seen Jake's kitchen knives. Clumsy fingers felt table cutlery and paper serviettes. She pushed the drawer closed with her butt and felt for the second drawer handle. Tugging it open, she gingerly felt for a thicker handle, extracted it and set it carefully on the counter. She turned to examine her tool.

Damn. A potato masher lay on the counter top. She looked through the contents of the drawer before noticing a kitchen knife in the dish drainer. She backed over to the sink and reached awkwardly for the knife. It was big and lethal looking and she was more likely to cut herself than the rope unless she could wedge it somehow and saw down onto it.

Excitement mounted as she clumsily set the knife at an angle within the drainer. Muscles straining, she manoeuvred a heavy cooking pot on top of the handle. Laboriously, she added further weight to the pot with a container of flour.

Sweating from her efforts, she backed towards the blade. Visions of blood pouring from her sliced wrists dried all the moisture from her mouth.

Don't think about it. Think of Tam. I've got to get to her first.

Because she knew exactly where her twin was hiding. From the information on her SIM card, Paul would learn only the general area.

Carefully lowering her bound wrists, she lined up the rope and the blade. She drew a deep breath and pressed down. Her first few passes were light and scary as hell. She lifted her arms and tested if there was any give in the rope.

Nothing.

Aligning her wrists with the blade again, she took a deep breath, pressed down and sawed back and forth. Sharp pain stung the back of her hand.

Shit. Don't think about it. Think of Tam. Breathe through your mouth.

She swallowed against her desire to vomit, and rubbed her bound hands against her hip. There was slight movement in the rope where before, there'd been none. Sucking in a mouthful of air, she set to sawing again.

With a sudden release of tension, her hands pulled apart. Her shoulder cracked at the change in position and she sagged onto the counter in front of her. Eyes closed, she massaged her bare wrist. The coppery tang and the slide of her still-bound hand over bare skin reminded her of the cost of her freedom.

Desperate not to see, she grasped her wrist and looked for something to cover it. She grabbed a tea towel from the hook beside the stove, held her breath and wrapped the towel around her wrist. Blood smeared her fingers and covered the palm of her other hand. Quickly, she thrust it under the tap and turned it on full.

Red rivulets ran down the plughole. Marcy gasped as fresh pain stung her hand and she blinked back stupid tears. At least she was free.

Shaking and gulping air, she refused to be sick. Nothing was going to stop her from saving Tam. She tugged open the lowest drawer. A small stack of clean tea towels filled one side. Grabbing a handful, she moved away from the kitchen and dried her hands, before carefully easing off the last loop of rope.

More by feel than sight, she rewrapped her injured hand. How much of a start did Paul have on her? She checked the time on the microwave and wondered how the hell she was going to reach Tam when she had no vehicle.

Shit. No phone GPS either. Oh, Tam, have I failed you again?

Chapter Twenty-Nine

Jake's phone pinged the arrival of an incoming message. He picked it up off the dashboard and flicked a glance at the number.

Marcy.

He scanned the road ahead and pulled into the next lay-by to read her message. A minute or two wouldn't make much difference to his interview. Delivery of the message had been delayed, probably by poor reception as he drove between coastal hills.

The text was sparse: *Tamsin hiding near our old home in hinterland of North Coast.*

Marcy had not told him much about her home, but bananas and a reference to Coffs Harbour lingered in his memory. He selected the Maps app and scanned towns and roads for a trigger name. Nothing jumped out at him. There was little he could do until after his interview, if he still had a career when it was over.

He tossed the phone onto the passenger seat. It bounced and hit the corner of his metal tool kit and the back popped off.

A minute, alien object fell from the phone onto the rubber mat.

He reached down and picked it up. *Shit! How long have they been tracking me and monitoring my phone?* The Bureau would be swinging into action, heading out to capture Marcy's sister, while he sat here like a stunned mullet. He picked up his phone, checked the battery and SIM card were in place, and refitted the back, minus the tracking device, which he pitched through the window.

He thumped his fist against the steering wheel, started the engine and roared across two lanes of highway. *Fuck the Bureau.*

He hit Marcy's number on speed dial followed by the speaker button. Danton and the Bureau would be pissed at him finding the bug but there were always other alternatives for tracking. He wondered if, even now, he was being monitored via the chain of highway cameras.

Marcy's voice mail activated and Jake swore as he was requested to leave a message. "Call me as soon as you get this. We have a problem." He stabbed the end call button and dropped the phone into his shirt pocket.

But by the time he approached the turnoff to the shack, she still hadn't called. Doubt niggled in his gut. What if it hadn't been the Bureau that had bugged his phone? The only time it had been out of his possession had been during his initial interview at central office the day he landed in Sydney. Protocol had required he empty his pockets at security. He was slipping; he hadn't checked it when he left.

He could barely entertain the other possibility and yet he

had to consider it. If Tamsin Westcott could be suspected of betraying her partner, wasn't it equally possible that Paul might have been bought off? And if that had happened, Paul had the knowledge to plant a bug and the skill to fake his own disappearance.

And Paul was alone with Marcy.

Jake planted his foot and raced along the single sealed lane towards the shack. How much time had he lost before the damned phone message had arrived?

He pulled up in a rush and jumped out of the ute. "Marcy? Where are you?" He rounded the corner of the shack and took the stairs three at a time. The front door stood wide open. "Marcy? Paul?"

Waves crashed and seagulls cawed but silence reigned in the shack. Pulling his gun from the back of his jeans, he scanned the beach and rocks before easing through the doorway. Back to the wall, he peered around the doorframe into the bedroom.

Rumpled sheets and broken bars in the bed frame looked like a bondage scene gone wrong. He glanced in the en suite before crossing the hallway to the living area.

A stool lay on its side and drops of blood lay like a trail from the edge of the counter to two mugs of coffee. He touched the side of a mug. Cold.

His gaze zeroed in on a bloodied kitchen knife wedged into the drainer by a motley collection of weights.

Beneath it, a small pile of rope coiled on the floor. One

loop remained intact, too small to fit Paul's big hands.

Jake picked it up and examined the ragged cuts. The tang of fresh blood assaulted his nostrils and he understood something of Marcy's haemophobia. This was her blood, drawn out of desperation to escape. Had she got away?

A lump formed in his throat, so big he could barely draw breath around it before his brain began coolly assessing the evidence. The unthinkable had happened. Paul had been seduced by drug money and sold out his partner.

And through his blind faith, Jake had given Paul the one sure means of regaining the stolen evidence from Tamsin.

Her sister.

Swearing an oath to find Marcy and bring her safely home with him, Jake raced outside and jumped into the ute.

He wouldn't let Paul get away with his filthy drug money. And he wouldn't lose Marcy. Not again.

Chapter Thirty

"I've got a fix on her general location." Iceman's voice was breathless, hurried. "I can't stay on the line for long."

Chan pressed the speakerphone button, leaned back in the swivel chair and pushed away from his desk. Through the picture window, he watched a cruise ship sail beneath the Harbour Bridge. "Where is she?"

"Somewhere in the north of the state."

"How far away are you?"

"Three and a half, four hours, tops. What do you want me to do?" A voice shouted in the background at the other end of the line and Iceman replied. "Yeah, coming."

A sense of urgency filled Chan. The woman was close. Soon he would have her at his mercy. Soon he would show her what her betrayal meant.

"Take the woman alive."

"And the sister? Do you want her eliminated?"

"Take her as well." She could be useful for leverage. Or maybe—

He'd never had identical twins before. Was the other one as

tantalising a prospect? The possibilities for his pleasure almost matched his need for revenge. Almost. "Take them both to Madame Wu's."

"Will do. Gotta go." Iceman ended the call. No one hung up on John Chan. Another black mark against his contact's name. One day soon, he would teach the man to respect his betters.

Chan opened the file on his contact and scanned the information. Iceman had a daughter. A pretty little blonde thing with blue eyes. He examined the photo closely.

Her fairness turned Chan off, but she might be useful as leverage. Her father would learn deference or the daughter would suffer. Chan closed the file and clicked onto the video of the woman and the agent making out in Nepal. He watched it play on a loop as he stroked himself hard.

Tonight he would teach the bitch a lesson. Tonight all that passion would be his.

Chapter Thirty-One

Marcy clung to the steering wheel of her rental car and tried to work out how much further the turnoff to the old farm was. In Nepal, she'd had a guide. The rest of the time, she relied on the GPS on her phone to counteract her abysmal sense of direction.

Her poor, shattered phone. She couldn't even call Tam to let her know of the danger heading her way.

Would Tam forgive Marcy for blowing her cover like this?

What else can I do? Tam might not suspect Paul until it's too late. I've just got to be in time.

A sign indicated a service station one kilometre ahead. She pulled off the highway, eased into a parking bay and turned off the engine. With hands that shook, she rubbed her face. Her right wrist throbbed and a small amount of blood had seeped through her hastily improvised bandage.

She gagged and stumbled out of the car. If she was to save her sister, she couldn't afford the luxury of being sick. Gulping down mouthfuls of diesel-laden air, she rested her forehead on her arm against the roof of the car. Listing her course of action would distract her from the smell of blood.

Strong coffee and a pain-killer, in that order. And a map.

"Dr. Westcott?" A light tenor male voice pulled her attention from her nausea.

Marcy turned quickly, regretting her haste as her head spun. She leaned against the car and held a hand to her head. Relieved to see a young man in his mid-twenties, dressed casually and smiling at her, she asked, "What do you want?"

His gaze flicked beyond her shoulder then he gave a small nod. "Please come with me. We have news of your sister."

\# \#

Jake changed down to third gear and took another curve, shooting past a single lane road before he realized it was there.

Reversing until he could see the signpost angled like a drunk—*Marianna Road*—he checked his GPS. Marcy's family farm should be a couple of kilometres down this road.

Whiz-kid Robbie at the Bureau had been reluctant to give him details but had finally revealed the address. He'd added that the property had been sold over five years ago but there was still an old farmhouse located at the far end of a dead-end road. The narrow, graded dirt road disappeared between lines of trees. He turned the ute and passed beneath the broad leaves of banana plants.

Overhead, a helicopter zoomed past, rotors beating the air. Jake peered through the trees. Military markings blazed from both sides.

The chopper veered away and headed north.

Jake continued until he saw a neat Queenslander house transplanted in the middle of a newly dug garden. The house looked like a recent arrival, and several small native bushes dotted the border. Was this Marcy's old family home moved to a better position by the new owner?

Movement on the veranda drew his attention. He pulled up in front and got out of the ute. A young German Shepherd bared its teeth and barked at him.

"Stand down, Ricky." The dog dropped immediately and his owner stepped into view. The man was in his mid-thirties, with a military buzz-cut and a hint of a limp as he walked to the railing and surveyed Jake. "You lost, mate?"

"I'm looking for the old Westcott farm. This it?"

"Who wants to know?" Suspicion and alertness tinged the man's voice, and a subtle shift in position as though he expected trouble.

"I'm Jake Harris, a friend of Tamsin's sister, Marcy. I said I'd look in on Tamsin since I was heading up this way on business."

"Don't know anyone by that name." He stepped back into the shadows and opened his front door.

A series of gunshots shattered the afternoon quiet.

The man's low-voiced command reached Jake. "Seek, Tamsin." The dog bounded off the veranda and raced up the road.

His owner reappeared with a rifle. So much for not knowing Marcy's sister.

"Is Tamsin up there?"

The guy looked at him, and raised the gun across his chest. "Tell me how you know Tam."

"I don't. But there are people who want to kill her. I can't let that happen."

Intelligent eyes coolly assessed him and the man nodded. "Neither can I. Let's go."

Jake reached for his guns and placed them close to hand as his passenger got in then floored the ute up the road. "How do you know Tamsin?"

"We're neighbours." With military precision, Jake's new partner checked his rifle and slipped a box of ammo into the pocket of his drill pants.

"Stop here."

The ute slid through loose gravel and came to a stop a hundred metres from a bend.

His passenger pointed, the gesture direct. He was army through and through. "You take the right flank. There's a gully you can use to get close to the house. I'll circle round to the left."

Jake watched his unlikely ally disappear into the trees like a combat soldier on patrol. Oddly, he felt like a mate had his back.

# #

Marcy struggled to contain her fear and frustration as three men surrounded her.

"We're to escort you to safety, ma'am." The youngest of the three smiled but the others, both older men, scanned the area.

"Please come with us."

"I can't. I have to—"

"You have to come with us now, Dr. Westcott." One of the older men took her arm while the other reached into her car and collected her bag and car keys.

"My name is Agent McKinley." The young guy looked mildly uncomfortable as he opened the plain side of an unmarked white van.

"You're with the Bureau too?" Marcy stopped short of climbing into the van. "I can't go back to Sydney. Not yet."

"We will be able to reunite you with your sister very soon but you need to come with us now."

Marcy touched his forearm and looked into his dark blue eyes. "You know where Tam is? Is she safe?"

"As far as we know, she is. Please get into the van, Doctor. There isn't much time."

Marcy climbed onto a bench seat and clipped her seatbelt. McKinley joined her as the door slid shut behind him. The van rocked as the other two agents climbed into the front and shut their doors. A dark-tinted glass panel separated them from their passengers but allowed Marcy a limited view of the road ahead. They turned out of the service station and headed north.

Tam is north. We're coming, Tam.

"So, Agent McKinley, what can you tell me about my sister?"

##

Running low and silently, Jake threaded his way through a wild remnant of banana plants. Up ahead, more shots were exchanged.

A rifle—that could be the neighbour he'd picked up—a shotgun, and two, maybe three pistols. Did one of them belong to Paul?

There were a lot of people at this turkey shoot.

Jake made his way around to the right, keeping to the gully until it petered out within sight of a wooden garage. Shots had been fired at the old farmhouse. Four shattered windows gaped above a spray of bullet holes. Peering through the undergrowth, he counted three armed men behind the garage. Paul wasn't one of them.

Beyond the far side of the yard, the ground fell away onto an overgrown terrace bordered by low bushes, and beyond that, banana trees. Had the soldier found Tamsin over there?

Jake moved into position behind the gunmen, wishing he had even a basic two-way radio. Where was Marcy's sister? Had she escaped the house in time?

A vehicle approached at speed, leaving a cloud of dust that rose above the tree line and hung in the still air. Silence surrounded the farm house.

One of the gunmen behind the garage checked his watch then, crouching low, headed for Jake's gully. Jake retreated into the bushes back towards the road.

A white van pulled up short of the house yard and two men

climbed out of the front seats. Agents Talisker and Phillips. What were the guys from the Bureau doing here? Talisker slipped from view until he rounded the back of van. Phillips paused beside the driver's door and lit a cigarette. He took a long drag and exhaled then turned and grabbed the handle of the side door. He slid the door open. Two soft *pffts* sounded and Phillips fell on his back.

Two holes, one in his forehead and one in his chest, bled thin red trickles. Talisker dropped to one knee and aimed his pistol at the opening.

Through the dust swirling in the doorway, Marcy emerged. Eyes wide, her hands clutched a shirt-sleeved arm wrapped around her neck. A snub-nosed pistol pointed at her right temple.

Jake's grip tightened on his rifle and he took aim. Marcy's captor stepped into view.

Robbie McKinley! Had he been monitoring calls from the back of the van when Jake received Marcy's text? But why was he holding Marcy captive?

"Let her go, Robbie." Bob Talisker trained his gun on McKinley from the shelter of the van.

A shot exploded close to Jake's right. Talisker dropped and rolled, clutching his shoulder. The gunman grinned and lined up the agent's fallen body for another shot.

Jake drew his pistol and fired. Out of the corner of his eye, he saw Talisker roll into a ditch.

McKinley spun around, holding Marcy's body as a shield between him and the undergrowth where Jake hid. Eyes wide, he was clearly on edge.

And unpredictable.

"Bring her here." A voice shouted from the direction of the garage.

McKinley backed towards the garage.

Shit. Last thing Jake wanted was Marcy in their clutches.

He steadied his aim and breathed out. He'd get one shot. He breathed in.

"Let her go." A huskier version of Marcy's voice rang across the clearing and a woman stepped into plain view. Hands raised above her head, she moved slowly forward. "It's me you want."

Jake fired. Two shots.

Chapter Thirty-Two

Marcy dropped to the ground and threw her arms over her head as guns blazed from both sides of the house yard. Sharp cracks that threatened Tam. The noise deafened, and almost defeated, her.

Afraid to lift her head, she peeked beneath her arm. Inches from her face lay the body of the fallen agent. His shirt had been pristine white when he climbed into the driver's seat. Now, it was red. Arms flung wide like a penitent, he stared sightlessly at the blue sky. A trickle of blood oozing from a hole just off centre in his forehead ran into his sideburns.

She bit her lip and forced back the whimper threatening to erupt into a scream. If she started, she wouldn't stop. Ever.

Finally, the shooting ceased.

Out of the bushes, Jake appeared, gun in hand. He grabbed her arm and, running low, dragged her into a gully. Marcy had no time to wonder how Jake came to be there, shielding her, rescuing her again. He thrust her behind him. Gun raised, he scanned the area ahead.

Needing to connect and feel warmth and life pulsing through him, she reached for his shoulder. But the hand reaching out was spattered with red drops.

So much red.

She blinked. Her horrified gaze trailed all the way along her arm. Red.

Copper-tanged, hideous stench filled her nostrils and her stomach heaved out her breakfast coffee.

Jake gripped her shoulder. "Breathe through your mouth."

She turned from the sight of her red skin and gulped in air laced with the ripe succulence of tropical fruit.

"Harris?" A commanding voice shouted across the house yard. Jake had help?

"I'm here." Jake's hand slid to her waist and his fingers curled into her body.

His touch grounded her, made her feel safe amid the terrifying events unfolding around them. Why had she doubted him? At every turn, Jake had been beside her. If ever she had taken his protection for granted before, she never would again.

She turned to tell him how wrong she'd been. That she trusted him.

"I've got Tam. Have you secured the sister?"

Who had Tam? Who was working with Jake?

The unseen voice raised questions Marcy didn't want to think about. She pushed her hair back with hands that shook—badly—and tried to piece it all together. How had Jake known where to look for Tam?

"She's safe with me." Jake flicked the safety catch on his

rifle. "Who got the other two shooters?"

"Some of your mob. I'll get the injured agent."

Booted feet crunched on gravel followed by a low murmur of voices.

"Where's Tam?" Her voice came out little more than a croak. She swallowed, cleared her throat, and tried again. "Jake, where's my sister?"

"She's safe."

Muscles quivered in her thighs as Marcy forced her legs to support her. If only she could command her jelly legs to move. "I need to see her."

Jake gently pushed her back against the earthen gully wall. "Not yet."

"Let me go!" She surged against his strength and twisted away.

His hand clamped around her upper arm. "Stay there and don't move. There're things you don't need to see."

Jake's grip was forceful and she grimaced as pain radiated down her still tender arm.

He frowned, wrapped an arm around her and held her. "Sorry, but I won't expose you to the aftermath of a gunfight."

"But Tam's out there. Tam needs me."

Jake's eyes darkened and his expression closed. "No."

"What do you mean, *no*? You promised to help find Tam then vanished without explanation." Nervous energy coursed through her body. Why wasn't he letting her go to her sister? "Is

Tam injured?"

"No, but there's blood and bodies out there."

Her heart took a dive into the pit of her stomach as the awful possibility took root in her mind. Had he intended to track down her twin while keeping Marcy out of the way at his shack? But Marcy was here, not quite as planned, and Tam had stepped out into the open, offering herself in exchange. Tam had stood there, gun dangling from her raised hands when—

Oh, Tam, what have you done? Marcy closed her eyes and prayed like she'd never done before.

No matter if Jake, Paul, and the whole bloody Bureau she'd been working for were after Tam, and the entire Chan drug cartel. Marcy would get her away. Hide her, even from Jake. Because no one was more important than her sister.

Blocked from Tam by Jake's intractable stance, unsure whether to shake him or pull him close, she clutched at his shirt. "Jake? Was this the business you set out to complete this morning?"

"Of course not. The time of my disciplinary hearing was changed. I was on my way to Sydney when I got your text. I turned around and came straight home."

Jake's hard body hemmed her in while he looked over the top of the gully at whatever was happening. A muscle ticked in his jaw and she sensed him withdrawing from her. His hand tightened on her shoulder.

Nearby, a car door slammed, followed by two more doors

closing a few seconds later. An engine started and tyres crunched before a vehicle headed back down the road. She craned her head to see. The white van she'd been brought in flashed past the end of the gully and gathered speed as it headed downhill.

Jake expelled a heavy breath, leaned over and wrapped her in his arms. "When I saw the blood and the rope back at the shack, I thought I'd lost you." He eased back and cupped her face. His thumb stroked across her cheek. Before her eyes, his Adam's apple bobbed up and down. "I couldn't bear that."

Without thinking, Marcy reached up to touch his face. Confronted by her blood-streaked hand, she choked and turned away.

Wordlessly, Jake stripped off his shirt. If he thought the sight of his bare abs would distract her—Marcy swallowed—he was right.

He tipped her chin up and gently wiped her face and arm. "Let's find you a shower."

Marcy nodded and stumbled out of the gully. Agents swarmed into the old home where her sister must have holed up for the last couple of weeks.

Tam!

Jolted back to the present, she gripped Jake's forearm. "Where's my sister?"

Jake's gaze roamed the yard before he led her to a Kevlar-vested agent. "Danton, Dr. Westcott wants to know where her sister is."

Danton examined her closely. "Uncanny. What we couldn't have done if we'd had both of them." His gaze flicked past her before settling back on her face. "Agent Westcott has been taken to a safe place for debriefing, Doctor. We'll contact you as soon as it's possible to speak with her."

"But—"

"I'm sorry. Your sister's work comes first, as it does for all operatives. Harris, please escort the doctor home."

Operative? Tam was an agent, like Jake. Marcy's brain refused to process the information. Tam was—just Tam, her twin.

Jake held the other man's gaze. "Has the threat been neutralized?"

"Yes. Simultaneous strikes."

Shivers goose-stepped down Marcy's spine. "Does your *spy-speak* mean the Chans are no longer a threat?"

"Correct, Doctor. Harris, I'll see you at your interview in the morning. Eleven sharp." Danton walked back to a group of men standing beside the front steps of the old farmhouse.

An agent emerged through the front door holding an old fashioned, anodised kitchen canister. The one her grandmother had used for tea leaves. He pulled the lid off and poked through the contents. "Any clue as to where she might have hidden it?"

Jake took Marcy's elbow and turned for the front gate. "Let's go."

She dug her heels in and pulled her arm from his grasp. Were these agents planning on turning the contents of her old home upside down? "What are they expecting to find?"

Jake frowned. "What's wrong?"

"Tell me what they think they'll find? Wads of cash? A thumb drive filled with incriminating lists of names and amounts paid? Why did they take Tam away? Couldn't she have just turned whatever evidence she has over to them?"

"That's not how it's done."

Bile rose in her throat. "You mean Tam's guilty until proven innocent?"

#

Jake understood why Marcy would see it that way. If their roles were reversed, he'd have defended Pete in the same way but it didn't make this situation any easier. "Your sister will be given every opportunity to explain her actions and turn over any evidence in the Chan case."

"What if she escaped before she had a chance to find anything? How can she prove her loyalty without evidence?"

"There's always something."

"Why did you say you were going to Sydney this morning?" Marcy's tone turned the question into an accusation.

Her words stung. A hell of a night had turned into a shit of a day and he was over it. "I *was* on the way there when I got your text message."

"So you turned around and arrived here like the cavalry before I did."

"Where are you going with this?"

"It's like this, Jake. I don't believe you. Ever since we met in Nepal, you've been chasing Tam. At first you thought I was her, or she was me. Anyway, you wanted to find her and grab the oh-so-important evidence she'd found at the Chans."

"That's not news. Tell me something I don't know, Marcy."

"You do know it was your *friend,* Paul, who tied me up and stole my sim card, don't you?"

Jake knew. But hearing Marcy's confirmation of Paul's treachery, his stomach took a dive. Had he trusted the wrong person? He checked out the faces of the operatives still in the yard.

"Do you know where Paul went after he left the shack?"

"No idea. Conversation wasn't on the agenda after he tied me up."

Okay, that was snarky but he welcomed it. Most people would be curled up in the foetal position after a shock such as she'd been subjected to. But not his Marcy.

She tipped her chin up and looked him square in the eye. "Where will they take Tam?"

"Headquarters. She'll be interviewed and held pending the outcome."

"Held?" Marcy paled and wrapped her arms around her waist. Damn it, he could have phrased it better, less frighteningly. That news shook her more than her own abduction and near miss had done.

But she would have seen through his attempts and cut to

the chase anyway.

"Where, exactly, is HQ?"

He could almost hear her brain cranking into higher gear. "Why, Marcy? Thinking of storming the building and rescuing your sister?"

Her gaze flicked away. "I have a right to know where my sister has been taken. You know, so I can bake a cake and smuggle a key in to her."

Bruised, frightened, and covered in Robbie McKinley's blood, she was undaunted by the worst life threw at her. Marcy would never give in while her sister needed her.

Like a freight train racing towards him, understanding hit Jake full in the chest. Feisty, passionate, and loyal, Marcy had wisecracked her way into his heart. She would move heaven and earth for those she cared about. She trusted slowly yet she had trusted him with precious information about her twin.

Had he blown his chance with her?

He wouldn't accept that. "No need. I'll drive you there. Maybe I can call in a favour and get you in to see her."

"Aren't you in the doghouse already?"

He shrugged. What was one more indiscretion on top of the balls-up he'd made in Nepal? "I owe you."

#

Jake folded his arm beneath his head and stared at the strip of artificial light falling through the curtains of Marcy's small lounge room. It was well after two in the morning and sleep eluded him. Every time he closed his eyes, the memory of Marcy with Robbie's gun held to her head played in his mind.

Robbie, who nobody had suspected.

Jake's heart stuttered at the thought of how close he'd come to losing Marcy. But hadn't he lost her anyway?

Marcy had barely spoken to him on the drive to Sydney. Their visit to headquarters had been less than successful and she'd retreated into her bedroom soon after their return to her apartment. The wonder of it was that she'd let him stay at all.

He might as well not be here. She didn't want him around.

Except that Paul had disappeared.

Paul, the unknown factor. Was he the rogue operative, or was Tamsin? Or neither?

Until Jake got a handle on that situation, Marcy would just have to put up with his presence.

The click of her bedroom door opening was followed by soft footfalls across the carpet and into the kitchen.

Jake watched through slitted eyes as she opened the fridge and pulled out a carton of milk. She took down a glass from the overhead cupboard and filled it halfway.

Jake tossed back his blanket and rose from the sofa. "Mind pouring me one as well?"

Her hand jumped and milk spilled over the counter top. With a muttered oath, she grabbed the dishcloth and mopped up the mess. "Geez, Jake, make some noise, can't you? I thought you were asleep."

"You'd know I was awake if we were in the same bed."

Her hand stilled. In the soft glow of the under cupboard LED lights, her knuckles whitened. "Don't. How can I—"

"Trust me? You're the scientist, Marcy. Look at the facts."

"I have. They don't add up to what you say." Finally, she looked at him with sad eyes. Betrayed trust, hurt beyond bearing gleamed back at him. "I told you where to find my sister and now she's in prison."

"Not in prison."

"She's locked away and I'm not allowed to visit her. I suppose you'll tell me that's protective custody like Nicholls put me in." She closed her eyes and drew in a deep breath. "I can't do this anymore, Jake. I need you to go."

"I can't. Paul is missing."

"Your dedication to your work is unquestioned but—"

"Fuck my work. I won't leave you unprotected."

#

A small part of her badly bruised heart latched onto his words and held them close. She was no longer just his assignment, *a job* to be completed and filed away. No matter that he'd killed men, Jake was a protector. Her protector.

Somewhere in all the craziness of her life, Jake had come to care for her.

If only—

But there was no use regretting what might have been. Trusting Jake with information about Tam had been unwise. Logic had always served her well in the past. It trumped foolish romantic notions every time. From now on her head would rule her heart.

"If you want to use me as bait to lure Paul out, then get on with it. But I don't want or need your protection any more. Watch from the street if it makes you feel better. Just—leave my apartment."

Bleakness flashed through his eyes as though her words had the power to hurt him. But that couldn't be because Jake never let emotion get in the way of work, and work always came first.

In spite of that her body swayed subconsciously towards him. She gripped the sink behind her, hanging on for dear life. Betraying her sister could not be forgiven. Her foolish heart would forget him. Maybe—one day. She lifted her chin and locked gazes with him.

In front of her, he morphed back into the hard, unreadable and unreachable mountain man. "Okay. You win. I'll be in my ute across the road."

She nodded, turned to the sink and rinsed out the dishcloth. In her peripheral vision, she watched as he pulled on jeans over his boxers, and grabbed his T-shirt. As he reached for his gun, he looked over at her.

How could she send him away?

How could she let him stay?

Shoulders hunched, she sagged against the sink.

"I'm leaving you my spare gun. Don't forget to flick the safety off if you have to use it."

She nodded but didn't speak as she took the pistol. Its weight dragged at the end of her arm and she doubted she had the strength to raise it, let alone aim at an intruder. But possessing it gave her a small sense of power. She set it carefully on the bench as Jake left, closing the door quietly behind him.

Marcy slid down the front of the cupboard and slumped against the door. Hugging her legs, she rested her cheek on her knees.

Their visit to the Bureau hadn't gone as Jake had predicted. And the encounter with Danton, Jake's Australian boss, had been beyond anything she could have imagined in a spy movie. He'd taken her aside for a brief, private word. Jake didn't, and couldn't know that on the pretext of filling in a form, Danton had asked for her help in uncovering the traitor in their midst.

"I'll allow your sister to make a call. One call, Doctor. It will be traced, and what happens after that will help us ferret out the traitor. I ask only that you don't insist on seeing her now."

"Do *you* think she's guilty, Mr. Danton?"

His half smile took the sting out of his words. "I hope not."

But with Paul still MIA, Jake's insistence on squatting in her apartment complicated things. It killed her to see the hurt in his eyes when she told him to go, but she had to know he was safe. Even if they had no future, she didn't want Jake putting his life on the line for her again.

If the traitor made a move on her tonight, she would face him alone.

Her gaze fell on Jake's gun lying on the end of the kitchen counter. LED lights glinted off the dark grey metal. She stood and trailed her fingers along the barrel then picked up the gun. The metal was cold in her hand. Wondering how she would find the nerve to point it at someone, she anchored her other hand beneath and raised the gun to the door.

Along with teaching her self-defence, it would have helped if Jake had taught her how to shoot. She dropped her hands and headed back to bed, the gun dangling from her right hand. She was debating whether to put it under her pillow or leave it on the bedside table when her new phone buzzed. Vibrations sent it skittering across the wood towards the edge.

She dropped the gun on the bed and grabbed the phone as it reached the point of no return. An unknown number flashed across the screen. "Hello?"

"Hey, big sis. You alone?"

Relief sapped the strength from her legs. She sank onto the bed and pressed the phone to her ear. "Tam! Thank goodness. Yes. Are you okay?"

"Yeah, I'm fine but I may be held a while. I'd love something to read. Danton tells me he'll let you visit tomorrow afternoon. Since you've just come back, do you have a traveller's tale about Nepal?"

Marcy's gaze dropped to her bookshelf. On the top shelf, her father's diary was tucked in between her bound thesis and her Nepal traveller's guidebook. They'd laughingly referred to their father's stories by that label. Did Tam really want to read their father's diary?

"Um, sure. I'll call in tomorrow morning with something to keep you going. Do you need anything else?"

"Nope, all good. And tell that ex-fiancé of mine that I forgive him if you see him. Do that for me?"

Marcy would see Paul in hell before she passed on that message but now wasn't the time to express that thought. "I'll do what I can, sis. Take care. Love you."

"You too. Bye." The line went dead.

Focussed on the diary, she tapped the phone against her chin then tossed it on the bed beside the gun.

Why did Tam want this book? What could be so interesting that—

Like a flash of summer lightning, Marcy couldn't believe she hadn't thought of it earlier. Fingers trembling, she pulled the diary from the shelf and felt along the tatty spine. It was nothing but book.

She opened the back cover and bent the spine past ninety degrees. A small cut in the end paper sent her scurrying to her beside lamp.

Beneath its light, she examined the cut. Something had been inserted and she had a sinking feeling she knew what it was. She pulled open the bedside drawer and took out a pair of tweezers from her manicure kit. With care, she eased the tweezers into the cut until—*there you are.*

She held it up to the light. Turquoise and amber patterned, it was slim-line and elegant and Marcy was in no doubt it was a thumb drive. But where had she seen that brilliant paisley pattern before?

A memory returned, of Tam thrusting the diary into the taxi. Her chunky bracelet was made up of turquoise and amber swirls and matched the pendant that nestled in the low V-neckline of her black evening gown. The slimline USB drive had been part of Tam's jewellery.

Marcy gasped and sank to the floor, her back against the bed.

Tam used me to get the evidence out!

Chapter Thirty-Three

Jake poured a cup of coffee, set the thermos close by on the passenger seat and settled in for a long night. He glanced up at the windows of Marcy's apartment then methodically checked the two streets within view of his corner position. Something was off, but he couldn't pinpoint what it was.

Thirty minutes ago, Marcy had turned off her bedroom light. Now, a soft glow emanated through the lounge room curtains. Was she unable to sleep like him?

He reached for his phone, his thumb hovering over her number. But she'd told him what she wanted. Him—gone.

His actions had all been to protect her, not to betray her trust. But that's what his unquestioning belief in Paul had led to. Loyalty—betrayal.

Two sides of the same coin.

The friend he knew would never have gone to the dark side. But was that just arrogant belief in his own judgment? And where was Paul now? Would he come for Marcy to get to Tamsin?

Adrenaline surged through his body. Stakeouts had never been this tough. But then, he'd never had the woman he loved as a target. He slammed his fist against the wheel and swore.

Fuck being given his marching orders. Out here on the street, he was all but useless to her. She could hate him all she wanted to—later. His hand grasped the door handle at the same moment he spotted a shadow slipping into the basement.

Jake was out of the car and halfway across the street before the basement door closed. He entered the basement and allowed his eyes to adjust to the low light. Keeping low, he dodged between parked cars until he reached the lift and fire stairs.

The lift whirred and clanked to a stop somewhere above. Four flights up, Marcy was alone and unprotected. Jake took the stairs, three at a time until he reached the last turn before her floor. Gun trained on the exit door, he scaled the final set of metal steps. Marcy's apartment lay to the left.

He cracked the fire door open and peered through the gap. Back to the wall, he edged along until he could press his ear to her door. Carefully, he tried the handle. It was unlocked.

Two voices murmured from inside the apartment. Marcy and a familiar male voice.

Jake braced himself, breathed in, and pushed the door wide. He surged into the entry, his gun covering the small lounge area. "Freeze."

Marcy sat on her sofa. And opposite, in the armchair, sat Paul. Neither stood or moved at his appearance. How the hell had Paul got in without Jake seeing him?" And why weren't they surprised to see him? Why— ?

"Took you long enough, big fella."

A fist-sized ball of lead dropped in Jake's stomach. In spite of his promise to protect her, Paul had got to her first. But the scene looked wrong, as if . . .

He looked from Marcy to Paul who sat, empty-handed, palms unnaturally still and resting on his thighs. Where was his gun? Jake glanced back at Marcy.

"So you worked it out too, Jake." Marcy's voice was tight and breathless.

"Worked out what?"

"That Paul and Tam were working together. Seems like we were both wrong. Come join us." Her lips shaped two syllables. *Bed—room.*

Jake glanced at the doorframe of her bedroom. Light spilled from within, but neither Paul nor Marcy moved. Jake looked at the scene reflected in the balcony window. The new angle revealed a fourth figure flattened against the bedroom door. Lamplight glinted off a gun in his hand.

Finally Paul turned to look at Jake. "Remember Ascot?" Jake nodded once. The fingers on Paul's right hand slipped one by one down the side of his thigh.

His thumb slid down and joined his fingers.

Jake dived, rolled, and fired into the bedroom.

At the same moment, Paul tugged Marcy onto the floor and covered her body with his.

A body slumped in a heap in the doorway. Jake trained his

weapon on the fallen man and cautiously approached. He kicked the man's gun aside and rolled him over. "Talisker?"

Jake knelt beside the agent and felt for a pulse. The kill shot had been clean. He checked the agent's pockets and coat then grabbed a towel off the nearby chair and covered Talisker's face and chest. Marcy didn't need to see this ugliness again.

Paul offered Marcy a hand to rise and they joined Jake in the doorway.

"Is he dead?" Marcy hung back, sneaking a peek around the doorjamb before she sat on the back of the sofa.

Jake positioned himself between her and the body. "Yes. Any idea what he was looking for?"

Marcy's gaze flicked to the coffee table. Jake had a sneaking suspicion she'd figured things out way ahead of them. By now, he was certain Tam had found and hidden the evidence from the Chan mansion. Otherwise, why would Talisker and the Chans have pursued both sisters? But what had Tam done with it?

"Tell me, Marcy. Talisker wouldn't have still been here if he'd found what he was after. Did he get it?"

She intertwined her fingers and drew a deep breath. Pushing off the sofa, she walked around and picked up a tattered book from the table. Almost reverently, she stroked a hand over the cover.

Her father's diary? With blinding clarity, Jake saw how brilliantly conceived Tam's plan had been. With the diary—and presumably the evidence concealed within—safely out of the country, Tamsin could lay low while the traitor risked exposing himself.

Marcy's gaze drilled into Jake and he had the sinking feeling she was sizing him up and finding him wanting.

Three quick steps carried her to him. She thrust the diary into his hand. "This is what he was after."

Paul tapped the cover. "Brilliant woman, Tam. She slipped the USB drive into the back cover before she returned the diary to Marcy who was on her way to the airport."

Jake opened the book and examined it. The slit in the back cover was just discernible, but whatever it had contained was no longer there. "Where is the evidence? It's not the diary itself." The idea was clever but anger surged within him. How could Tamsin have endangered her sister in that way?

Paul nodded as though reading Jake's thoughts. "We knew by the night of the party that we had a traitor in our midst. I even suspected Tam briefly. And she, bless her heart, considered the possibility I'd been turned. That was why she came up with the idea of enlisting Marcy's aid without me knowing, to put the evidence beyond Chan's reach."

Jake examined the inside cover again. Ingenious. "Where's the USB?"

Marcy's hand rose and her chin dropped. A thin gold chain dipped beneath her sleep shirt and Jake knew where she'd hidden it.

"I want Tam released. When she's free, I'll tell you where

it is."

Jake looked at his former partner. They could afford to let Marcy play out the game her way now Talisker had been stopped. "Sounds fair to me. Okay with you?"

Paul eyed Marcy. His eyes narrowed slightly before he met Jake's gaze. "Sure. Young Robbie McKinley surprised me at Tam's farm but you could have knocked me down with a feather when Talisker came through the front door tonight."

"So now you're on the good guys' side again, are you?"

Paul laughed. "Always was, mate. Sorry about tying your girlfriend up though. Shit, I was blown away when she turned up at Tam's hideout. I think you've met your match with Marcy."

"Do I get a look-in here, gents?" Marcy stood, hands on hips, and glared at both of them. "I demand an explanation of everything. And if I'm not satisfied with your answers, I'll"—she looked around, picked up Talisker's gun and pointed it at Jake— "I'll shoot you myself."

Palms out, Paul backed away, still grinning. "I'll phone Danton. Shouldn't take them long to get a clean up detail here."

Jake swallowed. Dammit, he should have taught her how to use a gun. "Put the safety on, Marcy."

She examined the gun. "Like this?"

"Yeah." He breathed a relieved sigh and berated his lack of foresight. Teaching Marcy how to use a firearm would be an excellent idea.

If he could convince her to give him another chance.

"How about I make a pot of coffee and the three of us talk and fill in the gaps? Is that okay, Marcy?"

Arms crossed, she barred his retreat from the bedroom. "How about you get on the phone and get my sister released?"

Paul strolled back and offered her his phone. "Danton wants to speak with you."

"What does he want?" She looked at the phone as though it might sting her. Biting her lip, she gingerly took hold of it. "Hello?" Phone pressed to her ear, she wandered onto the balcony.

Paul nodded towards the kitchen. "I need a coffee. Show me where everything is?"

Giving Marcy a bit of space was a good idea. And he needed answers from Paul that she might not like to hear. "Sure. Step this way."

He filled the boiler and plugged it in then opened cupboards until he found the crockery. John, Paul and Ringo grinned at him from three mugs. Marcy really had a thing for The Beatles.

"I can't find a coffeepot but there's a bottle of instant." Paul opened the bottle and grimaced at the aroma. "It'll have to do."

"Or you could go foraging for an all-night servo." Jake leaned back and examined Paul's face. Beneath the devil-may-care attitude, his skin was grey-tinged and he looked a little too lean. "On second thoughts, just answer this. Were you and Tamsin working together from the beginning?"

"We teamed up soon after you went to Afghanistan. Tam had connected with John Chan under the guise of planning a minor party for his sister and we built up our plan from there. He started getting suspicious that I seemed to be hanging around Tam so much. I improvised a very public proposal and we seemed good to continue our efforts to get invited into the Chan mansion.

"A couple of months ago, Tam landed the big gig—Chan senior's seventieth birthday bash at the mansion. We got a tip-off how to access the information and knew the party was our best shot to get into the office."

"What happened? How were you betrayed?"

"It had to be Robbie or Talisker. Tam was in the office copying data across to her USB stick while I kept John Chan and his brothers occupied. I spotted her slipping into the side garden and not long after, all hell broke loose. I guess we both just cut and ran but I didn't see or hear from Tam again."

Jake nodded. Paul's story tallied with Tam's version of events. "Who knew what you were up to?"

"Danton knew about our operation. Talisker was kept in the loop because he was being groomed as Danton's replacement. But my guess is Talisker was already on Chan's payroll."

"I don't understand how an agent of his long standing could be tempted."

Marcy appeared and stopped by the end of the kitchen bench. "Danton said Talisker needed money to pay off his wife's gambling debts. He'll be here soon by the way. Danton, that is."

She turned to Paul. "Go on. I want to know more about your plans with Tam."

Paul looked at Jake, who shrugged and nodded.

"There's not much more to tell. We had contingency plans but it all went pear-shaped so fast. I couldn't find Tam when the shit hit the fan. I got out and made my way up to Jake's shack."

"And Tam gave me the diary and let me leave the country with it."

##

Marcy's stomach cramped at the thought of the time bomb she'd carried into Nepal. Jake had been right to suspect her. She was involved, even if unknowingly. "Why didn't Tam tell me? I wouldn't have left if I'd known she was in trouble."

"You did help her by leaving when you did. And she trusted you with the most important thing she had. Cheers." Paul picked up his mug and raised it in her direction then wandered onto the small balcony.

Marcy turned to Jake. "But I could have—"

"Stayed? You would have tried to rescue her like you've been doing all your life. Your sister would have stuck around to protect you and maybe got herself killed. Giving you the USB drive put both you and it out of reach and gave her time to uncover and eliminate the danger." His expression gave little away, but the tension in his carefully casual pose betrayed him. What else was going on that he wasn't telling?

"That wasn't fair. She gave me no say in what happened."

"Tam made the difficult choice to see both the evidence and you were beyond Chan's reach. It was clever, but risky. By the time surveillance reported the taxi at the side gate and Talisker had guessed some of what happened, you were winging your way to Nepal."

Big sisters were supposed to look after their siblings, not the other way around. Tam had grown up and taken over her role while Marcy wasn't looking. She tried to pinpoint when the change had occurred but her head was fuzzy. She rubbed her eyes.

"How long will the clean-up take?"

Paul strolled back and chimed in. "Actually, best case scenario would be to take you to a hotel. Leave this to us."

"I'll pack a bag for you." Jake stepped towards the bedroom.

She grabbed his arm and pushed past him. "No. I'll pack it myself. Your choice of underwear left much to be desired last time." *One pair of undies and no bra.*

"Jake packing a woman's bag for her. I'd like to see that." Paul grinned, a knowing smile that made her wonder just how far Tam had carried the pretend engagement with him. Maybe she and her twin were both into bad boys.

But she couldn't be. She and Jake weren't going to happen because he would head back to Nepal, or Afghanistan, or wherever his work took him. No matter how much she wanted it to be otherwise, their worlds were too far apart.

"Your role in my family drama is over, Jake. Thanks—

again—for rescuing me. I hope when you return to Nepal that—"

His hands fisted and he frowned. "Not quite. We need to talk. I'll take you to a hotel and bring Tamsin over tomorrow."

A lump the size of Mt. Everest blocked her throat. They might have a few days before he went back to Nepal but then what? Jake didn't love her and no matter how much she loved him, there would be pain and another parting when each new hello became another goodbye.

As there had been with her father, until their final parting. Long distance relationships sucked, big time.

Jake's job would always come first; hadn't Danton told her that very thing about her sister? Saying goodbye each time he left would break her.

"Maybe—Paul could bring her?"

Chapter Thirty-Four

Two double knocks sounded on the hotel door. Marcy dropped the magazine she'd been flicking through and raced to open the door. "Tam!" She threw herself into her sister's arms. There'd been times recently when she'd doubted she'd see this day. Over Tam's shoulder, she caught Paul's mock salute before he sauntered back to the lift and stabbed the down button.

Stepping back, she held Tam's arms wide and examined her. "Tell me that hideous colour and cut are part of some bizarre disguise."

Tam ran a hand through her brown hair and grimaced. "It was the best I could do at short notice. You, on the other hand, look—hmm, I have to say different. You've lost that wide-eyed innocent look."

Marcy dragged her sister to the sofa and held both hands. "Four dead bodies and being shot will do that."

Guilt filled Tam's eyes. "Shit. I'm sorry, sis. So much for my grand plan to see you safe out of the country. I thought—"

"Hush. Getting shot was my own stupid fault." She was grateful her foolish action hadn't cost Jake his life. The thought of a world without him in it was unbearable.

"Planting the USB drive on you wasn't such a hot idea, but when I realized something was off, it was the best I could come up with. Your insistence on picking up Dad's diary was a golden opportunity."

"It was brilliant. Besides, Jake kept me safe."

"Jake Harris? I thought I saw him at the farm before the guys whisked me away in the van. How did you meet him?" Tam sank back into a corner of the sofa and wrapped her arms around her legs.

"I was his assignment. Nothing more." She stalked to the window and, through blurred vision, ignored the view of Circular Quay. *There can't be anything more, not when his job is more important than me.*

Tam came to stand beside her and put an arm around her waist. "You never could tell a lie. You're in love with him." Tam tipped her head until their foreheads touched. "Oh, sis, that is one doozy of a fall."

Marcy sniffed back her tears and shook her head. "He's not in love with me though. Why would he be? I was just a job. Anyway, you know what I think about commitment. He'll be heading back to Nepal after this and there's an end to it."

"Aren't you supposed to be in Dolpa now?"

"The company withdrew my funding. Don't ask. It's embarrassing." But she'd cherish the memory of that first kiss forever.

"Look, we've got all morning to ourselves before Danton needs to debrief us. Reckon we can wangle a couple of facials and a manicure downstairs?"

She looked at her twin and the gleam in her eye and sighed. "Is there any chance I can talk you out of it?"

"None. Come on."

#

Jake sat at Danton's desk waiting for the chief to arrive. At the very least, he'd be hauled over the coals, and losing his position in the Asian arm of the Bureau was a possibility he had to consider. The organization demanded the highest level of commitment and until Marcy came along, he'd given it his complete focus.

But now, contemplating the possibility of not returning wasn't as difficult as he'd once expected. He'd changed, found closure, and Marcy was the reason.

And he was going to make things right for her. After all, if Danton couldn't pull a few strings, he'd be very surprised.

Danton entered and sat across from him. The chief placed a red manila folder on the desk and looked at it for several seconds, sat back and met his gaze. "Are you still up for the job in Asia, Harris?"

"Sir?"

"You're a top agent and the most effective regional manager we've had. Why wouldn't I want to keep you there?"

Jake frowned. Danton's opening was way off what he'd

expected. "I made a rookie mistake by getting involved with my target. I think that disqualifies me from control of further operations in that arena."

"Granted you chose an unusual method of flushing out the cartel, and I wouldn't advocate teaching the technique to new recruits." Danton sat back and folded his hands on the desk. "But you pulled off a real coup, kept Dr. Westcott alive and delivered a key piece of evidence that will close the Chan operation."

"Nicholls relieved me from duty." Much as Jake disliked the man, he respected the decision. Under the circumstances, he'd have done the same.

"And I'm reinstating you. Unusual methods aside, you're a valuable part of this team, and I want you with me."

Tension drained from Jake's shoulders and neck. He still had a job and that meant choices. He wouldn't make the wrong one again. "I heard that John Chan escaped when the team hit the Chan mansion."

"Yes. We'll get him, but I want you and Paul to work the case together. Tamsin Westcott needs to stay clear. From what she's told us, the man is borderline, sanity-wise. And it's clear he was grooming her to become his mistress." Danton leaned back in his chair and folded his hands over his small pot-belly. "So, will you continue working for the Bureau?"

"On one condition. Dr. Westcott has suffered considerable loss because of my—method. It's only fair for us to make it up to her."

"And you think I can correct the situation?" Danton's lips twitched. Clearly he'd seen the video. "You do realise Talisker, not the pharmaceutical company, sent that message rescinding her research grant, don't you? My guess is he hoped to force her hand and make her return early, which she did."

"So her grant is still active? Great. If you can fix things for her to return to Nepal and continue with her research, then you've got me. I'd like to be the one to tell her."

"Sure." Danton stood and moved around to Jake's side of the desk.

Jake stood and looked his boss in the eye. "There's just one other thing I'd ask of you."

Chapter Thirty-Five

Marcy checked the gauge on the incubator and added the reading to her clipboard notes. Losing her grant had felt like failing her mentor, but when Professor Summers' laboratory technician left abruptly with acute morning sickness, Marcy had been given the chance to make it up to him. At first, the university had been reluctant to take her back in any capacity, but the elderly academic who had championed her initial research had gently insisted, and here she was.

In a laboratory doing someone else's work.

The door at the far end of the L-shaped laboratory hissed open and firm footfalls entered. "Professor? I'm checking the readings now."

Jake rounded the corner and stopped at the end of the bench where she was working. "Professor Summers let me in. Hello, Marcy." He shoved his hands in his pockets and leaned against the bench. Eyes the colour of dark chocolate ranged over her face, drinking in every detail before his dark gaze settled on hers. Delicious and dangerous, Jake sent her heart rate skyrocketing into the stratosphere.

Heavens, how she longed for his touch, for his lips following the path his gaze had taken. A trail of molten heat arrowed south and she pressed her thighs together. There were enough rampant pheromones on the loose in the breeding cages without adding her lust for Jake into the mix.

She planted her feet and gripped the edge of the bench top. Cold metal bit into her fingers and she landed back in reality with a thump. Tipping her head, she tried to work out what was wrong with the image in front of her.

"You're wearing a suit and tie. What's happened?"

Jake slipped a finger into his collar, flicked the top button undone and loosened the conservative black-and-red striped tie. "Nothing's happened."

"What's with the suit?"

"A man tidies up a little, puts on his work clothes and you complain. And here was me thinking you might prefer the more civilized, city version of me."

Stubbled mountain man versus neatly suited businessman? Truth to tell, she didn't know which version of Jake she preferred. Both made her mouth water. "I'm sorry. Guess I'm not used to the fresh-shaved, neatly-pressed look."

She did a double-take as his words sank in. "Hang on, since when do field agents in Nepal wear suits? Oh no! Don't tell me Danton fired you?"

Her throat tightened. Jake needed wide open spaces and freedom. Stuck behind a desk in an office, he'd slowly suffocate.

Jake rubbed the back of his neck. "Thanks for the vote of confidence."

Heat rushed up her cheeks. "I didn't mean to imply—"

"Don't worry. I expected to be moved but Danton wanted me to stay on the Asia desk. I refused."

Mystified and more than a little concerned, Marcy closed the gap between them. "I don't understand why you'd do that. The mountains mean everything to you."

"I thought so for a long time. But when I was offered the chance to go back and expand my area of operations, I realized there's something far more necessary to my life."

Suddenly Jake was within her personal space, his cologne teasing her senses. Combined with his suit, she was confused. When had Jake concerned himself with fashion in any form? Subtly, beneath the hint of *Cool Water*, Jake's unique scent reached her. Reassured her that he was still the same man she'd fallen in love with. "Nothing is more important than being where you want to be."

"Exactly what I told Danton. And where I want to be is wherever you are. I love you, Dr. Westcott." He trailed his fingers down her cheek to her lips and his thumb rubbed lightly across her bottom lip.

Nerve endings sprang to attention and she leaned closer.

"Maybe you slipped me some of your aphrodisiac because I've never wanted to spend all my time with one woman like I do with you."

She stiffened. The loss of her grant still rankled. "That's not funny, Jake."

"I just thought you might like my services"—he pulled a folded sheet of paper from his breast pocket, opened it and held it up for her inspection—"when you return to Dolpa."

As she scanned the page, elation bubbled up within her. "My grant—you mean, it was never rescinded? But how—?"

"We think it was Talisker's doing, to get you back to Australia. It worked." His mouth tightened and his eyes narrowed.

A shiver ran down her spine. If not for Jake, she probably wouldn't have left the mountains alive. She reached up and ran a finger across his forehead, smoothing away his frown. "But the bad guys didn't get what they were after. The good guys won, and it looks like I can return to Nepal and continue my research."

"I came to offer myself to you in whatever capacity you'll have me. Guide, lover—partner?"

Whatever she'd expected to hear, it wasn't this. Only in her dreams had Jake been all hers. She shook her head. "Are you suggesting we move in together?" For the moment, that was all she could concentrate on.

Jake pulled her into a loose embrace. "Will you? I can't stand another day without you in my life for good."

Tears pricked her eyes but she clung to logic. "And when the wanderlust grabs you later—what then?"

"It won't."

"My father couldn't fight it. He didn't love us enough to be there when we needed him.”

“I’m not your father, Marcy. I took the job as Danton’s deputy because I love you. Wherever you are, that’s my home. And if that means we have to live in the city, just expect me to take you camping often so I can make love to you under the stars.” He stood and held her hands, waiting for her answer.

“I love you. God, how I love you!” She flung her arms around his neck.

With a muttered oath, his arms circled her waist and he lifted her off the floor. “Is that a yes?”

“Yes.”

“Great. Because we’re leaving on the three o’clock flight for Daydream Island.”

She leaned back and looked up into his eyes. “Jake Harris, are you trying to take charge of my life again? I can’t just up and leave the professor like that. There are observations to take and notes to make and—”

“But it was the professor who suggested you needed a break.”

“Honestly?”

“Well . . . there may have been an element of persuasion in our discussion, but hey, I’ve packed a bag for you.” His eyes glinted with mischief.

She thumped his shoulder. “You did not just say you packed for me again. Last time you forgot to pack my underwear.”

“Ah, I’m sure I’ve got everything you’ll need this time.”

He dug into his trouser pocket. "See."

Slowly, he withdrew his hand. From the tip of his forefinger, her lacy black undies dangled. He raised his treasure to eye level. The desk lamp shone through the open weave and patterned the lower half of his face. His lips parted and she groaned, already imagining the tug of his mouth as he kissed her everywhere.

His attention returned to her face. Wicked thoughts of naughty nights danced through her head as he slid his free arm around her waist and held her against him.

"Am I convincing you yet?"

She pressed against his erection and wriggled her hips. "I could be persuaded—if the rest of your packing is as good as this."

He looked from her face to the scrap of black in his hand. "This is it. Did I pack too much?"

The End

Thank you for reading 'High Stakes'. If you are able to leave a review on your e-store or Bookbub or Goodreads, this writer thanks you.

Want to read Paul's story in 'The Singapore Trap'?

Click here: https://amzn.to/2yIojOh or check my website for more details: https://www.susannebellamy.com

When Paul Rimmer follows a lead that takes him to Singapore, he joins forces with Lin, a local undercover officer, in the bid to track down the new head of a drug cartel.

Beautiful Lin is a distraction. Is she running interference for Chan, or chasing him down? Can Paul trust this his new partner or will she trap him?

Extract:

Chapter 1

Sydney, two years earlier

Paul Rimmer confirmed his teams were in place around the perimeter of the warehouse and brothel owned by the Chan family. More teams awaited their signal to begin a combined multi-pronged raid on the Chan mansion and three sites in Sydney where illegal businesses operated.

Paul had asked for, and been given, leadership of the teams hitting the Rocks locations. Both sites were links in the cartel's drug chain, but details about the brothel angered and sickened him. Girls abducted and illegal immigrants caught in virtual slavery, two of the Chans' favourite staffing methods. It sickened him that it happened at all, and the thought of it happening to any one of the women in his family made him want to go all Rambo. Was that because he had four younger sisters and a stack of female cousins?

Both Paul and his partner, Tamsin had risked their lives to get the information, and Tam's even twin sister had been caught up in their sting, but now, Bureau agents were about to close the net. Determined not to let a single member of the drug cartel escape, the planning had been meticulous and limited to a very small group. Two moles within the Bureau had been killed during a recent raid to rescue Tamsin, and now Danton, the Bureau chief, wasn't taking chances.

"Where there were two, there may be others. Until we've had a chance to clean out any other rotten wood, eveything stays within these walls, got it?"

Now the plan devised by Danton along with Paul, Tamsin, and Jake Harris was underway.

Paul raised his communication unit and gave the signal. "Red team in position. On my word . . ." He drew a deep breath. "All teams are go."

Cordoned off and locked down, the streets around three sides of the warehouse and brothel exploded with dark-uniformed officers hitting their assigned points of entry.

Paul led his team through the front door. A small reception area was unoccupied, but a security camera tracked their progress into a spacious L-shaped club lounge. Blacked out windows were mostly hidden by heavy red drapes, while several decadently padded couches were set at strategic points around the room. All were angled towards a low dais, which Paul saw as he turned the corner into the long leg of the L.

Two men seated on couches raised their hands. Considering the girls positioned beside and behind one, with a third girl on the floor between the legs of the other man, Paul dismissed them as clients. The third girl looked up at Paul and his team and the only sound in the room was the soft pop-slurp as her lips left her client's cock.

But they weren't the main reason Paul was here. Leaving the men and girls to the sweep team, Paul signalled his partner, Perkins. They moved into position on either side of the dais, guns at the ready. A dark-green feather boa lay abandoned on the highly polished floor.

Paul's gut tightened at the sight.

The girls servicing the two clients were little more than teenagers, and this dais was apparently a stage for clients to view a parade of women and make their selection. *Like a bloody meat mart.*

Perkins led the way along a short besser-brick hallway with a single door at the far end. Unpainted and poorly lit, it was clear the hallway was only used by the working girls as a passage from the lounge to the rooms where they plied their trade. According to the building plans the door led to the business side of the brothel; a selection of theme rooms catering to all tastes and wallet sizes.

Gritting his teeth, Paul opened the door. Six doors with another wider hallway that connected back to the lounge punctuated a small, tastefully decorated foyer. Rich clients were given the royal treatment when they came into this part of the brothel. Upstairs, another team would be picking up clients and working girls from the cheaper rooms.

Methodically the two officers worked their way through the rooms, taking one side each. Paul disturbed two men attended by a single woman in the first room; the middle room was vacant. In the third room, styled as a dungeon, a client, bound and leather-clad, was being beaten with a riding crop.

Paul nodded to Perkins that he'd take the last room. Information said this was John Chan's private room, and the last intel report had indicated he had left home for an evening at the brothel.

Moving into position, Paul pushed the door wide and did a sweep around the spacious, high-ceilinged room, finishing with his gun aimed towards a king-sized bed. A young woman sprawled naked and alone on the bed, her dark hair fanned across the pillow—beautiful and unmoving.

Not the reaction Paul expected.

Cautiously he made his way to her side and set his fingers on her neck.

Dead.

Her wide-open eyes stared sightlessly at the distant ceiling. Partly concealed beneath her shoulder, a ripped plastic bag suggested how she'd died.

Perkins appeared in the doorway. "Anything?" He approached the bed. "Aw, shit."

Paul gently closed her eyes. "I want Chan in handcuffs

before we leave."

"Sounds kinky, boss."

Sometimes humour helped them confront the worst of humanity. And then there was now.

Paul gritted his teeth so hard his jaw ached. "Not now, Perkins."

Perkins flicked a glance at the dead girl. "You're right. Sorry."

They left the room and met up with the second team in a pincer movement near the stairs, their search netting the brothel's Madam Wu, several employees and a handful of clients, but Chan wasn't among them.

Paul pressed the button on his comm unit. "Blue team, have you got John Chan? Was he with his father? Over."

Jake's disembodied voice crackled over the comms. "Negative. Chan senior is in custody along with his very angry wife and assorted family members. She's screeching up a storm. Chan junior isn't here. What about at the warehouse? Over."

Perkins called the warehouse team and shook his head. "Not there either."

"Damn it. Do you want to let Danton know, or do you want me to tell him?" Paul knew neither of them wanted to be the one conveying that news, but Jake would be more worried about getting home to protect Marcy if Chan had slipped the net. "I'll do it. Over."

"Thanks, mate. Over and out."

They returned to the room where the dead girl now lay beneath a sheet. One of the sweep team twitched a corner to cover the girl's foot.

Had Chan managed to slip out before the raid? But how, and why hadn't he been spotted? Paul frowned and turned to see Perkins examining a mirror.

"I can't see the benefits of this myself." Perkins stood in front of the oversized mirror, set so clients could enjoy watching themselves as they performed on the bed. "Unless you're a selfish, narcissistic prick."

"Not for me either, but intel indicated this room was the one most often used by Chan. His *private playground*." Paul tipped his head up. From the dark ceiling, hooks and chains hung down, indicating something of the darker sexual tastes of their quarry. His glance landed on the now-shrouded figure and disgust mixed with bile in his gut.

"I reckon Chan has got away."

"But how?" Paul nodded towards the dead girl. "That method's one of the violent, sick dude's preferences. He was here, I'm sure of it. We're missing something."

"What, like a secret door out of here?" Perkins snorted. "Been reading crime novels, mate?"

Paul's gaze narrowed on the mirror. He approached the glass and pressed his fingers along one edge. "Could be a two-way mirror."

"Makes a sick kind of sense I suppose. One bloke pays to do it and another pays to watch."

"Instead of being impressed by the brothel's business model, try looking for that secret door *you* suggested might be—"

Click.

The mirror moved slightly away from the wall. Paul bent to examine the glass near his hand. Fingerprints smudged one spot on the otherwise clean surface. "Perky, I apologise. You were on the money with that secret door wisecrack."

Paul let his team know what he'd found and then he and Perkins turned on their night-vision goggles and stepped into a narrow, rough stone passage.

It lead down and angled sharply to the right twenty metres on. A heavy metal door, old and flaking but still solid, barred their exit. Paul set his shoulder against the metal and forced it partially open with a squeal of unoiled hinges. It stopped where a lump of broken concrete caught and held the lower edge.

Ahead of them, the lights of Sydney Harbour danced across the water. Boats sailed slowly past sending small waves crashing against a jumble of rocks below Paul's feet. The narrow opening was hemmed in on both sides by buildings that reached to the water's edge and Paul visualised their location as seen from the water. Unless Chan had wings, the harbour was the only way out from this remnant of Rocks' history.

Perkins stood by Paul's side looking out. "How the fuck did he escape? There's no watercraft close enough to pick him up."

"Unless he was tipped off. Maybe we have another mole to ferret out."

Chapter 2

Sydney, present day

Paul knocked on the open door and strolled into Jake Harris' office. Two years into his job as second-in-charge at the Bureau and he looked right at home, although Paul knew his one-time partner escaped to remote camping sites with Marcy more weekends than most couples.

"You wanted to see me?" He dropped into a chair and got comfortable.

Jake tossed a folder across the desk and leaned back. "Tell me what you think." The casual pose didn't fool Paul. Jake's dark gaze was hooded, but his tense jaw spoke volumes.

Paul flicked the cover open and looked at a long-distance photo, shot with a zoom lens, enhanced and cleaned up, but still lacking something in clarity. The background was out of focus, but enough to see the wall behind was grimy, with security grills over a pair of windows.

He picked the photo up and peered at the three-quarter-face

image. A thrill raced down his spine like the feel of a perfect wave building beneath his surfboard.

Finally!

"I spy with my little eye . . ." Paul tossed the photo down. It slid and stopped halfway between them. Their gazes met and any attempt at humour vanished. "This is Chan, and yes, I'm sure, if that's what you were going to ask. Where and when was this taken?"

"Geylang district in Singapore, two days ago."

"Geylang? Isn't that a red-light district?"

"Pretty much. Fitting for Chan, although the source of this photo doesn't believe he's living there."

"Are you giving me this assignment? Please tell me you are." Losing Chan two years earlier still stung. He needed to make things right, especially for the dead girl. Her image haunted his nightmares in times of stress. If Paul had been so inclined, he'd have said her ghost followed him, demanding vengeance.

"Yes. Tamsin told Marcy and me she's pregnant. Fairly early stages, but her doctor has some concern about her health. Marcy didn't elaborate."

"So she's out of contention. Damn."

"I know you two work well together, and I'm convinced there's merit in mixed teams. However, would you agree to working with a local officer in Singapore?"

"Not keen, but I'll do it. At least he—"

"She. Mixed gender teams are my preference and so I requested their best female operative."

"At least *she* will have local knowledge. My experience of Singapore is limited to transiting through Changi Airport twice on my way to and home from Greece."

"Good. I'll set up a meeting with Tamsin. See if she remembers anything about Chan that isn't in the reports."

***

Tamsin Westcott curled her legs up and held a cushion

against her still-flat stomach and sipped her steaming green tea. "Thanks for moving the meeting to my apartment, Jake, Paul. I can't seem to move far without either wanting to throw up or crawl back under the doona."

"No problem, Tam." Paul thought she looked peaky. The oldest of his sisters had *glowed* when pregnant with his niece, but Tamsin had admitted to having a rough time of her pregnancy. "Your reports were comprehensive. You always were more thorough than me, but I'm looking for any small, personal details that might help locate Chan. Odd preferences for food, recreation . . . You know the sort of thing I mean."

Tamsin's nose wrinkled and she set the mug of tea down. "Perversions. That's what he likes, and the more awful you might think it, the more he'll like it."

"So the girl in the brothel—"

"Yes. Perverse, extreme, highly dangerous, although never to him. Pretty sure he's a sociopath. He's fascinated by creatures that kill with poison."

"What, like scorpions?"

"Probably not exotic enough for him." Jake scrolled through the file on his iPad and enlarged an image. "His Sydney apartment yielded a large aquarium of highly dangerous tropical fish. Look at this." He passed the device to Tam who passed it on to Paul.

"Ugh, is that a tiger fish?"

"The big ugly thing with razor-sharp teeth? I believe so. It's like an African piranha. There was no evidence to suggest Chan brought it into the country legally." Jake took his iPad back from Paul. "Tracing him via his taste for the perverse might not be of much help in Singapore without the help of your contact."

Tamsin met Paul's eye and grinned. "I wonder if she'll be as accommodating as me?"

"I only did the things a fiancé is expected to do, including proclamations of love when Chan was around."

"Putting up with those pet names was the hardest undercover role I ever had."

"What's wrong with Babycake?" Paul grimaced. Maybe he had been pushing Tam's buttons with some of the rubbish he'd dished up. "Anyway, it won't come to that. Chan knows me. He won't be fooled again by that routine."

Tam's gaze settled on him and she reached out to touch his arm. "Be careful, Paul. Chan's more likely to feed you to his tiger fish this time."

"Thanks for the vote of confidence, partner."

Jake typed on a fold up keyboard and then looked up. "Anything else, Tam?"

Twenty minutes later, Jake stowed his iPad and rose. "Thanks for the extra details, Tam. Something there might give Paul the break he needs. Now, Marcy told me to ask if you're free for a barbecue on Sunday. She said to just show up if you're feeling up to it."

"Thanks, Jake."

"Am I invited too?" Paul collected their empty mugs and carried them through to Tamsin's kitchen.

"Come Sunday, you'll be in Singapore."

Read on for the first chapter of 'The Emerald Lei', set in Hawaii in 1960

(originally published as 'Winning the Heiress' Heart')

Chapter One

Hawaii 1960

Lucien Martineau pushed open the back door of the plantation house. 'There is Nuthin' Like a Dame' blasted from the kitchen radio along with his cook's slightly off-key singing. Luc hung his fedora on the rack, dropped his suitcase by the door, and sniffed appreciatively. *Roast pork.*

"How long till dinner, Annie?" He leaned around her ample frame and filched a taste of chocolate cake batter from the mixing bowl. *My lucky day when Annie came to work for me.*

She turned, hand on hip, and raised the wooden spoon like a pointer at his chest. "Where you been, Luc? Jack Lyons rang hours ago. Been ringing twice a day since you left. Couldn't get hold of you at that hotel you stayed in."

He paused, hand hovering over the rim of the bowl. Muscles tensed, his heartbeat sped up, hammering like a drum roll in his chest.

The plantation estate sale! Had Benson agreed?

As nonchalantly as he could manage, he leaned back against the counter and folded his arms. "What did he want?"

"Said there's a tenant in the Benson house, that English heiress the papers wrote about, and she needs a hand. Said you were the one to help her."

"Tenant? He's leased the house then?" Jack had earned the bottle of imported single malt Luc had promised if he'd sealed the deal. He pushed off the counter, grabbed his hat, and was almost out the door when Annie called after him.

"Yeah, *heiress* tenant. Dinner will be ready in an hour. Come home any later and I feed that pork to your dog."

Luc zipped back and kissed her cheek. "You're looking at the new owner of the Benson plantation, and that pork will be waiting for me to celebrate when I get back."

Laughing aloud, he skirted the table and raced out the back

door. He bounded off the veranda and up the track linking the two estates. If Jack had found a tenant for the house, Benson must have accepted his offer for the land. Which would give him twice the property his father had owned, *and* the best plantation on the island. That meant the Tourism Board contract was as good as his. The contract was in the bag.

His foreman, Sam, met him halfway up the track. "Welcome back, boss. Good news?"

"Yep. You can start clearing that track to connect us with next door."

"Benson sold it to you? I'll get the boys right on it."

Giddy with elation, Luc strode up the hill, brushing past long-fringed palms. Late afternoon sun cast a golden light over the field of spiky leaves, and he paused to admire the rows of plants curving down to meet the track. Hawaii joining the Union was momentous, and if his research was accurate, the Island would be seeing a steady rise in the number of tourists visiting. Soon he'd be bringing in visitors from mainland USA and reaping the benefits of Statehood.

A pity his father hadn't seen eye-to-eye with him about this project. It was one of only a handful of disagreements they'd ever had. But that didn't matter now because Benson had finally forgiven Luc's ill-advised proposal to his daughter, Genevieve, and agreed to sell him the place.

He breathed deeply; the sweet scent of pineapples and success surrounded him. For the first time in years, a sense of hope filled Luc's chest. Finally, everything was working out.

Three distinctive notes of birdcall trilled and were answered from deep within the palm-filled ridge separating his plantation from Benson's. A machinery track had to go through the lower slope to link the fields but otherwise, this forest remnant would remain intact.

Adrenaline pumped through his body as he took the short cut through the palm grove. What a celebration he'd plan. Details for a tourist itinerary jostled in his mind. The two new teenage boys he was mentoring could be trained as guides, and he'd put in the order for the people mover tomorrow. Until it arrived from the mainland, they'd make do with smaller groups in Jeeps.

As Luc crossed the ridge and strode downhill, he wondered why Jack had asked him to help the new tenant. Pity his excitement at the news had stopped him from thinking clearly before he left his house. A phone call to Jack might have easily sorted the problem and he could have been toasting his good fortune right now.

Once he found out what the new tenant wanted, however, he'd head home and have that whiskey to celebrate. Soon.

He rounded the last bend in the track, emerging on the western side of Benson's plantation house. Sunlight bathed the roof in golden light, imperceptibly releasing its hold, until only the weather vane glittered in the last rays. Wide verandas cast deep shadows, but a flash of white near the front door caught his attention.

He climbed the side steps, strode around the corner and crashed into a ladder. Unbalanced, the ladder wobbled. Barely noting his stinging shin, a startled gasp was his only warning before a body dropped into his arms. A very feminine body, all curves and satiny skin and long, auburn hair.

Instinctively, his arms tightened. His right hand slipped down bare thigh below a pair of tan shorts and held tightly while his left hand shaped the curve at the side of her breast. Milky-white skin, soft and smooth as satin, warmed beneath his tanned hands. Slowly, his gaze travelled up the length of woman in his arms.

Strands of auburn hair slipped off her face as she raised her head, and her perfume, complex and elegant, tantalized his nostrils. It had been too long since he'd held such a delightful armful. Luc adjusted his grip and the slide of his hand along silky skin fired up desires he'd ignored since the Genevieve debacle. By rights he should have been embarrassed but right now, an apology was the last thing on his mind. Delicate features, a turned up nose and startled green eyes looked into his. A gentleman would immediately release her. A gentleman would apologize for causing her fall. Instead, he held her against his chest and grinned.

A gentleman missed out on all the fun.

"Hi there. I thought I was the one dropping in."

Rosy-pink flared along her high cheekbones but she gave him a quick smile. "My apologies. I don't usually fall into a man's arms at our first meeting."

Cool and cultured, her English accent explained her delicate colouring. But what was an English rose doing in the middle of pineapple fields?

"Then I am honoured to be the exception. Are you okay to stand?"

"I'm fine, thank you."

Reluctantly, he released her and hooked his thumbs into his pockets.

She took a step back before holding out her hand. "I'm Evangeline Abbott. You must be *Monsieur* Martineau?" Her accent on the French title and his name was that of a fluent French speaker.

He shook her proffered hand, holding it longer than politeness dictated. Warm and soft, it fit snugly within his. "Please, call me Luc. A pleasure to meet you, Miss Abbott."

A pleasure indeed. His skin tingled with the memory of her body plastered against his. It had probably cut Jack to the quick having to ask for Luc's assistance. Knowing his friend's love of beautiful women, Luc had no doubt that, given half a chance, Jack would have monopolized her attention. He'd thank Jack later for sending him up to meet the new neighbour. "You've a fitting name for a newcomer to our little paradise."

A small frown knit her brow and she tipped her head to the side. "Abbott?"

"Eve."

Her smile tightened and her gaze narrowed on him, cool and assessing. Had he overstepped some undefined boundary? The odd image of a door closing between them settled in his mind. "Don't you like compliments, Eve?"

"Not particularly, and I prefer Eva—to my friends. Mr Lyons said he'd ask you to call on us."

Us? She was married? Disappointment stabbed and he clung to the smile he'd worn since Eva Abbott had landed in his arms. Of course some lucky man would have put his ring on her finger long ago. No wonder his compliment had drawn such a cool response. "I gather Mr Abbott wants to speak with me. Is he home?"

"Mr Abbott?" She frowned before a broad smile took its place. The cool mask fell away and her expression lit up as she pronounced his name. "Oh, you mean Sebastian?"

That Sebastian was the love of her life couldn't have been clearer. Love like that had skipped Luc's family. A band tightened around his chest and threatened to suffocate him. He didn't understand that sort of smothering love. He didn't *do* love.

Eva giggled and his attention snapped back to lush pink lips curved in a smile and the hint of a dimple on her left cheek. Her green gaze met his. "He's not quite eighteen yet, but he'd be chuffed you thought him older."

"Chuffed?" He shook his head and wondered what had happened to his grasp of English. "Forgive me, but I don't understand what you want from me. I thought Mr Abbott wanted my assistance?"

She looked away and her right hand toyed with her left, rubbing her ring finger. It was bare, but she twisted her fingers around it as though she was used to playing with a piece of jewellery. "There is no husband, *Monsieur* Martineau. Just me. Look, would you like a drink while we talk? Mr Lyons said you'd be able to help me with Seb. He's the reason I wanted to speak with you."

Luc nodded and his smile firmed. She wasn't married. There was no husband. Just a teenager who needed help. Jack must have talked to her about his work with Acky and Moe. Was this Seb at risk, too?

Intrigued, he followed her straight back and softly swaying hips as she led him down the wide hallway and through the library. Half-unpacked boxes littered the polished wooden floor. Several contained expensive, leather-bound books, the type of volumes passed down from one generation to the next. The sort of treasures one would ship to Hawaii if they were planning to make a permanent home there. The possibilities opened up by his newest and nearest neighbour were looking better by the minute. "Are you planning to stay a while?"

She turned a steady gaze on him. "Indeed, I hope so. We've sold everything in England."

"A major move then. Do you miss it? Your home, I mean."

She looked through the window. Beyond the house, dusk was quickly falling. She touched her fingers to a pane and Luc sensed she was seeing a remembered scene. A soft sigh fluttered away, so soft he wasn't quite sure if he'd imagined it. "I miss the garden at Bellerose most. Gardenias and roses scenting the night air. I doubt they will grow, let alone thrive, in this hotter climate."

"You might be surprised what flourishes here." Including an English rose, if he had his way.

She blinked, as though the sound of his voice had woken her from her reverie and dropped her hand to her side. "Perhaps. Shall we?" Straightening her shoulders, she led the way into the sparsely furnished reception room.

Gut and fists clenching, he stopped in the doorway. *Not this room.*

The last time he'd been in this room, he'd proposed to Genevieve Benson and she had dumped him. Her dismissal ghosted through his mind and his jaw tightened.

"With a divorce in your family and a mother who's the

scandal of the island? How could you ever think I'd consider marrying you, darling? We've had a good time, Luc, but you're not marriage material. Although if you make an indecent amount of money, I'm sure some woman will be only too happy to overlook your shortcomings."

Eva's voice intervened in his dark thoughts. "I'm sorry I can't offer you a selection yet but I have a tolerable sherry. Will you have a glass while we talk?" She stood by the sideboard and waited, hand on a crystal decanter.

Luc forced himself to step into the room and walk to the nearest armchair. Desperately, he scrambled to collect his thoughts. *Never again.* Love was for fools. He looked across at Eva Abbott's curves. A breeze drifted through the open window and carried her scent to him. His arms still held the ghost of her body against his. An affair, however, would be very pleasant.

"Thank you, yes. And my friends call me Luc. I hope we'll be friends—Eva?"

"Perhaps." She poured two glasses of golden sherry and carried one to the small table beside him, carefully placing it within easy reach. "Maybe you'd like to hear the favour I have to ask of you before you offer more."

He sipped the sherry. "Spanish?"

"You've a discerning palate, Mr—Luc."

"I'm more a Scotch whisky man but I appreciate quality, wherever it's from. So, this favour—it has to do with Seb?"

"How did you—of course, Mr Lyons told you."

"I haven't spoken to Jack but his message said you needed my help. I assumed he mentioned the program I've been piloting with the island boys."

She sat and folded her hands neatly in her lap. "He did and it sounds like the answer to my prayers. Please, tell me more. You work with them on your plantation, don't you?"

"They're boys at risk, some of whom would likely end up in jail, but I teach them the ins and outs of growing pineapples and the everyday workings of a plantation. Whether or not they choose to stay with me afterwards, they all develop skills that make them employable."

"Mr Lyons said you've had a great deal of success. He was talking about you turning the lives of those boys around. That's very commendable." She gave him a silent toast and sipped her sherry.

He shrugged then grinned inwardly, aware of the irony. Compliments made him uncomfortable, too. "I offer them the opportunity. If they put in the work, they succeed and they learn that working brings its own rewards."

"I haven't heard of another program like it before. It sounds wonderful, and exactly what Seb needs."

"Bit of a hell-raiser, is he?"

"Not exactly but—he needs more discipline than I can give. Frankly, he needs a man's guidance. I've done my best but I'm not his father."

"Seb's your brother?"

She paused before answering quietly. "Nephew. Phillip— my oldest brother—was killed recently." She dropped her gaze to her white-knuckled hands and drew an audible breath before slowly releasing it. "He was a test pilot. When his plane crashed, I became Seb's guardian." She pressed her lips firmly together before quietly clearing her throat.

"My condolences. That's a difficult task, especially when you must also be grieving for your brother. Do you not have other family to help?"

She raised her glass and sipped before carefully replacing it on the side table. Arms folded across her stomach, she stared at a spot on the rug between their feet. "Harry, my other brother, was lost when his ship was torpedoed early in the war, and Seb's mother and my parents died in the London bombings. The war deprived me of most of my family."

Jaw tight, Luc nodded and frowned. Loss and grief were

probably the story for many British families. "The war tore many families apart."

"Pearl Harbour must have been as bad. I guess you know what it was like." Finally, she raised her head and made eye contact.

His stomach clenched as vivid memory rolled back the years. He knew. Twelve years old and free as a bird, he and Jack had camped overnight in Keaiwa Heiau National Park. Early the next morning, they'd used his birthday gift of binoculars to identify the silhouetted shapes of the American Fleet anchored in the harbour. Instead, bombs rained from the sky and fire lit the water. He doubted the memory would ever fade. "They were terrible times."

"Seb's the only family I have left. I'm doing what I can but lately he's become...difficult."

"He's a teenage boy. Most go through a rebellious phase. I sure did." He smiled. Perhaps the personal remark would lift her anxiety.

She gave him a distracted half-smile and interlaced her fingers in her lap. "I understand he's grieving for his father—they were very close, you see—but I fear he might follow in Phillip's footsteps."

"Flying, you mean?"

"I couldn't bear to lose him, too. He's got the same…reckless attitude Phillip had. Combined with a young man's sense of his own invincibility, well… That's part of the reason I decided to sell and come to a new country, somewhere very different from England."

"And take his mind off flying?"

"Yes."

Hesitant to give offence, at the same time he understood the challenge Eva had undertaken. A few tips on raising a young man wouldn't go astray. "Sometimes you have to compromise. It's much better than butting your head against a brick wall."

Her green-eyed gaze flashed with fire, putting him in mind of a lioness protecting her cub. "What are you suggesting I do? Let him take flying lessons?"

"I wouldn't presume to tell you what to do. Just don't hold the reins too tightly. Teenage boys need space to grow into young men." And the chance to make their own mistakes and work out who they are. He'd plant the seed of the idea for now and offer to help if she wanted it.

Slowly she nodded. "I remember how it was with Harry. Tell him not to do something and for sure it was the one thing he would do."

Luc's respect for Eva grew. Taking on responsibility for her teenage nephew was a huge commitment, as was moving them both to a foreign country. A simple offer would ease her concern about her nephew. "How can I help? You want me to give Seb the same training I give the boys in the plantation programme?"

Her body stilled and her gaze settled on him. In her eyes he discerned a yearning to give her nephew the best she could. Right now, it seemed the most important thing in the world to help her achieve that peace of mind. And give him a reason to see more of her? He wouldn't mind that either.

In fact, he planned to see a whole lot more of Eva Abbott, nephew or not.

Even across the intervening yards between their chairs, her tension was palpable. "Would you consider taking him on?"

"I don't see why not. Soon, I'll have a great deal more work with tour groups visiting and if Seb trains up well, he could work permanently for me."

"That's very kind of you, but I hope with the training you give, he'll learn enough to take over the running of our plantation before too long."

"Your plantation? You plan to buy property here?"

"I already own a place. I signed the deed for this plantation yesterday."

ABOUT THE AUTHOR

BOOKS BY SUSANNE BELLAMY

<u>Rural fiction</u>

<u>Hearts of the Outback</u> (6 book series)

<u>Individual titles – Hearts of the Outback</u>
Just One Kiss
Heartbreak Homestead
Long Way Home
Winds of Change
Wild About Harry
The Cattleman's Promise

<u>Home to Lark Creek</u>
A Promise of Home
Hard Road Home
Turn Left for Home
Home from the Hill

<u>Bindarra Creek Romance</u>
Second Chance Love
Pearls and Green Beer (novella)
In the Heat of the Night

<u>Through Escape Publishing</u>
Starting Over (Also appears in print bind up: Heart of the Town - four book anthology)

Engaging the Enemy
Her Christmas Kisses

Contemporary romance:
White Ginger

Romantic suspense:
The Emerald Quest (originally published as Winning the Heiress'
Heart)
High Stakes

Novellas:
A Taste of Christmas (in A Season to Remember)
One Night in Sorrento
One Night in Tuscany
Romancing the Holidays (limited release)
Be Mine Valentine (limited release)

Visit my website for more information about my books at:

http://www.susannebellamy.com/books-by-susanne-bellamy.html